MAD *about the* BANKER

PIPER RAYNE

Mad About The Banker

ISBN: 978-1-987925-27-2

 This book is a work of fiction. Names, characters, places and incidents either are products of the author's imagination or are used fictitiously. Any resemblance to actual events or locales or persons, living or dead, is entirely coincidental.

Cover Design by:
RBA Designs

Line Editor:
RJ Locksley

Proof Reader:
Behind The Writer

Interior Design & Formatting by:
Christine Borgford, Type A Formatting

Who knew my brother's friend could be Mr. Right, and not just Mr. Right Now?

My brother refused to introduce me, so I blame him. If he'd just caved, and introduced me to Jasper, I wouldn't be in this mess. I mean, really, what's the big deal? I'm not interested in the guy's looks.

Oh no, I want his cold hard cash. (Be honest, you were expecting that other four letter 'c' word weren't you?)

Now, before you go getting all judgy, I'm not a gold digger. I have a legitimate business opportunity for Jasper to invest in. The problem is that my stick-up-his-ass brother is embarrassed that his twin sister invents kick ass sex toys. His problem, not mine.

So, I took matters into my own hands. Defeat isn't a word in Lennon Hart's dictionary.

Using my stealthy P.I. moves, I narrowed my search to a time and place where I knew I could find him. It was completely innocent. A chance meeting that would give me the opportunity to pitch my business.

It wasn't until I sat down across from the gorgeous panty soaking man in front of me, that I realized I wanted so much more than just his money. I could very well want his heart if I wasn't careful.

Apparently my P.I. skills aren't as stellar as I thought because Jasper had his own secret—and it changed EVERYTHING.

MAD *about the* BANKER

To the wild child in each of us.

chapter
ONE

I SLAM MY PORTFOLIO down on the mahogany table at the Thirsty Monk. Whitney's blue eyes widen and Tahlia's white wine splashes in her glass. Her manicured hands stop it from spilling. Of course. I shouldn't be surprised because her life is working out fucking fantastic.

"What's wrong?" Whitney asks, leaning forward in her ivory blouse and matching pant suit.

My two best friends sit at the table, eyes zeroed in on me. They have everything going for them. Their dream careers, check. Dream guys, check. Okay, other than the fact that they each found their unicorn cocks, I'm not that jealous of the monogamy aspect of their life. I mean, one day, they'll probably be envious of my ability to nail a new guy every week, but right now they're thoroughly enjoying the one magical cock in the universe that can deliver the type of orgasms every girl dreams of—hence unicorn cock.

"Another bank shot me down." I sit my ass down in the booth and let out a long sigh. "I thought San Francisco was supposed to be liberal? Every banker has a rod up their ass, when if they'd just change it out for one of my dildos they'd probably be on their knees begging to invest in my sex toy company." I slump in the seat.

Whitney raises her hand for the waitress.

A minute later, a whiskey neat is sitting in front of me. Yeah, we come here a lot. It's where Whitney and Cole first met, not to mention it's Cole's bar that he bought from his dad's empire. Long story, but just another example of how everyone gets their dream, except for me.

I down the glass, enjoying the burn as it travels past my throat. I've probably been indulging a little too much lately, but there's no one counting my drinks. Might as well add 'drunk' to my list of flaws.

"Another one?" Tahl's lips dip down and she reaches across the table to touch my hand in sympathy. "Do you want me to look at your business plan?"

She offers with every decline and I refuse each time. She worked as vice-president of her father's sausage company—I know, I can barely say that with a straight face—and now she's started her own successful party-planning business. She'd probably redo everything I have, but I went to college too. Switched my major from art to business. Maybe not magna cum laude like Tahl, but I like to think I'm not the dullest pencil in the box. Plus, there's a satisfaction of doing this on my own, without the help of my friends.

"No. I got it."

The perky red-headed waitress drops off another whiskey neat, which I quickly lift to my mouth.

"Cole's outdone himself with this one." I raise my cup up in the air and Whitney proudly smiles at my compliment toward her boyfriend.

"He'll be here in a few, so you can tell him yourself." She sips her own mixed drink which I'm sure contains Rock Hard

Whiskey—Cole's distillery.

"Great." Any hint of excitement in my tone is void.

"Lucas is, too. We thought we'd all go to the movies tonight," Tahlia says, excitement bouncing through every octave in her voice.

Another fifth wheel date? No thanks.

"I might have other plans." I eye the new bartender.

Whitney and Tahlia both turn their heads and swivel back my way with huge grins.

"Slade," Whitney sighs. "He's new." Her voice is slow and sultry.

"Hey, Cole." I wave at the door like he's actually here and Whitney's back snaps straight, her eyes searching for him before they zero in on me. "You shouldn't be ogling other men, Whit," I say with fake seriousness.

"I'm sure he looks at other girls," she comments, leaning back in her chair and sipping her drink.

"You think?" Tahl asks, clearly not as comfortable with the fact that her lover dearest Lucas' eyes could stray for a second.

Whitney's brows crinkle. "Tahl, you don't mind staring at Slade, do you?"

Tahlia gives him another look over at the bar before turning her attention to us. "No, but I'm not thinking about going home with him."

Whitney laughs and I sit back, enjoying the exchange between my two friends, who have never truly enjoyed having casual sexcapades. They're the ones who want marriage, kids, a house. I'm the odd man out when it comes to the three of us.

"Of course not. It's like when you go to a strip club. You look, but you're more than happy to go home at night," Whitney says.

I scoff. "But I bet you bang your boyfriend like a naughty, naughty girl after the guy at the club has got you all horned up."

Both their eyes zoom to mine and I raise my eyebrows in a challenge. They know I'm telling the truth.

"No," Whitney argues, while Tahlia takes refuge in her glass of white wine.

"Hmm . . . I think one of us does." I laugh.

Whitney turns to Tahl, but she's so busy guzzling down her Moscato, she pretends she's not paying attention. Whitney dips her head lower so she's in Tahlia's line of vision.

"Once, okay. It was Chase so it doesn't count." She sips her wine again, her face matching her red blouse.

"You can't erase your past, Tahl, but I'm looking at you in a whole new light." I raise my glass to her and sip my whiskey.

She rolls her eyes and stares off, forever the débutante who is too self-conscious to be unleashed. "New topic, please," she mumbles.

"Let's talk about the fact that you gave me one of your sex toys and only told my boyfriend about the app." Whitney's drink slams down on the table and she gives me an admonishing glare.

A roar of laughter throttles out of me. "He finally did it, huh?"

I'd secretly told Cole that he could control the toy with his phone. It's the impromptu sex toys that I love so much.

"In the middle of dinner with my grandparents! Now they think I loooove tuna casserole. Thanks." Whitney tilts her head, but I'm too busy laughing to really see if she's mad or not.

"Great though?" I ask and Tahl leans forward, wanting the answer as much as I do.

"Fucking awesome." The corners of Whit's lips turn up. "Brilliant, of course."

"So, write me a review on the product," I remind her and she nods.

"I'll have Cole write one up too. I'm not sure which one of us got more pleasure from it." The waitress brings another drink over to Whitney and then places chips and salsa on the table. Must be happy hour. "Make a guy version so I can give him a little payback." She wiggles her eyebrows and I nod, agreeing.

"Payback for what?" Cole asks, leaning over and giving his girlfriend a kiss.

"Hey," Lucas says, leaning down to give me a one-armed hug and then moving toward Tahlia.

"Hey, guys," I say, but each of them are busy saying hello to their unicorn cock owners.

Lucas unbuttons his suit jacket, shrugging it off and placing it behind him on the chair. After he sits, he leans over and kisses Tahlia.

"Hey, baby," he says and she places her hands on his cheeks, leaning into his touch.

Damn, they make monogamy look good.

"So, Cole. Whit was just telling me about the app." I stifle a laugh with my hand.

This is where I should probably just leave and let them do their coupledom crap, but hearing a little praise about my sex toys takes precedence after the shitty week I've had.

"Classic. Seriously, Len. You have a gift." Cole smacks his hand on the table, rearing back in laughter.

"What am I missing?" Lucas asks, taking a swig of the beer that the waitress just brought over.

Like I said, we're here a lot.

"You didn't give them one?" Cole asks me, as though it's the latest toy on the market that everyone can get their hands on. That's the idea, but capitalist motherfuckers are making it difficult.

"Nope, just you two," I say.

"Oh, you gotta give him one." Cole swings his gaze to Lucas. "There's this toy that you have the girl wear and then an app controls it. Whitney practically had splinters under her fingernails from gripping the table so hard." He's like a kid who's met his idol, pulling out his phone, demonstrating the pressure to Lucas.

"How did you get her to wear it?" Lucas asks and Cole eyes me.

I shrug. "I told Whit that it was just supposed to keep you mildly stimulated throughout the night so there'd be more urgency when you got home."

Tahlia's wide gaze shifts to Whitney. "You wore it when you were having dinner at your grandparents?"

"I was trying it out. I didn't believe it would work and Cole was pushing me to wear it." She glares at him from the corner of her eyes and he wraps his arm around her shoulders.

"It worked." His eyes light up and the entire table laughs.

I love my friends and their boyfriends are great extensions to our group. Each one I'd have picked out for them myself.

"I want one," Lucas pipes up like I'm the ice cream truck and he's six.

"Invest, Mr. President." I love referring to Lucas like that because he hates it. But c'mon. He's now the president of what was Tahlia's family's sausage business. The jokes practically write themselves.

I cock my eyebrow at him and he glances to Cole. "Did you?"

Cole shrugs. "I believe in enhancing my sexual experiences." Cole acts all proper, or Webberly, as I refer to it. Cole comes from San Francisco royalty—the Webber family.

Lucas looks at Tahlia and then to me. "Sold. Come by the office tomorrow."

I smile. No way would I ever let my best friend's boyfriends give me money. Money and friends do not mix.

"Don't forget the toy though." His eyes light up and Tahl elbows him in the ribs.

He slides closer to her, his lips moving to her ear and whispering. Whatever he's saying, she's smiling and her face is getting closer to the shade of her blouse again.

"Care to share?" I ask.

Tahlia shakes her head.

"So, the movie." Lucas changes the topic just like she did and I smile because he knows Tahlia so well. No way she wants to discuss her sexcapades in front of all of us.

"I'm out," I say, standing up and grabbing my portfolio from the table.

"Why?" Whitney whines.

All their eyes are fixed on me.

"Because I'm sick of being the spare." I eye Slade at the bar and pat Cole's shoulder. "I like your new bartender." I waggle my eyebrows and he laughs.

"He's under strict rules not to touch the customers," Cole adds, his face too serious for his own good.

Back in the day, Cole was a bigger player than Dan Bilzerian. Haven't heard of him? Google and you'll understand my point.

"Oh, Cole. You should set a better example then." I smile sweetly between him and Whitney.

Whitney laughs because I've got him there. The two of them met while Cole was working the bar. He rolls his eyes, shaking his head.

I laugh and walk away, sidling up to the bar as two stealthy blue eyes peer into mine.

"What can I get you?" Slade asks, his voice deep, gruff and powerful.

I lean forward so only he can hear me. His arms rest on top of the bar, the wood holding his weight so he can get closer. "You, naked in my bed. Oh, and of course your cock in my mouth."

chapter TWO

I'LL GIVE SLADE SOME credit. He waited until Cole left before he followed me to the bathroom. Even then, he stopped at second base, not allowing me to detour him further when I pulled him into the stall.

Later, when the redhead said someone should leave early since it was so dead, he jumped at the chance, hopping over the bar, taking my hand in his and escorting me out of the Thirsty Monk. I like a man who takes action.

On the taxi ride back to his place, his tongue was lodged in my throat, his hands up my shirt. Things were hot and I was more than eager to feel his rippled stomach under his white t-shirt.

"You're so damn hot," he whispers now in the stairwell of his apartment building.

I jump in his arms, his hands gripping my ass, mine fisting his long dark strands.

Our lips lock and he weaves us from one side of the wall to the other on our way up the staircase. He's strong and that turns me on more than the bulge in his pants. Stopping outside a door, I unwind my legs and slither down his body until my feet are planted on the ground. His lips stay on mine while he fumbles with the lock.

"Finally," I say, sliding past him into his apartment.

I take no time to investigate the place. As long as the door is locked behind us, I'm good with whatever. The door slams shut, his fingers hook in my belt loop, pulling me toward him, and when my lips land on his, his fingers are unbuttoning my jeans. My own fingers slide down his white t-shirt, feeling the ripples of his abs while I match his objective—to become unclothed as fast as possible.

He pushes my pants down along with my panties and I toe out of my flats and shimmy my jeans off the rest of the way. I'm hot and ready.

His hands mold to my bare hips as he backs us until I fall into a soft couch. Standing above me, he slides his fingers down his zipper. I lick my dry lips, waiting for the glimpse of the cock I'll feast on tonight.

The bulge in his underwear isn't as big as I felt grinding against me up the stairs, but maybe he's not fully hard yet, which I'm more than happy to lend a helping hand with.

Look, I should tell you now that I make no apologies for my open sexuality. I'm a single, adult female—why shouldn't I enjoy getting it on as much and as often as I'm able? Because some man tells me it makes me a slut? Or because some uptight woman who doesn't know her clit from a light switch thinks it's wrong to enjoy sex?

Screw that. I don't mess with taken guys and as long as everyone's a willing participant then I'm down for a little fun. And hopefully an orgasm. Because who doesn't love those?

Anyway, where were we?

I eye Slade with my sultry blues, widening my legs for him to stand between them. Hooking my fingers on the waistband of his boxers, I slide them down his legs as I promise him with my eyes how much fun we're going to have tonight. The anticipation to feel what I'm working with is too strong and so I glance down, finding a thin penis that gives no tingle between my legs. His fingers weave through my short dark hair and he urges my head back up to his eyes.

I'm sure this guy has been the running joke in his locker room and I'm not some bully or tease, so I plaster on a smile. It's not how big it is, it's how he uses it . . . right?

"Go ahead," he says, grinding his hips toward me so that his dick might reach my lips—if it had another three inches.

I size him up again, trying to figure out how a guy over six feet, with huge muscles and a ripped stomach, could have such a disappointing package. He's fully hard now, the tiny mushroom facing upward.

My hands are shaking slightly as I wrap them around him, my fingers overlapping, and I pump.

He groans. "That's it. Mouth, you little bitch," he says, shaking his hips again, and my hand unclenches before I squeeze so hard he falls to his knees.

Now, I'm all for dirty talk and the right guy can boss me around in the bedroom with zero complaints from me. But there's a way to make it hot and there's the douche way. Slade is being a douchebag.

"I don't take directions well," I comment, leaning back to wait for him to apologize.

"Oh, you want to play hard to get?" A knowing smile crosses his lips and I raise my eyebrows.

I think we're on different pages.

"My pussy is spread-eagle on your couch. I don't think this is exactly hard to get."

He grabs my arm, urging me back up to the edge of the couch, and he places my hand on his pencil penis.

"I promise, I'll make it worth your while." He shimmies

forward, and for the first time in years, I'm not horny with a dick in front of my face.

"Let me guess." I stand up, making him stumble back. With his pants still around his ankles he can't get his footing and ends up falling to the floor, but he sits there, not attempting to pull his pants up.

Grabbing my own pants and panties from the floor, I put them on while continuing to talk. "I'll blow you and you'll expect me to swallow, which I'm not opposed to, but then you'll tell me you need some time to recover. Have you never heard of ladies first?" I button my pants, slipping on my flats, finally able to look around the space I'm standing in the middle of.

Doilies on the table.

Vases of flowers.

Little ceramic statues of kids.

Flower fabric couches with pink drapes.

"Oh. My. God. Where are we?" I ask and step to the door, placing my hand on the doorknob.

"My place," he answers with a shrug.

"And who else's?" I narrow my eyes.

His gaze casts down for a moment but then meets mine with a ring of fury around his pupils.

"You're just a tease. Girls like you think you have so much control, but all you are is some whore guys use to get their rocks off." He stands to his feet, pulling up his pants.

"If you'd treated me with any respect, I would have been a sure thing. As far as being a whore, I'm going to let that slide since your hard-on probably isn't giving you enough testosterone. But let me be very clear." I step closer to him, staring up so that he knows how serious I am. "You ever disrespect me again and I will wrap that pencil-thin penis of yours around a twenty-pound weight and let go."

He laughs, a hollow and overly sarcastic one. "I'd rather

have a small dick than be the pass-around girl."

Before I can stop myself, I cock my arm back and punch him in the face. He holds his cheek and points to the door.

"Get the fuck out!" he yells and a door clicks from down the hall.

"Stevie?" an elderly lady says.

"Go back to bed, Gram."

"Is everything okay?" She rounds the corner in a pink night coat and her hair in rollers. Her eyes widen at me and then she scowls at Stevie, aka Slade. "I told you no girls." Her shaking finger points to him.

"I'm out," I say, springing the door open and leaving the apartment before Granny gives both of us a beatdown. The door shuts behind me and I hear him apologizing and her yelling.

Crisis averted.

I hit the street and try to decipher where I am exactly, and notice that the night must still be young because couples are walking hand in hand down the street with takeout containers. Another group of people look like they're just getting the night started as they file out of their apartments.

I take a few steps to the corner crossroads and read the street signs. Slade's grandma lives way too close to me and I hope I never cross her in a dark alley.

After walking a few blocks I find my usual Starbucks and open the door, allowing the warm, comforting smell of coffee to surround me. I wish I had my sketchbook. Drawing has always been how I relieve stress. Maybe I can design a toy that could help men like Slade in the Nanometer Peter club.

I head to the restroom first to use the facilities and then wait in line. Most people ahead of me order iced teas and other drinks that aren't hot or loaded with caffeine.

Missy, the usual barista, smiles up to me when I step up. "Bad night again?" she asks, one side of her lips cocking up.

So I may come here too often after a bad night. Which seems to be happening way too often lately.

"Needle dick," I deadpan.

She cringes and a deep laugh rumbles from behind me. I glance over my shoulder, finding a man. I grant him a half smile and he winks, his lips only turning half wattage.

"Grande black," I say.

"Name?" She arches her eyebrow, waiting to see what's coming.

"Katniss Everdeen."

She laughs, punching it in, and I hand her the cash. "I volunteer as tribute," she says and we both share a laugh now. "It'll be right up."

"Thanks, Missy."

I tuck the cash back into my purse and pull my phone out to distract myself, checking my Facebook notifications. Whitney and Tahlia have both been posting about their date nights. A twinge of jealousy flares and once again I'm reminded that one thing isn't like the other when it comes to my group of friends.

I mean, they'll forever be my friends, but once they get married and start having kids, we probably won't have much in common. Pretty soon, I'll just be the crazy aunt who shows up at birthday parties and all the kids wonder who I am. No, I promise myself. They'll always know me and I'll be the cool aunt who gives them expensive gifts because I can afford it. I'll be the one they look up to because I travel all over the world, live life by my own rules and have affairs with exotic men.

The man behind me leans against the counter and I glance up to see that he's on his phone. He's smiling as he types away. His suit jacket hangs open and his tie is loosely undone, but his vest is still buttoned. Who still wears a full three-piece suit? I have to admit though, it looks hot as fuck on him. His hand rises and he weaves his fingers through his already dishevelled brown hair. The sparkling of cufflinks catches my eye and I wonder what kind of job he has that he's this dressed up. Aren't most companies going to business casual nowadays?

I picture him behind a boardroom table barking out orders and the mental image of him having a very powerful job ignites a tingling between my legs. I bet this guy is packing and would know how to dominate me in the bedroom.

"Katniss Everdeen." Missy's singsong voice rings out.

Before I turn my attention to her and my coffee, the guy looks up and our eyes meet. A smile plays on his lips and I'm not sure if it's from the texts he's receiving or if it's for me, but no matter what, it lights up his face, raising him up the attractive meter until the bell rings on top.

The tingling turns into an ache down south.

I snap my eyes away from him and grab my coffee. "Have a great night, Missy."

"See you tomorrow," she says and I nod because I'm here at least once if not twice a day.

Moving over to the counter to pour in my Splenda and milk, I try not to feel the small hairs on the back of neck snap to attention. Nor do I admit that I feel his eyes on me. Instead, I busy myself pouring and stirring. If he wants me, he can make the first move.

"Peeta Mellark." Missy's voice rings out again and then she chokes out a laugh.

I whip my head around and find a set of hazel eyes set on me with arched eyebrows. The amused smile on his lips is even more prominent than seconds earlier. My gaze whips over to Missy and she's smiling from ear to ear, pointing to his back. She wraps her arms around herself and kisses the air. I roll my eyes and when the guy turns around to see where I'm looking, she quickly straightens her back and pretends she's organizing the straw compartment.

"Have a good night." She uses her sweet-as-pie voice and the man nods, stepping toward me.

I swallow the lump in my throat. I have no time to try to figure out why I'm suddenly nervous. No matter how hard I try to relax, I can't control my heartbeat. Only five steps separate us so I don't have time to think about why this guy is bringing out a side to me that rarely, if ever, makes an appearance.

I wait for him to say something, but he doesn't.

Instead, he slides next to me at the condiment stand and a waft of his cologne breezes past me. The scent is intoxicating. It's musky and all man. I cross my ankles, pressing my thighs together.

He busies himself with the sugar, no milk, and he stirs it for an unusually long time. His phone chirps as he's placing the lid on top of his coffee.

I'm about to stop him, but something holds me back and I cower down, fascinated by his hands. Strong and manicured. Never would I have thought manicured nails would turn me on.

All movement stops and I look up to find his eyes on me. He slowly appraises me from top to bottom and back before he leans in, his lips only an inch away from my ear. Our bodies aren't touching and somehow that's hotter than if he'd pulled me into him.

"I thought you'd want to know . . ."

He trails off and the scent of his cologne has my eyes drifting closed while I wait with anticipation to hear the end of his sentence.

" . . . you have toilet paper stuck on your shoe."

He pulls away and my eyes snap wide open. He winks and before I can say anything, the door chime rings and he's eyeing me through the window as he talks on the phone and I frantically try to remove the toilet paper with my other shoe.

God, no wonder he was staring at me.

"Holy shit," Missy says, her hand over her heart.

I grip the counter behind me to stay upright—half from embarrassment and half because my knees are still weak. "Who was that?"

"I think he's your Peeta Mellark," she says with a dreamy edge to her voice as she leans over the counter.

I shake my head. "Oh, Missy. Lennon Hart doesn't get to have a Peeta Mellark. She just gets to screw around with a lot of Gale Hawthornes."

One thing I can't deny, he turned me into a fumbling mess and he only uttered a handful of words. Now there's a man who can boss me around in bed.

chapter THREE

I WALK THROUGH THE doors to Venture Bank and wait for the receptionist to stop typing and actually look at me. Eventually, she takes the pen out of her mouth, her fingers stop moving and she fixates on me. Her gaze roams me up and down.

Yeah, I know I'm hot, but I'm over my lesbian phase so she can look but she can't touch.

"How can I help you?" She uses her pen to scratch her scalp under her pile of auburn hair.

"I'm here to see Jacob Hart."

She eyes my t-shirt with disdain and I roll my eyes. She's probably some stuck-up, snobby woman who's never been fucked properly in her life.

"And you are?" She picks up her phone, her fingers poised to dial Jacob.

"Lennon Hart," I say and her back straightens, a smile replacing the scowl. "His sister."

"Oh, let me ring him."

"Thank you."

I take a seat in the small waiting area with four chairs and an array of magazines. I've never been to my brother's office before, but it's a nice place. He's vice-president and about as opposite of me as you can get. Everyone's always thought twins must be alike, but Jacob and I couldn't be on farther ends of the spectrum.

Just as I expect, he comes out himself to greet me.

"Thank you, Mrs. Mendez," he says with a smile and then sets his eyes on me. "Lennon." He nods his head, turns on his heels and walks back to his office.

"Thank you, Mrs. Mendez," I say sweetly and she gives me the polite smile, placing the pen back in her mouth and typing away.

Jacob waves and speaks pleasantries as we weave our way through the desks until he reaches his office. He opens his door and waits for me to go in first.

"No hug?" I ask, plopping down on a chair in front of his desk.

He shuts the door and rounds his desk to sit in his enormous chair. Overcompensating much?

"Is the big chair to make up for other inadequacies?" I ask and his eyes bore into mine with no reflection of the humour I was going for.

Debbie Downer.

"I've told you never to come to my office." He clasps both his hands together in front of him.

"Oh, come on, bro, you know you love me." I cross my legs and shrug my shoulders as if telling him, *This is me and you need to accept it.*

"I do love you, Len." He looks out his glass window. "But this is my place of business and I worked my ass off to get where I am. The people here don't really understand people like you."

"People like me?" I'm starting to be offended between my

brother and that jackass Slade.

"Look at you." His hand floats down my body. "Your skin is a damn art show. Your jeans are ripped. Your toes have skulls painted on them. And the shirt. What the hell is that? A rooster with a unicorn horn." He shakes his head with the same look he used to have when our mom forced him eat oatmeal.

"First of all, my tattoos are an expression of my personality. Ripped jeans are in, Mr. Brooks Brothers. As for my shirt, it's a unicorn cock. You wouldn't understand, you're a guy." I uncross my legs and bring them up to the seat so I'm cross-legged.

"Unicorn cock? Is that the name of one of your new sex toys?"

Actually, that's not a bad idea.

Jacob's phone rings and he picks it up. "Please hold all calls, Mrs. Mendez." He listens for a second. "Tell Jasper I'll call him in five minutes. Thank you." He hangs up.

"Jasper Banks?" I ask with an innocent bat of my eyes.

"No," he deadpans and I can't help but be hurt that my brother is trying to lie to me. Isn't that some sort of twin no-no?

"Mom taught us not to lie, Jacob," I remind him and he rolls his eyes. Jasper isn't a common name like Mike, so I know it's got to be the guy who mentored my brother out of college.

"Len, you are not getting Jasper Banks' phone number," he says with annoyance. Jacob let it slip once that Jasper had moved on from conventional loans and he's a partner at a venture capital firm now. I may have bothered him for an introduction a few times. The difference this time is that I'm sober and not rambling on about how my family doesn't understand my vision.

"Then why don't you invest in my business?" I ask him, for the millionth time. There was one week I messaged him ten times a day. Needless to say, he blocked my number after five days. Then I told my mom and the next day she made him unblock me in case I had an emergency and couldn't reach him.

I know how to work my family.

"I've told you before, I can't have my name associated with something like that. It's a bunch of dildos and vibrators. Use your head." He taps his temple to drive the point home.

"Now you're getting mean." I act upset, although I'm used to Jacob—this is him. He's strait-laced and above board while I'm crazy town soaked in a vat of gasoline.

His shoulders sag, the need to never see me upset setting in. It's been that way since we were eight and he pushed me off a swing and I broke my arm. He'll forever feel guilt for that. Not that I don't use that guilt to my advantage every now and then, like right now.

"Listen, I know you want to start this company, but I don't understand. The tattoo shop does great. And if you remember, I gave you the first loan for that place."

My feet drop to the floor and he stands, making his way around his desk and sitting down next to me. "Len, I believe in you, but you have to understand I can't exactly approve your loan here when I was just promoted to VP. How would that look? Give me some time and I'll see if I can figure something out."

I look up to technically my younger brother by six minutes, who constantly acts like my older brother. "Why won't you just give me Jasper's number? He might be interested."

He shakes his head and releases a sigh.

A knock on the door interrupts us.

"Come in," my brother says and in walks a woman close to my age. Her wrap dress is flowery and flows nicely over her petite frame. I notice that she has a matching pair of flats on. I also notice that she's looking at my brother in a way that isn't entirely professional. She's cute and I decide right there that I like her.

"Oh, I'm sorry," she says, her gaze tipping down when she spots me. "I didn't know you were with someone." Her eyes meet mine and she's appraising me, but I see no judgment there. I snap my head in the direction of Jacob, whose gaze hasn't left her since she opened the door.

"It's okay, Megan, this is Lennon, my sister."

The despair in her eyes fades and she walks over to me with a bounce in her step, her hand in front of my face within seconds.

"I'm Megan Channing," she says.

I shake her hand. "Lennon."

"It's so great to meet you. Jacob doesn't say much about his family, but you guys have the same nose." She looks from me to Jacob and back.

I take a quick glance at Jacob's desk and spot his cell phone sitting there and an idea begins to form. I lean back in my chair. "What do you do here, Megan?" I ask, knowing just how to get under Jacob's skin.

"I'm a teller."

"A teller? So Jacob is your boss?" I ask and her lips dip. For a second, I feel bad for putting her in the middle of my sibling fuckery.

"Yeah." She nods, appearing a little unsure.

I look at Jacob and raise my eyebrows. "Interesting," I say and he huffs.

"Give me a second, okay?" he says to me and waves Megan over to the door.

His phone chirps on the desk and I lean forward, seeing Jasper Banks' name light up on the screen.

Seriously, this is going to be easier than getting Professor Hendred to change my grade freshman year of college. Don't judge.

"Don't," Jacob warns when I reach for the phone.

Damn it. My brother knows me well.

"Megan, just give me a few minutes," he whispers.

I stand, pretending like I'm getting ready to go. I look from the two secret lovers to the phone. Jacob has his back to me now, his hands on her arms. Seems there's trouble in paradise.

I press the home button on the phone and the phone lights up, displaying a few texts he's gotten this morning. Boy, Megan sure has been busy on her phone this morning. Jasper is the text at the top and I slide the phone closer to me to catch the words *Richmond's at eight tonight*. Well, that was easy.

Jacob swipes the phone and tucks it into his pocket. "You're not getting his phone number," he says, his blue eyes that match my own piercing into mine.

I roll my eyes. "Just making sure you didn't miss any important phone calls." I turn my head to find Megan's no longer here. "Screwing the help, Jacob?" I shake my head. "I had higher expectations of you."

"Don't you have a dildo to sell?" he says and I pick up my purse.

"I think I'll go hit Megan up. See if she's in the market." My footsteps move away from his desk and he follows me, probably making sure I actually leave.

"Don't you worry about her, she's more than satisfied." He smiles and I'm surprised he didn't grab his junk in his hands.

"From what I remember . . ." I don't actually say anything but scrunch up my nose and shake my head while I raise just my pinkie finger.

"We were five the last time you saw my dick," he says, reaching past me to open the door. "Bye, sis."

"Let's get together tonight. I can get to know Megan better?" I ask.

His unamused eyes linger on mine again. Seriously, Megan needs to do her job better because it's obvious that my brother needs to get his rocks off. He's way too uptight.

"I'm taking Megan out for her birthday. Just the two of us."

"Where?" I ask, acting the part of the caring sister. I push aside the guilt I feel at knowing I just want to be able to pinpoint his whereabouts this evening.

"It's private. Listen, I'm bringing her to Dad's retirement party. Run interference, will you?" He changes the direction of conversation, but I know my brother wouldn't take a girl he's interested in to a bar, which means I can *accidentally* meet Jasper tonight without worrying about running into him.

"Sure thing, little brother." I squeeze his cheek and he groans. "See you."

He shuts the door and I start walking. My phone dings before I'm even through the doors of the bank.

Jacob: Love you. I'll look into another option.

I smile.

Me: Love you. No problem, I think I might have a lead.

A cynical laugh escapes from my throat and my phone dings again.

Jacob: In the last minute?

Me: See you next week.

Jacob: Lennon.

I laugh again because he knows me too well. Climbing into my unicorn van, I turn up Eminem and pull away from the curb.

Tonight, I'll finally meet one Mr. Jasper Banks and he's going to be the one to solve all my problems.

chapter FOUR

"I NEED A NICE pant suit. One that screams serious, conservative, but a little sexy, too." I push past Tahlia and into her condo.

Lucas looks up from the television.

"Hey, don't mind me, just grabbing something. The Cincinnati bowtie can commence in ten minutes." I wave to Lucas.

"I don't even want to know what that is," Tahl says behind me.

"Where's my toy?" he asks and I dig into my purse, tossing it to him.

He examines the packaging with a huge smile on his face then throws it back to Tahlia. "Put it on, baby." His smile could compete with a kid's on Christmas morning. He pulls his phone out while we leave the room.

I walk into Tahlia's bedroom and she rolls her eyes at me. Tossing it on the mattress, she moves to her closet, stepping in.

She and Lucas moved in together last month and with his income, they can afford more, which means she finally has a walk-in closet. Lucas' suits line the left side and her dresses and blouses the right. Every high-priced high heel is perched on shelves in the back next to Lucas's mismatch of sneakers and loafers.

"Must drive you crazy."

She follows my line of vision to the shoes. "We fight about two things. Family dinners at my parents' house and that." She points and her face scrunches up as though it smells like a garbage truck in New York City on a hot summer day.

"He doesn't like the fam, huh?" I ask, my hands digging through her clothes.

"No, he does. He doesn't mind going. It's me. He's found some common bond with my dad and it's so annoying." She huffs and pulls out a black silk suit.

Now I'm the one scrunching up my nose. She hangs it back up. "That's awesome that they get along, Tahl."

I truly am happy that everything turned out so great for her, and yet that twinge of jealousy unexpectedly stabs me in the chest again.

What the hell? I'm happy, too. I don't even want what she has.

She shrugs. "So, what's this for?"

I sit down on her closet floor. Yes, it's that big.

"I'm meeting with an investor tonight, but it's at a bar."

Her eyes narrow and she pulls a light pink suit out, pairing it with a navy blouse.

I shake my head again and she huffs and hangs it back up.

"A bar? Are they legit?" She rifles through her clothes some more.

"Oh, he's legit. He just doesn't know I'm coming."

Her eyes shoot to mine. A look of worry crosses over her face.

"Relax. It's fine." I hop up and start rooting through her clothing. She leans against their built-in dresser in the middle of the closet.

"I don't want you to be disappointed." Her voice is soft and I should expect nothing less. She's my best friend. "I was talking to Lucas—"

"No, Tahl." I raise my hand and squash the topic of any of my friends helping me.

"Come on, Len. We're friends and we want to help. Lucas has the money," she pleads, but I won't hear of it.

I have faith in my ability and this company, but there are too many factors that could go wrong. If this fails, I refuse to let my friends take a hit in any way.

"I appreciate it. I do, but no." I pull out a Chanel pant suit. "Can I borrow this?"

"Of course, anything." She crosses her arms, clearly not understanding why I won't take her boyfriend's money.

My shoulders deflate and I wait for her eyes to reach mine. "Listen, Tahl. I need to do this on my own."

She nods. "Okay." She takes the pant suit from me, placing it on the dresser. Taking my hands, she squeezes. "Never be too proud to ask for help though, okay?"

I nod this time and our conversation ends with an understanding that nothing will change. I'm not taking her or her boyfriend's money.

"Babe? Are you wearing it?" Lucas hollers from the other room and when we enter the living room, his finger is on the app screen.

She playfully smacks him in the head and his shorter, now gelled hair doesn't move. "We have a guest."

"Lennon's not a guest," he jokes and I sit down on the chair across from Lucas. He places his phone down.

"Oh, I have the best necklace you should wear with that outfit." Tahlia rushes back into her bedroom, leaving Lucas and I alone.

Lucas sits up, resting his elbows on his knees, and glances

back to their bedroom door. "So, Lennon. I've been thinking."

I place my hand up in the air. "Your girlfriend beat you to it."

His eyebrows scrunch and for the first time I notice how perfect they are. I wonder if he threads or waxes. Maybe he got laser hair removal?

"I want to invest. I need to invest my money somewhere. Might as well be your company."

I appreciate my friends wanting to help me out, and it would be an easy to accept Lucas's and Cole's money, but no. I have my pride.

"I'm meeting an investor tonight." I hold up my crossed fingers. "Let's hope he loves sex toys as much as you and Cole."

Lucas picks up his phone, presses the app and Tahlia comes out holding the vibrating toy in her hand.

"Seriously, Lucas. Wait until Lennon leaves." She tosses it on the table and I wonder if she'll ever wear it for him. Although I'm fairly sure they have a kinky sex life behind closed doors. Tahl just likes to act like she can take it or leave it, but I can't imagine there's ever any headache nights with Lucas.

He laughs and she comes over, handing me the necklace.

"Who's the whale?" Lucas asks, crossing his leg on his ankle and placing his free hand on Tahlia's leg.

"His name is Jasper Banks," I say and Lucas' eyes light up.

"Seriously?" he asks. Tahlia and I both look at him, not understanding his reaction.

"Yeah." My voice sounds small. "Do you know him?"

He nods and a smile crosses his lips. "I went to school with him. He was a year older than me, but we were in the same fraternity."

Damn it. I didn't have to sneak behind my brother's back. I had a connection to Jasper all along.

"How perfect. Lennon, tell him you know Lucas." Tahlia practically bounces in her chair.

"You've already pitched?" Lucas asks.

I bite my lip and shake my head.

"Why are you meeting in a bar then?" he asks and I'm starting to feel a little foolish about my plan.

"Um. He doesn't know who I am, but he was my brother's mentor. I saw a text he sent to my brother and I'm going to the bar hoping to corner him."

Lucas laughs again and though I've always loved how easy-going Lucas is, right now I want to sew his lips shut.

"You know he's a control freak, right? Not to mention a pompous ass? He'd shred you in front of a crowd of people without even blinking," Lucas says.

I slump back in my chair. "He's a jerk?" I ask because I don't know much about him other than the fact that he invests in companies others don't. I mean, he got a kitchen gadget on the HSN and made the inventor a shit-ton of money.

Lucas nods and Tahlia's excitement dims significantly. Her eyes bore into mine, silently asking me to allow Lucas to give me the money.

"Well, I can be a bitch and if he doesn't like the idea and tries to embarrass me, he'll have a challenge on his hands." I stand up and drape the pant suit over my arm.

"Be careful, Lennon," Tahlia says, unwrapping herself from Lucas and walking me to the door.

"Hold up." Lucas stands and pats Tahlia's ass to get her to slide out of the way. "Let me walk you to the elevator."

Lucas grabs the door and Tahlia leans in, giving me a hug.

"Good luck. Not like you need it because you're going to knock this Jasper guy off his ass when he sees you." Her arms tighten right before she lets go. "Call me when you're done."

"I will. Thanks for the pant suit and I'll get it dry-cleaned."

She giggles and shakes her head. "No, you won't, but it's nice that you think you will."

I roll my eyes because she's probably right.

Lucas walks with me side by side to the elevators. I'm about to tell him I don't need a babysitter, but when my hand moves to hit the button he stops me.

"Lennon, I meant what I said about investing. If you're worried about putting Tahl and I in a bind if the company fails, you don't need to." He looks pained, as though he doesn't want to throw his eight-figure bank account in my face.

Jesus, what if it's eight figures? I should get Jacob to do some digging. I shake my head, immediately dismissing the thought.

"It's not that I think you two would be eating ramen noodles for the rest of your life if it doesn't work out. Money and friends don't mix."

He nods, his eyes focused on the ground. "Let me come with you tonight. I'll introduce you. We'll act like it was a coincidence."

Of course Tahlia fell in love with this man. How could she not?

I shake my head. "No, Lucas, but thank you."

His shoulders falter and he tucks his hands into the pockets of his worn-in jeans. "Okay." He looks resigned.

This is the difference between him and Tahlia—he doesn't push, which I appreciate.

"Thank you, though."

I move my hand to press the elevator button and this time he allows me, but continues to stand by my side. The elevator dings and when I enter, he holds the door.

"At least use me as a reference. Tell him you know me and I swear by your products." He flashes a panty-melting smile of white teeth. Well, panty-melting for Tahl, not me.

"Are you willing to write a review?" I joke, but he nods his head.

"If this new toy gives me as much fun as it did Cole and

Whitney, hell, I'll buy you a billboard."

The doors move to close and I wave.

"Bye, Lucas, thank you."

"Good luck," he says, waving back.

Pompous control freak or not, Jasper Banks better watch out, because he's never seen the likes of Lennon Hart.

chapter
FIVE

I CLIMB OUT OF the Uber in my Chanel pant suit and heels. Well, okay, Tahlia's Chanel pant suit and heels, but tonight I'm making this outfit work for me. I hate the fact that I'm changing myself into someone else, but this is my last resort.

I've never been to this bar before and from the outside it appears way higher-end than I thought it'd be. As far as I know, Jacob doesn't really spend his money on frivolous things, which makes him a good banker, I suppose. He's more of a beer guy than a guy who can recite the wine menu. Sure, he's stuffy, but not nose-in-the-air snooty.

I step through the door and the inside of the place is dark with crimson walls and black tables and chairs. Businessmen fill the seats with jackets strewn on the chairs behind them. The gleam from their expensive watches and cufflinks sneaks out from under the sleeves of their suit jackets as they pick up their highball glasses that contain alcohol without any ice. The number of women in here is low. I count only five to the men's twenty. They too are dressed up for the business world and I thank God

I made one good choice and borrowed an outfit from Tahlia.

I sway my hips on the way to the bar and slide onto a stool. The bartender, who is probably a few years younger than I am, approaches me immediately. God, I wish I could take off my jacket, but that would leave me in a sleeveless blouse and I'm not sure this crowd would appreciate my tattoos. Once again, I'd be in a situation where 'one of these things is not like the other'. Cue the *Sesame Street* theme song.

"What can I get you?" He leans across the bar, invading my personal space. He's cute and normally I wouldn't mind, but I'm trying to be Miss Proper here. Miss Proper doesn't flirt with the cute bartender while she's on a mission to save her not-even-a-real-business-yet business.

"Scotch. Neat," I order and he nods, and places a glass on the bar, pouring the scotch in front of me. "Thank you." I slide my twenty across the table and he leaves it there to go help out another customer.

I sneak a few peeks of the group over the rim of my glass, trying to figure out which one is Jasper. It's seven fifty, so technically there could be ten more minutes until he arrives, but I doubt a man like Jasper Banks is ever late. Nor does he accept tardiness in others, I bet. I've never met Jasper and when I Googled him, no pictures come up. How in this day in age do you not have one picture on social media? Sure, there's plenty about him, but not even a picture at a charity gala. Does the man not believe in giving back? Nothing private is mentioned about his life and everything is strictly about his business. So I search for a guy around Lucas' age, only a few years older than myself.

All the blue-hairs I omit. That leaves me with ten men still in the running. Unless he's prematurely gray. It could happen. I knew a guy with a full head of gray at the age of thirty. I used to call him the Silver Fox.

From my vantage point I can't get a really good look at

all of the men and I resign myself to the fact that I'm going to have to work the room. Each of these men looks like matching game cards in a game of memory. Expensive suit, yes. Gelled hair, yes. Flashy watch, yes.

The bartender slides the twenty my way.

"Ladies' night, drinks are on the house." He winks and I'm unsure if that's just for me or for every woman.

I mean, shouldn't there be a sign outside stating this very convenient fact? Maybe because this is such a classy joint, they let word of mouth do the work rather than an advertisement that could drag in *any* women to their place. Me being the perfect example.

"Thank you," I say, tucking the money in my purse and then handing him a five-dollar bill.

He nods and the door behind me opens. I turn in my stool to watch a bunch of women walk in, all done up—dresses, hair, jewelry adorning every limb and more make-up than a Mary Kay factory.

This group of clones is a little odd and why do they arrive together? Maybe it's a bachelorette party.

I check my phone and see there's five more minutes until eight o'clock. I need to be prepared to make a good first impression.

I take a deep breath and knock back the remainder of my Scotch. The friendly bartender fills it up immediately. He's very attentive.

At eight o'clock on the dot, a man comes into the bar from the back, locks the front door, then claps his hands to get everyone's attention. All heads turn in his direction and as I examine all the other faces, none of them hold any surprise, as I'm sure mine does. They're all the opposite—smiling, the women on the edge of their chairs, the men putting their jackets back on.

What am I missing?

The man in charge looks to be in his fifties with gray hair and beard. He glances around the room and spots me. "Looks like we have some new people tonight."

Fear grips my throat that he's going to single me out and ask me something I can't answer. Oh, shit, is this a speakeasy or some private party that I'm crashing? Just then someone knocks on the glass door. The man turns to open it and shakes hands with the person who's entering.

You have to be shitting me.

In walks the guy from Starbucks the other night.

Makes sense. This is definitely the right kind of place and people for him. He never looks around the room, but takes a seat at a table with two other guys. They all shake hands and say their hellos before returning their attention to the man in front.

"I'm fairly sure that's everyone for this evening." He claps his hands again. "For the new members, I'm Gage, and I'm your speed-dating leader for tonight."

Speed dating?

Umm . . .

"The tables are set up through the curtain." Gage motions with his hands to a curtain-covered doorway on the far side of the bar. "Rules are the same, guys stay, girls hop. You have five minutes at each table. First names only. No specifics as to where you live or work. There's a list of questions to ask printed out on the table in case conversation proves to be a challenge. Fill out the questionnaire sheet at your last table and come back out here. We'll announce any matches after and you're more than welcome to find out more about one another at that time." He waves his hands frantically in the air to get everyone moving once he's done speaking.

I stand, figuring this is my time to cut and run.

"Um, Gage." I touch his arm and he slowly rotates his head my way. "I think I'm in the wrong bar," I say, ready to slide past him to the door.

"Oh, sweetie, I knew you hadn't registered, but we had a cancellation so why don't you stay? Free of charge." A gold cap emerges when he smiles. "There's a connection in the air tonight, I feel it."

I scoff. "I'm not really looking for a connection." From the corner of my eye I catch the man from Starbucks stand and he follows the crowd to the back. Why does a man like that need speed dating? "Can I ask you a question?" I lean closer and he does too, like he's the paparazzi and I'm about to tell him where Rihanna and Drake are out clubbing tonight.

"Anything."

"Is Jasper Banks here?"

I have to be at the wrong bar. Although I have no idea what he looks like, I can't imagine Jasper Banks would need to resort to speed dating.

A full-watt smile emerges on Gage's face and he nods. "He is. Do you know Jasper?"

The caterpillars turn into butterflies in my stomach. Finally.

"Could you point him out to me?" I ask and a devilish look gleams in his eyes.

He shakes his head.

"No?" I clarify, my own lips pressing into a straight line.

"You'll have to find out for yourself. Best way to do that will be to go in that room and take a seat at a table." He walks away and exits the room behind the curtain.

The bartender clears his throat and my gaze detours to him. "If you don't find what you're looking for in there, I'm free."

From the smug smile on his lips I'm guessing that he probably gets propositioned often and never goes home alone after one of these functions.

"I'm good, but thanks." I tuck my clutch under my arm, and my heels click on the floor while I head toward the curtain.

THE LIGHTING IS DIMMED back here. Black sofas line each wall, with small tables in front of them and chairs on the other side.

"Women take a seat at one of the booths," Gage instructs and I wonder why we have to be on the booth side.

All the women get giddy like it's picture time at prom while I sit down, cross my legs and lean back until this torture is over.

Once I find Jasper, I'll stalk him when he leaves and confront him then. I mean, surely blackmailing him that he does speed-dating will get him to invest.

"Now, men sit in the chair closest to you," Gage says and chairs slide out, men sit.

Lucky me, I get the best-looking one.

Kidding. Haven't you realized? Luck is not on my side.

I get the creepy older man with a pinkie ring. Do men still wear these? Then again, he could be Italian. I should play nice.

I sit up in my seat, folding my hands together and resting them on the table.

Gage walks over to a huge clock on the wall, presses a few buttons and then he screams, "Begin."

"Hi, I'm Bill." He places his hand out and I shake it.

"Lennon," I answer before figuring out I should have used a fake name.

"Is this your first time?" he asks. "I've never seen you here before."

I nod. "Yeah."

"There are usually more people here, but with the holiday . . ."

"Memorial Day?" I ask.

"I'm looking to take someone to my house in Napa this weekend. Have you been?" He smiles brightly.

At first I think creep—he's inviting me on a weekend trip after one minute, from what the clock says—but then I think it's sad really. He wants to share his life with someone and can't find the right person. I can see if that's something you want in your life and you can't find it, it would be upsetting.

"I have. It's beautiful. I can't imagine having a house there."

His eyes light up. "I have a winery. Small and serene."

"Do you bottle?" I ask. This fascinates me.

"Only enough for myself and friends. If you ever make it up there, check out Ginger's Winery."

"What a great name."

"I named it after my wife. She died five years ago." His eyes zoom down on the table. He is lonely.

My heart pricks. Here I am judging this man and he's been through more than I might ever be. *Food for thought, Lennon.*

"I'm so sorry," I say and the buzzer goes off before he can say anything.

He nods his head and I slide down the booth to the next guy. When I glance down the row of tables my eyes lock to a set of hazel ones that unglued me more than I care to admit last night. What I'm starting to notice as his humorous smile comes out to shine again, but this time he shoots me a wink that seriously has my engines purring down below. Who is this man?

The buzzer rings again and I have no choice but to look in front of me to my speed-dater companion. He's younger than the first guy, but looks way too strait-laced for me. He's J Crew to a tee. Sweater vest under his jacket and although he's got that swanky retro thing going for him, he opens his mouth and I think I just ran nails over a chalkboard.

"I'm Bec," he says. "Short for Beckett Humphrey III."

Rich boy and wants to stake his claim immediately.

"Lennon," I answer, shaking his hand. It's soft and moisturized. No pinkie ring, but a nice wedding ring tan line.

He catches me examining his hand and pipes up, "She divorced me two weeks after our honeymoon."

"When was your honeymoon?"

"Last month," he deadpans and I swear tears well up in his eyes.

"And you're here why?" Okay, so I probably should have taken the sarcastic tone out of my voice.

He crosses his arms. His jacket even comes with reinforced elbows. What are people doing with their elbows that they need extra fabric as back-up there? "I'm trying to forget the bitch."

Man, this is a hot mess of a place.

"Let me give you a hint. Head over to Sundowners. You need a hook-up, not a girlfriend. Play around there for a while and when you're finished, come back here to find your one and only," I offer and this information piques his interest. "Or there's always Tinder."

"I've known her since I was in seventh grade. She was my first." His whining mixed with screeching must be what a dog whistle sounds like to a dog.

"Oh, Bec, go get yourself some experience. The only way you're going to do that is if you fuck a truckload of different girls. You're young. At least you look young and now is the time to find out what you like."

His eyes widen and he's like a dog where he's all invested in what I'm saying right now.

"What are you doing after this?" he asks and my eyes veer over to Hazel Eyes'.

"I'm here on a different mission. Sorry."

"Oh," he says. I reach over and pat his hand.

Gage scrambles over, crouching down. "There's no touching except for one handshake in the beginning."

I nod. "Okay." I raise my hands in the air, but I'm thinking the conversation to my left is going stale because they're staring at us.

The buzzer rings. Thank God.

"Good luck, Bec," I say and slide.

The song *Slide to the right, slide to the left* rings in my head and I giggle a little myself.

"What's so funny?" my third date asks and I wave him off.

"Just a song in my head."

"Oh." He puts his head down and again my vision veers, but his eyes are set on the woman in front of him. Hazel Eyes is still two people down from me and I'm anxious to hear what's about to come out of his mouth.

Two more guys and two heartbreaking tales of scorned men later, I'm right next to him. He's my next date. I can practically feel my body buzzing being so close. He's given this date his full attention whereas the prior two our eyes locked on occasion. The playful smile on his lips is constantly teasing me. I wonder what I have to do to make it not so playful.

Instead of looking at him, I look to the woman across from him and next to me. She's a blonde, big breasts and flirtatious personality. No touching, my ass. I'm about to call Gage over because she's discreetly touched his arm no less than five times. Worse is the fact he hasn't pulled away. He could easily move his arms under the table, but he's like a statue, with an upturned smile the entire time. He likes her and for some reason a stab of the jealousy knife pierces my heart and it drops in the pit of my stomach.

It's then when the jealousy washes over me that I realize I'm worried about this man I know nothing about when Jasper is somewhere in this room.

Priorities, Lennon. Priorities. My eyes search out again and I figure out the next five guys after Hazel Eyes are Jasper's age and then after them it's all white hair. So in the next half hour I should have a face with a name.

Buzz.

"Pleasure meeting you." I nod like a Southern belle at the ball of a duke.

Slide to my left and his hand is already out before I can situate myself.

"Katniss." He nods.

"Peeta."

His hand is rougher than Bec's but softer than Bill's. No jewelry on his fingers, no tan lines that suggest he's recently divorced. An expensive-looking watch that Tahlia would probably know the going rate for. The thing that makes that ache between my thighs deeper is the skull-and-crossbones cuff links. This man is not who I've typecast him as. Today there's no vest under the jacket and he's sans tie. Part of me wonders if it's stuffed in his pocket and he came here right after work.

"So, are you willing to give me your real name?" he asks, his voice a deep rich tone that makes me think of barrels of whiskey.

"Lennon," I say before I think it would have been fun to play a game where we don't know each other's real names. "You?"

I ask because I'm not about to give him something for nothing.

"Jasper."

No fucking way. Shit just got real.

chapter SIX

THE SUAVE GUY FROM Starbucks is Jasper Banks. The one male specimen on this entire planet who has the capacity to unnerve me.

I situate myself in my seat, and his hazel eyes focus on my actions.

"Is it hot in here?" I fan my face with my hand. It wasn't hot a second ago, but suddenly I'm my grandma in the dead of winter standing in front of a fan to cool off.

"A tad, maybe." His lips quirk up, knowing exactly why I'm perspiring like a hooker in church. "So, Katniss?"

I laugh and he leans back in his chair, his hand lying out, his manicured nails tapping down on the black table.

"I was feeling extra feisty that night."

"Why?"

"I feel feisty a lot." I shrug, not willing to turn this man away by divulging I was with someone else.

Seriously, Lennon, get it together. Who cares?

Why do I care if he thinks I'm a slut? It might actually help with my cause—you know, experience.

The war inside of me continues to waver while he patiently waits for my real answer.

"Someone just got me angry."

"Ex?" he asks, his voice holding a hint of gruffness.

"I don't have any exes." The truth sneaks out.

"Surely you're not a virgin?" The light-hearted smile comes out to play once more.

"Do I look like a virgin?" I waggle my eyebrows.

There you go, girl, you're on your way back.

"If I thought you were a virgin, we wouldn't be here right now."

"Why is that?" I arch my eyebrow and a low chuckle escapes his throat. Damn, I want my tongue down that throat and I want to swallow down his groan.

"I don't think I could do what I want to do to you with a virgin." His tongue snakes out of his mouth and he wets both of his lips.

My shaking hand moves toward the glass of water and I bring it up to my lips to quench the thirst burning for him. I shrug off my jacket before I sweat through Tahlia's expensive suit. His eyes zero in on my arms. Shit.

This man has knocked me off my game. I'm not supposed to be flirting with *Jasper*, but I definitely want to flirt with the guy I saw at Starbucks. It's like a tug of war between the devil on one shoulder and the angel on the other.

"Why do you think I would have allowed you to do those things to me?" My voice should not sound this weak, I just gave myself a pep talk.

A confident chuckle leaves his kissable lips. "Do you really think you wouldn't?"

Damn it, this man has got me all out of sorts. Where is the buzzer and why is not ringing? I've been waiting for twenty minutes to get in front of this guy and now I can't wait to get away from him so I can collect myself.

"Well, I'm not like other women. I'm not one to lie there and wait for you to come." Jesus, it's like I can't stop myself.

"That's exactly what I'm hoping for." His eyes tease promises of what he'd do to my body. I squirm in the seat, the vinyl doing nothing to dull the ache.

"I doubt you could handle me."

He raises both his eyebrows and the buzzer goes off. I move to slide over, but he grips my hand and this time around I'm not tattle-telling to Gage because his touch is warm, comforting and domineering. Just what I crave.

"I'd have you on your knees after one kiss," he promises, his eyes widening in invitation.

Losing all my power to speak, I dislodge my hand and slide to the next guy, who's looking between me and Jasper since our eyes haven't left each other's.

"Excuse me, it's my turn," the girl to take my place says in a bitter tone.

Jasper winks and then focuses his attention to the next woman, whose finger instantly twirls her hair.

The further I get away, the more I come together, that unnerving woman stranded at the table across from him. Five men later, and I only have to stare at the back of his head. Who does he think he is? *You*, I think to myself, but I shoo that thought from my mind because I am not like him. I am not expectant like he is. I don't make people feel uncomfortable.

Yes, you do. Whitney's and Tahlia's voices ring in unison in my head. How the hell did they get in there? Quickly, I realize that he's the male version of me. Strike that, he's better than me. His lines are panty-soaking, his purposeful touches like direct hits in Battleship. Well, he sank my battleship, because my entire outward shell of a character is cracking as a result.

The idea of sleeping with him is at the forefront of my

mind, but so is my business. I didn't expect to share a connection with him—it's never been quite like that with anyone else before. I guess I need to decide which I want more—Jasper in my bed, or Jasper in the boardroom?

AN HOUR LATER, GAGE walks in with a small piece of paper in his hand. I wonder if Jasper picked me, too? I only picked him because hello, I need to spend some more time with him so that I can talk to him about investing in my company. That's what I tell myself anyway, because when I was writing his name down the only thing in my head was the way the material of his suit jacket hugged his biceps and the way his eyes sparkled when he flirted with me.

"We only have one match this evening," Gage starts. "Jasper and—" A woman on the other side of the room stands up immediately and begins sauntering toward Jasper. Did they discuss picking each other? Because she's very expectant. "—Lennon."

The woman's head whips over to me when I let out a little yelp of excitement.

Relax, lady. From the stink-eye she's giving me you'd think I just stole her boyfriend.

Jasper's eyes do that twinkling thing again as he stands up, ignoring the woman when he brushes past her. My mouth waters when I notice the way his broad shoulders fill out his suit jacket. God, I need to get my head on straight before I try to convince him that I'm a commodity he should be investing in.

He makes his way over and holds his hand out to me once he's standing in front of me.

"Jasper, if you'd like to go to the back room," Gage offers but Jasper shakes his head without removing his gaze from mine.

"We're heading out." He tips his head, questioning if that's okay.

I hop down from the stool, grab my clutch and accept his hand.

"Have a great night." Gage winks as I walk by him. "Told you," he whispers.

We step out of the bar and into the night. The air still has a chill to it since summer hasn't fully arrived in San Francisco. Jasper still has my hand in his as we walk in silence down the street.

This is the part where I should come clean—tell him about my sex toy business I'm trying to get off the ground and ask him if he's interested in investing. It suddenly all feels too real and for the first time maybe ever, I clam up. How do I bring it up? Will he look at me and laugh in my face? Lucas' words about Jasper ring like warning bells in my head.

Then again, I think he might want to try a few out with me the way he talked earlier because there is one hundred percent without question something between us. Something different than anything I'm used to, and what if bringing up business fucks that up? On any other night, with any other guy I wouldn't give a shit. But something . . . something in my gut tells me not to be so flippant where Jasper is concerned.

"Did you have a car?" he asks, dragging me from my thoughts. I haven't said a word this entire time. The man probably wonders if I'm a mute.

I look around and realize that we're at the opening of a parking garage. "No." I shake my head.

He glances up at the garage and then down to me. Letting my hand go, he scratches his fingers along the back of his head, seeming conflicted.

"Is there a problem?" I ask. Shit. Did I read him all wrong? That almost never happens. If there's two things I'm good at it's knowing which men are the gay ones at a bar and which are the ones who want to fuck me. Maybe I'm losing my touch.

Jasper exhales a long breath. "Coffee. How about some

coffee?" he asks. The look in his eyes from earlier—the one that told me he wanted to be balls deep inside me until I was screaming his name—is a distant memory, replaced by a more resigned expression, but I'm not sure why.

"Um, sure."

He nods, takes my hand in his again and walks us across the street to Starbucks. The place is practically dead since it's almost eleven. You can tell the employees are annoyed by our presence since one of them is already mopping the floor and the other one is packing up the garbage. The two of them exchange a look. Yep, sorry, baristas, we're going to be *those* people tonight.

We walk up to the counter and the girl there smiles wide. Compared to the other two this girl looks so happy she has to be winning Employee of the Month from them each and every month. "Welcome to Starbucks," she says in a peppy voice I thought was only reserved for that My Little Pony show my niece watches.

"Can I have a grande black?" I ask.

She punches the order in. "Name?"

"Vivian Ward."

The girl smiles, probably assuming that is my actual name. I'm not old enough to remember *Pretty Woman* and I'm sure she's not either. The only reason I know the name is because Tahlia has forced me to watch that movie five hundred times.

I walk down the way while Jasper orders, waiting by the other end of the counter. He pays and meets me a minute later.

"Did you want to sit?" he asks and I almost chuckle at the horrified look of the employee who's mopping and silently praying I decline.

"How about a walk around the city instead?"

I don't miss the way the high school kid's shoulders relax when I respond. He probably has some hot date tonight. Don't worry, dude, a cock blocker I am not.

"I haven't walked in this city in ages," Jasper says with a smile that shows he's excited.

"Vivian Ward," the barista calls out, and places my drink on the counter.

I move to the milk and sugar, but Jasper is right next to me.

"So, where is that name from?" he asks, his cologne overriding all other senses.

"You don't know?" I ask, stirring my milk into the cup.

He shrugs and a second later, the barista calls out, "Edward Lewis." Jasper's eyes widen and the usual full of fun smile emerges.

I laugh, shaking my head, thinking that he might just be someone who can compete with me.

After he makes his coffee the way he wants it, we file out the door and hear the snap of the lock sliding into place a second after it closes behind us.

Jasper checks the door. "No wonder we were getting the evil eye, they must close at eleven."

I chuckle. "I caught on when the guy mopping was crossing his fingers after you asked if I wanted to sit."

We walk a few paces down the sidewalk before Jasper says anything else. "I remember I worked at this sub shop in high school and kids would come in five minutes before close on purpose so we'd have to take all the deli meat back out and then clean up all over again." The annoyance rings through in his voice.

"I worked at a dry cleaner in high school. My hours were good, but some of the clothes . . ." I do a full-body shiver and he laughs while nodding. "I still remember reaching in to check the pockets of one man's suit and pulling out a condom. Used."

"Oh, God," he says with a look of disgust and covers his mouth.

"Yeah, that's not something you easily forget."

"Oh, high school jobs. They did suck."

We walk a few blocks, reminiscing about how awful high school was. Finally, we reach the Pier and his hand slides into mine. The warmth from his skin radiates up my arm. We stop at the end of the Pier and I take a seat on the bench there.

I cross my legs and fidget a bit. Now would be the time I should bring up the business, but part of me—a big part—wants to prolong whatever this is that's happening between us.

He sits down on the bench beside me, his coffee cup clasped in his hands, concentrating on his white lid instead of the bay.

Fuck it. It's now or never, as they say. I inhale a deep breath and open my mouth to speak, but Jasper beats me to it.

"I have a confession."

"I'm not a priest," I joke and he glances over at me, chuckling while he does.

"You are something rare though." He says the words I've heard many times, but he doesn't have that angry or annoyed look that normally accompanies them. His voice almost sounds wistful, as if he enjoys that about me.

"That's what everyone says." I shrug, trying to play it off.

He shakes his head. "I think it's what I like about you."

My heart does some foreign flip thing in my chest. What the hell, heart? What's that about?

"Usually it's what people don't like about me," I admit. I manage not to let any of the hurt I feel deep down show in my voice. There's nothing that turns a guy off faster than baggage—or babies.

"Can I be honest?" he asks. I nod and he shifts in his seat so he faces me. "I want nothing more than to take you to my condo and fuck you with my tongue, my fingers and my cock until your voice gives out from screaming my name."

Whoa.

I blink.

And I blink again.

"Oh," is my über-intelligent response.

Meanwhile wetness pools between my thighs and my nipples peak beneath my bra because the truth is I want that too. So bad. More than I want to pitch my business to him. At least in this moment.

There's something enticingly erotic about a man as put together and sophisticated as Jasper saying dirty, filthy things to me.

"But I'm not going to," he adds—completely serious.

If I was a cartoon character a little sad face emoji would be floating above my head right now. Jasper just stuck a pin in the balloon that held all my pent-up sexual energy.

"Why?" I sip my coffee so that my lips have something to do other than frown.

"Because I don't want this to be over." His eyes dance with sincerity and a dash of mischief.

"Why do you assume it would be over if you did everything you just told me you want to?" I tilt my head, ready and waiting for him to typecast me. Good luck with that. My family has been psychoanalyzing me for years and still haven't figured me out.

"In my line of work, I have to be able to read people. In a short amount of time. Usually in less than half an hour. If I predict wrong, they lose and I lose. I don't like to lose, Lennon." He's morphed into this intense, serious guy, all that playfulness from earlier now hidden well below Earth's crust.

"Okay. I'm not sure what that has to do with me." This is the part where I should ask what he does because I'm not supposed to know.

"You'd probably come back to my condo, we'd fuck, you'd show me a few tricks—and I have no doubt they'd be spectacular—but it would be one and done. I think you probably avoid seconds and I think after having you I'd feel like a starving man if you wouldn't let me be a repeat offender."

Most girls probably want flowery words and heartfelt emotion, but Jasper is speaking my native tongue. Who would've guessed that he's a sweet talker in his own way?

"So, you think I'm easy?" I counter.

He shakes his head. "I think you're free."

"With my body?"

He chuckles. "Okay, let me start this over."

His hand grips the back of his neck again before he places his coffee at his feet. Next, he takes mine and places it beside to his. His eyes lock with mine and his large hand moves up to cup my cheek. Before I have a chance to realize his intentions, his lips are lightly brushing along mine. Then his tongue slides between my parting lips, gliding along mine. Jasper brings his other hand to my hip, locking me into place. His fingers rub along my bare skin right above my waistline and goose bumps race up my spine.

I knew he'd be an amazing kisser, but it's the need I feel pulsing out of him that sets me aflame. A groan rises from his throat when the craving becomes too much and his urgent hands singe my skin with want until he seems to purposefully calm them.

He wants me and doesn't want me at the same time.

Jasper is totally muffin' bluffin' me.

Slowly, his tongue leaves my mouth and I wish it wouldn't end. My hip grows cold when he pulls away and I want to yank him back to me after he creates some distance between us again. Then he picks up my coffee, handing it to me and then grabs his own, sipping it.

What the hell just happened?

"Do you understand?" he asks.

"I understand that you just soaked my panties and you aren't going to finish the job. I understand that you're a pussy tease." So maybe I'm a little bitter. Even if I shouldn't be because wasn't I telling myself a few minutes ago that something like this could not happen?

"I barely know you, yet you're the most intriguing woman I've ever met. Believe me, Lennon, I want nothing more than to have you come apart underneath me, but I know once won't be enough. So I'm going to do something I haven't done since college."

"I'm guessing it's not tying me up and flogging me," I deadpan.

His flirtatious smile emerges. "Will you go out with me next week? On a date?"

My breath hitches and my heart picks up speed. I'm not sure I've felt this way since Jimmy Twendle asked me to homecoming my freshman year. For the first time in a long time, I'm excited to not be sleeping with someone. Scratch that. For the first time in my adult life.

"I'd love to," I say and yep, if we were in a cartoon right now I'd have big heart eyeballs because I'm looking over at him like he's the only thing I see.

He smiles and then his phone rings from his pocket. Pulling it out, he holds up a finger to me. "One sec." He stands and as he's walking away, he answers. "Jasper Banks."

As soon as there's some distance between us, it hits me like a hammer to a nail—I'm not supposed to date him. My entire plan just flew off the edge of the pier, sinking to the depths of the ocean.

How did he make me forget that I don't want him to spend money on a date, I want him to spend money on dildos?

chapter SEVEN

I RING THE DOORBELL to my brother Kurt's house and hear the little footsteps getting closer before the door swings wide open.

"Auntie Lennon!" My niece Katie jumps in my arms and my nephew Ethan, not far behind, clamps onto my leg.

"What's up, you two?" I laugh and limp into the house and let Katie slide down my legs once I'm in the foyer.

From here I can already hear the commotion in the kitchen—the clanking of dishes and silverware, the arguing about arrangements.

Katie quickly wraps herself around my other leg and soon I'm teetering back and forth as I make my way toward the noise.

"Has anyone seen Katie and Ethan?" I ask when I reach the kitchen.

Kurt glances down at my ankles, laughing. "Man, are you pregnant? Because your cankles are bigger than Tina's when she delivered."

I stand there and wait for it to happen. Not a second later, Tina comes by and hits him across the head.

"I'm kidding," he says, following her into the dining room.

As those two start bickering, Jacob rushes over and grabs Ethan off my leg and tips him upside down, swaying him like a pendulum. Ethan squeals.

"Katie, want some cookies?" my mom asks and Katie jumps off me and onto a stool by my mom at the breakfast bar.

I take the tour and say hello to all the family members present here today trying to make my dad's retirement party from the police department the best ever. I finish up with my mom.

"Hi, Mom," I say and kiss the top of her head since she's shrinking in her older age.

"Lennon, sweetie." She pats my hand, clasped to her upper arm, until she notices my t-shirt that says, 'I ENJOY LONG WALKS TO THE BAR.' "Nice of you to dress up for us."

I roll my eyes but she misses it because Katie grabs her attention away, wanting her to pour her some milk, so I snatch a cookie and sit down at the table.

My family doesn't make me feel like an outcast, but I'm misunderstood at the very least, the black sheep at the worst. The circle to the square. I'm the wacky family member no one likes to admit they have who's always up to something. In short, though I love my family, I just never really fit in with them growing up.

Besides Jacob, my twin, there's Kurt, who is ten years older than me and married to his college sweetheart, Tina. Mark, my other brother, is four years older than me and he's been married to his high school sweetheart since eighteen. Kurt and Mark followed in my dad's footsteps as police officers and both of their wives stay at home. None of them have a ton of money, but they're rich in love, so if I was ever going to consider a settled-down life, my brothers and my parents are the poster people to show it really can work.

"What did you do last night?" I ask Jacob, taking a bite of the cookie. "Or more who did you do?"

My mom swiftly smacks me in the head. It's a family thing.

"Sorry."

Jacob looks over the rim of his laptop and rolls his eyes.

"I think Megan's cute," I say, knowing what will happen next.

Jacob shoots me a look and I grin.

"Megan?" My mom bites on the piece of cookie crumb I gave her, leaving Katie on the stool and making her way over to the table.

Ethan runs up and grabs a cookie off Katie's plate before running away. She's whining when Tina comes back into the kitchen.

"Oh, stop it, you two," Tina says, taking the rest of the cookies away and placing them by the sink.

This is my chaotic life and we're missing my dad and brother's family.

"Who is this Megan, Jacob?" my mom asks, nudging my feet off the free chair.

Jacob gives me another look like he's going to kill me, but this is payback for him not giving me Jasper's number. If he had, maybe I wouldn't be as conflicted as I am right now.

"She works with me." He brushes the question off, but anyone can tell his cheeks are getting pink.

"Why are you blushing?" Kurt points out and Jacob buries his head back in the computer.

"I'm not. I have to work on this proposal." He types away in quick succession while my mom eyes him for an extra-long beat just to make sure he's aware that she knows something's up. No doubt she'll be showing up at the bank Monday morning. Somehow, I manage to suppress my internal chuckle.

"It's not my proposal, is it?" I ask in a hushed whisper so no one will overhear.

Jacob rolls his eyes again before concentrating back on

the screen.

"What proposal?" my mom asks.

Damn it. My mom always did have the uncanny ability to overhear everything I didn't want her to.

Ethan stands below her, shaking an orange in her face, so she takes it and starts peeling it.

"For my company," I say.

Up until this point, all my family knows is that I have a new venture I'm excited about. Jacob is the only one who knows the nature of the business and although I know any of the women in my family would fall in love with my products, I'm not sure I'm ready for that conversation.

Jacob looks up, leans back in his chair and crosses his arms over his chest. "You don't know, Mom?"

Oh, so now he has time to focus on the family conversation?

Her head snaps up from where she's peeling the orange with her hands and she focuses her attention on me. "The tattoo parlor?" she asks. "Are you expanding?"

Her eyes almost light up because at least that would be something. Telling people that her daughter is a tattoo artist is about as fulfilling as saying your kid's a musician for a living.

"Nope." Jacob pops the 'p' and I narrow my eyes because I know he's about to out me.

Can't say I blame him though. I've already done the same to him and I did put the grenade in his hand. He just has to pull the pin.

Ethan stands next to my mom, gaze fixated on the orange, bouncing on his feet while he waits.

"Let's go in the other room." I motion to the living room and my mom glances down to Ethan.

"Katie and Ethan, go upstairs and watch a movie," she orders. She quickly finishes peeling the orange and passes it to my nephew. Both kids whine but follow their grandma's orders, because you don't cross my mom. At least when you're seven and four you don't. Once you're my age, you like to test the invisible fence and see if the shock is as painful as you remember. Hell, I've been testing my pain threshold since I was eight. Maybe Katie will take after me and she can be the one constantly being told to calm down and to keep her dreams based in reality.

Tina and Kurt join us around the table and Jacob closes the lid to his laptop. He smiles as though he's holding back the punch line to a killer joke.

"Hello!" Mark bellows from beyond the kitchen at what I'm assuming is the front door. I've never been so happy to see my brother because maybe his entrance means I'll be forgotten.

"Mark, sit," my mom says, pointing to the chair next to Tina. "Lennon has an announcement."

He eyes me. "This should be good," he says with a laugh and sits down where instructed, placing his hat on the table.

"It's not an announcement," I moan.

My three brothers all exchange looks.

"Can we guess?" Mark asks. We both got the sarcasm gene in our family. "Pregnant?"

"By the priest?" Kurt adds.

My mom scowls and they all sit back, knowing they're crossing a line. My family is as Catholic as the Pope. Oh, you know what I mean.

"Lennon has a business venture and she's trying to get your brother to invest in her."

Kurt and Mark look to Jacob, who widens his eyes: *Watch this, Mom's going to nail her to the cross. Literally.*

"Mom, nothing is set in stone. It can wait until I have more information."

She places her hand on my bobbing knee. "Sweetie, if it's important to you, then it's important to all of us. We want to support you." Reverse psychology. She's good. But every time I fall for it, the judgmental eyes and long sighs happen regardless.

"Um . . ." Jacob's smirk annoys me and I can't wait to show him how wrong he is about my business. "It's more of an adult entertainment business."

Tina sucks in a breath and her eyes widen.

"Lennon, prostitution is illegal in the city of San Francisco," Mark says, and although I'm not entirely sure if he's joking, I assume he doesn't think that badly of me.

Jacob chokes out a laugh before my mom shoots him a warning glare.

"Adult entertainment," my mom says with zero enthusiasm.

"Oh, jeez, Len, I have a bachelor party for a buddy coming up and I don't want see my sister on the pole." Tina smacks Kurt across the head.

"Do you think I would really do that?" I half yell and they all remain silent. Fuck a duck, they do. "Well, if you think I'd sell my body for money, then me starting a sex toy business shouldn't really surprise you."

I stand, my mom's hand falling from my knee. I need a minute to push back the hurt and the shame so they don't see it. There's no way I can look at them right now, but the silence resonating around the table tells me I've stunned them. Lennon strikes again.

When I open the fridge door, my mouth waters for the beer, but I grab a diet soda instead.

"Sex toys?" my mom asks first, probably confused.

I turn to face the firing squad.

"Like the parties?" Tina asks and Kurt's head whips around to her in a panic, his expression saying, *Don't act like you know anything about those things in front of my mom.*

Mark leans back in his chair, just like Jacob, waiting for the show to begin.

"Yeah, Mom. Battery-operated toys that help spice up your

love life in the bedroom." That was conservative enough, right? I focus my attention on my sister-in-law. "No, Tina, it's not a party thing, I've actually developed some myself."

Her eyes widen, clearly impressed. I feel like saying, *Yes, I am smarter than you all give me credit for.*

"Why?" my mom asks and you'd think I just confessed to eating all the hosts for the Christmas Eve Mass.

"Because it interests me, Mom. Because I use them." I shrug.

Her hand covers her heart briefly and I'm surprised that after all these years I can still somehow manage to shock her. She recovers quickly though.

"If you had a man you wouldn't need a toy," she says. "I don't understand why you can't be more like your siblings. What happened to you in the womb?" She places her head in her hands and Jacob places his hand on her back while Kurt slides over to where I was sitting to comfort her on the other side.

All the while Tina eyes me with a Cheshire grin and I know she'll be hitting me up later for some samples. That right there is why I want to make a success of this business. Women shouldn't have to feel ashamed that they enjoy sex and want to have it. Besides, there's a huge market for it and although my mom doesn't want to admit it, she'd probably have a shit-ton of fun with my products. Not that I want to think about my parents that way because . . . yuck.

"Mom," I sigh, hitting Kurt until he slides over to his original seat and stops kissing Mom's ass.

She looks up and there's no tears, no sign of sadness because this is her. I love her, but she's dramatic. Even more than me, I sometimes think, and that's saying something.

"I'm a good person. I give spare money to homeless people, I allow my elders to walk through doors in front of me, I'm kind and considerate. I support myself with what I earn. The type of businesses I own doesn't change who I am inside."

She nods, but doesn't believe what I'm saying. All she cares about is what she has to tell her church friends. She has two police officer sons and a banker son, but the tattooed, sex-toy-selling daughter negates the previous three.

"It's just . . . I was just warming up to the tattoo thing."

Oh, to be my mother and only worry about dinner on the table at five, a happy husband and bragging to her friends every lunch on the third Thursday of the month.

"I'm sorry I always disappoint you."

It's true, I am sorry for disappointing her, but I'm not sorry for who I am. That ship sailed when I was thirteen and my date to the school dance tried to corner me in the hallway. That's when I realized that I wasn't the preppy, wholesome girl I was always being told I had to portray—I was anything but inside.

"Listen, I gotta go," I say and stand. Might be a record—it took less than an hour for me to be uncomfortable enough for me to want to leave.

"What about Dad's retirement party?" Mark asks. "Maybe you could do the parting gifts?"

Jacob coughs out another laugh and Kurt is too busy listening to Tina whisper something in his ear to bother paying attention.

"Enough. Sit down, Lennon," my mom says. "You aren't going anywhere." She points to the chair and I slump down into it.

"Maybe we should plan this for another day," I offer, but her black hair, not unlike my own, is already swishing side to side.

"Nope. This is the only day we can do it this week. The date is almost here and I want this finalized."

So I stay seated. And we talk. Ironically about parting gifts. Instead of anal beads we're doing boxes of chocolates. Instead of lube, we're doing small bottles of sanitizer. Good options, for a good Catholic man who worked hard every day of his life.

"So." My mom looks at her to-do list and back up to us.

"We still need to find a way to get Dad there."

No one wants to take responsibility for this because getting my dad out of the house on his day off is about as difficult as luring a lion away from a fresh kill.

"Why don't you do it, Ma?" Jacob asks, his computer back up and running since the 'Lennon's Disappointing Choices' show is over.

"I need to be at the restaurant to set everything up. What about you, Mark?"

"I'll be coming right from the precinct. I'm hoping I don't get stuck," he says.

"I'll talk to the chief," she says, her pencil back on the paper.

"Mom," Mark whines like she said the principal and not his boss. If Mark was the President of the United States I think she'd go to the United Nations. The best thing about my mom is that she's bold and afraid of no one. Where do they think I got it from?

"Kurt?" she asks.

"We have dance for Katie right before and Ethan has baseball. There'll be no time."

She looks to Jacob, but he's armed with an excuse. "It's my Saturday to work, but I'll be on time."

She huffs. "Okay, well, I guess I'll have to be the one then. I'll sort it out." She scribbles notes on her piece of paper.

I'd be offended she didn't think to ask me, but I'm used to it.

"I can do it," I offer and a long stream of breath flows out of her mouth. "What?" I can handle driving my dad to a restaurant, for Christ's sakes.

"I doubt he wants to go in your monstrosity of a vehicle," Kurt says.

"Dad loves my van. He laughed his ass off when I first showed him."

My van is wrapped in a design that features a unicorn

shitting and puking rainbows. It's fun and unique and I mean, who has a hate-on for unicorns? Come on. It may be a tad excessive, but the more everyone tries to shove me in that perfect box, the more I claw myself out.

"In front of all his friends? I doubt it," Kurt adds.

"Are you sure you can get him there on time?" my mom asks, every wrinkle she's earned grooved even deeper in her forehead while she looks on at me.

"Yes," I deadpan. "I *am* a functioning adult."

A bunch of sighs ring out over the table. If they aren't careful, I'm going to call out each one of them on the skeletons they lock in their closets. Maybe Mom would like to know how Kurt used to sneak girls in through the back door after my parents were asleep so they could 'spend time together'. Or perhaps she'd find it interesting that Jacob used to write his own notes to skip classes so he could hook up with Jessica Townsend?

"Okay, Lennon, I'm putting you in charge of bringing Dad," she says with resignation ringing throughout her voice. "We'll have to have an excuse for it."

"How about I just ask him to dinner?" I say.

"He'd be suspicious," Mark says. I eye him and he shrugs. "Name the last time you and Dad did something together."

I rack my brain, not coming up with anything. "Believe me, I can convince him. I'll get him there and he'll be surprised when he walks in. Promise." I point to each one, prepared for them to make a bet.

Then Jacob's phone rings and even with the evil eye from my mother, he still grabs it and begins to walk away from the table.

"What's up, Jasper?" he says.

My stomach tightens, my heart flutters in my chest and I swear my palms sweat.

"You're flushed." My mom touches my forehead with the back of her hand, but I shake my head.

"I'm fine."

It's near impossible to stay seated in the chair and not be able to hear what Jasper is saying to Jacob. There's no way Jasper's figured out that we're related. I mean, he doesn't even have my last name. Still, I worry that somehow he knows and the only problem with that is that my brother will inevitably fuck it up for me and it's still too early. There's something brewing between Jasper and me and I haven't had time to figure out how to bring up my business to him.

While my mind whirls like a tornado, Jacob walks back in the room, his phone already tucked into his pocket.

"Was your phone call that important?" my mom asks.

"Sorry, it was my mentor. We're working on something together."

Phew.

"How is Jasper?" Mark asks.

"You know him?" I ask and everyone looks over to me, questioning my outburst.

"We all do," he says like I'm a dumbass.

"He came to the house for dinner a few times," Kurt adds and my shoulders fall.

"Why wasn't I invited?" I ask and Jacob's lips curl.

"You were too busy," Jacob adds and then turns his attention to Mark. "He's good. Actually, he mentioned that he met someone last night."

Mark smiles. "That's awesome."

Jacobs nods. "Yeah, but you know Jasper, it would take a lot for someone to truly win him over."

"Why?" I ask, interrupting their conversation.

The two exchange a glance and then turn to look at me again. "He's not just going to fall for some girl because she spreads her legs for him."

"What are you guys talking about?" I ask, but my mom

slams her pencil down on the table.

"That's enough of that kind of talk, Jacob," she admonishes. "We're done here, everyone. I have to get home to your father before he starts to suspect something."

We all stand and Jacob packs up his computer. Mark calls into his radio that he's off lunch. Kurt grabs an orange while Tina rushes to a crying Ethan in the other room.

I'm still at the table, watching it all in slow motion, hoping someone explains what they were talking about, but everyone ignores me.

Maybe Jasper just isn't into committed relationships? Suits me fine.

Still, five minutes later I'm driving away, my mind still plagued with the thought that there's more to Jasper than I first thought.

chapter EIGHT

"I'M RETURNING THE PANT suit for a dress." I shove the pant suit into Tahlia's open arms and walk into her condo, past the living room and down the hall toward the bedroom.

"Um, okay," Tahlia says and follows.

Lucas and Cole are playing Xbox when I pass—somewhat ironically, it's a boxing game. The two are perched on the edge of the couch, their thumbs pressing the buttons rapidly, and their eyes haven't strayed from the screen for a second. Who'd think they're both in their thirties?

"I'm done watching them play this stupid game." Whitney rises from her chair and joins us. "What do you need a dress for?" she asks when we reach the bedroom.

"A date."

"Date?" she says in a singsong voice. If I had anything suitable for a dinner and play, there's no way I'd be here telling them about my date. The last they heard, Jasper was to be my investor, not my date.

"Yeah."

"With who?" Tahlia asks and I shake my head, but she runs and gets in front of her closet doors. "No access unless you give us the password."

"Password?" I ask.

"The name of the guy." Whitney comes to stand beside me. "Who's the lucky guy who gets to see you in a dress?"

Exhausted and probably needing a little advice from my friends, I save us the ten minutes of me trying to weasel my way out of telling them, or me wrestling Tahlia to the ground so I can get into her closet—Lucas and Cole would like it too much. "Jasper."

"Jasper Banks?" Whitney's eyes stretch wide.

"How do you know?" I ask. But I already know. I turn my head to look at Tahlia, the big mouth.

"I thought he was going to invest in you. I was excited," Tahlia defends herself, unblocking the closet doors to allow me through. She drops the pant suit in the pile of shirts on the floor.

"Hey, I got that dry-cleaned," I say and a surprised look crosses her face and she scrambles to pick it up.

"Sorry, I just assumed." She hangs the outfit up and I see her cringe and exchange a look with Whitney. They might as well put me on the same boat as my family and sail me off to Neverland.

The two of them sit on the floor while I rummage through Tahlia's closet.

"How did you go from 'invest in me' to 'stick it in me?'" Whitney asks and laughs at her own joke.

"How long have you waited before asking that?" I ask with a smirk.

"Hey, I'm quick-witted, okay?" Tahlia and I just stare at her and she rolls her eyes. "A few minutes."

We laugh and it feels good to release some of my anxiety with laughter. Ever since Jasper texted me last night to let me know where he was taking me, my entire body has been stiff and my mind has been preoccupied. It's so bad that when I went to yoga class this morning I couldn't even flirt back with the hot instructor like I usually do.

"What about this?" I hold up an elegant black dress. It's nothing like me and not what I would normally wear. Then again, I've been to the theater once in my entire life and it was in high school when Tahlia's parents invited Whit and me.

"It really goes with your shirt," Whit says with a laugh.

I glance down to my 'How I Cut Carbs' t-shirt with a picture of a pizza roller underneath and shrug.

"Nah. Not you." Tahlia stands and I hang the dress back up and sit down next to Whitney.

As Tahlia slides the hangers back and forth, inspecting each dress, Whitney places her arm over my shoulder. "Tell me about him."

Whitney and I went to Berkeley together. She saw the one time that I tried to seriously date someone freshman year, only to find out that he had a girlfriend. I'm not sure if Tahlia knows about that or not. I've never told her.

"I don't know enough yet, but he's intriguing," I respond.

Whitney dips her head and looks at me from under her brows.

"He's intense and playful but serious, too. I know nothing about him and what I do know, he doesn't know I do," I admit and Whitney's eyes narrow a bit.

"He doesn't know you want him to invest?" she asks.

I shake my head.

"Len, are you going to tell him?" I can sense her displeasure.

"I don't even know what's going on with us at this point and I think as soon as I agreed to the date, that was me choosing him over the business, as lame as it sounds."

Tahlia stops what she's doing and studies me for a minute.

"You really like this guy." She looks at me as if I'm some mythical creature she's only ever heard tell of.

"I didn't say that," I snap, feeling the need to defend myself for some reason.

"You don't have to." Whitney squeezes my shoulder.

I ignore what they're saying and try to move the conversation on. "Anyway . . . I'm not going to pursue him as an investor anymore. I'll have to figure something else out." I sound more sure of myself than I feel, but I can't shake the notion that there's something between Jasper and me that needs to be explored. I've always been a person who goes with her gut and that's what I'm going to do.

"Lucas can invest," Tahlia offers and I roll my eyes.

"Not an option," I say, as pleasantly as possible. This topic seems to never die.

"So you're interested enough in this guy that you're letting your business take a back seat to your personal connection," Whitney clarifies. Damn her and her investigative reporter instincts.

"He'd assume that I sought him out, which admittedly I did. Then not only wouldn't I get him to invest in the company, but I wouldn't get him. I'm not even sure if I want him, like *want* him for the long haul, but I didn't tell him the other night and so here we are." I ramble on while Whitney's mouth hangs open and Tahl's hand pauses on the hangers above her head.

"Oh. My. God." Tahlia's mouth moves, but she's still as a statue.

"It happened," Whitney says, so sure of herself.

"What?" I look between the two, wondering what their problem is.

"You've met him." Whitney glances at Tahlia and she nods in agreement.

"Who?"

"Your unicorn cock," they say in unison.

"Hate to break it to you, ladies, but I've yet to sleep with him." Ha. I mentally high-five myself for pointing out how wrong they are.

Whitney shakes her head slowly. "Now I know for sure you found him."

"The whole idea behind the unicorn cock is that you found the one *cock*, not guy."

Whit shakes her head. "It's him. I know it."

I stand up and grab the first dress I see, a navy one with short sleeves, and head to the bathroom.

A small part of me thrills with the idea that maybe they're right, but an even bigger piece of me panics.

Lennon Hart is *not* a one-man kind of gal. If Jasper is more than just some guy, where does that leave me?

chapter NINE

THE V ON THE black dress I stole from Tahlia dips all the way down to my waist, clearly giving a view of my less than ample boobs, but all in all, I'd bang me.

Tossing my lipstick, my phone, my keys and a tampon into my purse (but seriously, fuck me if my period decides to arrive tonight), I take a deep breath to calm my nerves.

Usually, I wouldn't care that I live in a studio apartment where I literally fuck where I eat—really, it's like two steps from the bed to the stove—but Jasper probably lives in a penthouse. I mean, the way his suit fit him perfectly tells me it's tailor-made especially for him and he probably spends what was my entire inheritance from my grandma on his clothing over the course of a year. So I want to be armed and ready to go so I can slide out into the hallway and my place will remain a mythical, imaginary land to Jasper.

Knock, knock.

Shit. I'm not ready. Story of my life.

I grab my clutch from the counter and hop over to the door on one foot while I try to put on my strappy sandals. My hand is on the door handle when I realize that I left my shawl on the table.

"Be right there," I say, scrambling back for the shawl that will cover the majority of my tattoos.

Right before I open the door, I pause, take another deep breath. This is just a normal date. Not a big deal.

My hand covers the doorknob and it feels like slow motion when I turn it and open the door. Jasper in a suit isn't a new look for me, but Jasper freshly showered, clean shaven and smiling is. His gaze slides down and back up my body.

I swear there was something I was going to do when I opened the door, but hell if I know what that was. All I can think about is how badly I want to grab the lapels of his jacket and drag him to my bed. Too forward?

"May I come in?" he asks and without thought I slide to the side, opening the door wider for him.

Then I come to my senses and my hand shoots out to push on his chest.

"No!"

He raises an eyebrow.

"I mean, we don't want to be late."

He places his hand over mine, easing it down to my side, and strides into my apartment.

"It's not much." I follow behind him like a yipping Chihuahua on his heels.

He nods to himself as he glances around. "It's you."

"As in I look like I'm poor?"

He turns around and places his hands on my shoulders. "I meant it's eccentric." He grabs my shawl, sliding it from my arms. "It's warm tonight, no need for this. Plus, if need be, you'll have my jacket."

I never thought I'd be a girl who'd swoon. I figured if a guy offered me his jacket, it'd be a leather jacket—preferably one from a motorcycle gang. Or like, maybe he'd be referring to a condom as a jacket for his dick and be passing it to me in the heat of the moment. But Jasper Banks has accomplished what very few before him have. He's made me blush.

I glance down at my tatted arms, unsure, and then back up to him. "I love your skin, Lennon." He tosses my shawl to the side so it flutters down onto my couch. "I'm dying to find out the meaning behind each and every one of these." He trails his finger slowly down my arm and goose bumps break out down my skin like a wave cascading into the shore.

There's no way this guy's for real. He wants to take me to the San Francisco Playhouse in all my tatted-up glory? And everyone calls me crazy.

"Now that I know where you sleep, we can go." He spins on his heels and walks the short distance to my front door.

"You wanted to know where I slept?" I ask, locking up my apartment door.

"I'm a visual kind of guy." He winks and I know for sure now that the thong between my legs has zero chance of staying dry tonight.

We take the elevator down to the lobby, and when I say lobby, I mean past the mailboxes with overflowing piles of junk mail.

"I'm cabbing it tonight," he says as we step out into the night. He holds his hand out to hail our ride.

I guess I'd assumed we'd be taking his expensive sports car. Surely, a guy like Jasper Banks owns a two-seater that goes zero to sixty in four seconds.

A cab pulls up to the curb and Jasper opens the door for me. I slide in, trying to be extra ladylike and not flash him the goods before he's even bought me dinner—not that that's ever stopped me before. Once he climbs in after me, the space becomes cozy and it's hard not to be aware of how close he's sitting to me.

"5A5 Steak Lounge," he directs the driver who nods and

pulls off the curb. Then his attention turns to me. "You aren't a vegetarian, are you?" The panicked look on his face is amusing.

"No." I shake my head. "Vegan," I say.

He grimaces and shifts to pull his phone from his pocket. "Where do you like to eat?" His thumbs move across the screen and I place my hand on his, waiting for him to look up at me.

Once he does, I feel bad for making the joke because he looks almost nervous.

"I'm kidding. I love meat." I waggle my eyebrows so my double entendre is clear.

He smiles and a laugh escapes his throat. "Good to know," he says with a grin and slips his phone back in his pocket. "Probably something I should've asked before making the reservations, but I hate French food and I'm not a huge fan of Asian."

"You don't like Asian food?"

He shakes his head.

"Isn't 5A5 Steak Lounge also Japanese?"

A smirk crosses his lips and he nods. "All you'll find on my plate is a steak and maybe a potato."

"I'll take you to a place one day and I bet you you'll change your mind."

He shakes his head again. "Tried them all."

"You're thinking sushi and Chinese food, right?" I turn in my seat to face him as the cab driver whizzes through the hilly streets.

"Maybe." He acts coy but I can tell that I'm right.

"We'll go to a Korean Bar-B-Que I know. I promise, you've never had anything like it before." I remember the first time a guy in our dorm took Whitney and I to that place. I'm surprised I didn't walk out mooing when I left from the amount of meat I ate.

"So, you're committing to a second date before you know how the first one ends?" His eyebrows quirk up and I giggle like the schoolgirl I am tonight.

"I guess I should wait, but following the rules has never been my style." I shrug.

He leans in close, his fingertips running along the length of my thigh. "Does that mean you go to second base on the first date?" he whispers in my ear, igniting a rush of goose bumps up my neck.

I turn and our faces are millimeters away from one another.

"Oh, Mr. Banks, if you play your hand right, you might score a home run."

The scent of his cologne increases, as though it becomes stronger when he's turned on.

"I always play to win." He winks that damn hazel eye at me.

I may be playing out of my league.

chapter TEN

"BANKS," JASPER TELLS THE hostess after we walk into the restaurant.

I've been to fancy restaurants before. I've been to Tahlia's family's country club, but this restaurant is beyond beautiful. The large circular room is filled with booths and dark wood tables paired with cream cloth-covered chairs. There's a long bar on one side of the room with a large screen behind all the bottles. The image on the screen is a fire and it's hard to drag my eyes away from the flames as they flicker and lick up to the ceiling. The entire restaurant is filled with a warm glow from the many recessed lights. My only complaint, if I had one, would be that I wish we had more privacy.

The hostess flings her brunette hair over her shoulder, swivels on her stilettos and sways her ass while guiding us to our table. I'm sure she finds many a rich boy to fuck in the coatroom, but bitch can back off because it's not going to be with Jasper. Standing at the edge of the table, she clutches the menus to her chest, waiting as Jasper holds out my chair for me. Once he's seated across from me, she hands us each a menu, bending a little further down for Jasper. I don't wait to see if he takes the bait and looks down her loose blouse.

I glance over the menu until the hostess has left and then raise my eyes in his direction as he places the menu down on his bread plate.

"I assume you've been here before?" I ask.

"I have. The prime rib is my favorite." He busies himself by placing the napkin in his lap and I follow suit and do the same.

"I'm a filet kind of girl." Even though I've decided on what I'm going to have, I continue to read over the menu, considering trying something I never have. Who knows if I'll ever go to a restaurant like this again?

"Yes, you are." He smiles.

"What does that mean?" I tilt my head.

"Filets are feminine without an ounce of fat on them. They're lean and petite but hold a punch. And they melt in your mouth."

I laugh. "I've never been so happy to be compared to a slab of meat."

The corners of his lips turn up. "I do try to be unique."

"That you do." I place my menu down on the table.

Our waiter, who introduces himself as Leon, comes over. "Good evening." He bows slightly at his waist. His hair is salt and pepper, his white shirt crisp and his pants pressed. I bet he's been doing this for awhile.

"Good evening," Jasper says in return, nodding his head.

Leon relays the specials and asks us what we'd like to drink. I defer to Jasper, allowing him to dictate the bottle of wine, which he does without looking at the menu.

While we're waiting on the wine our conversation stays on course as we discuss my tattoos and my work at the studio. It isn't until he asks me about my family that I realize I haven't thought this through.

"Any brothers or sisters?" he asks.

I grab my water glass to coat my suddenly parched throat. "Brothers," I say.

He nods. "You're the only girl?"

"Yep."

Leon comes over, shows Jasper the bottle of wine and does the whole opening rigmarole that they do at places like this. Jasper tastes and then nods to pour, which Leon does, starting with my glass.

"What were we saying again?" Jasper asks after Leon takes our order and leaves. "Oh, yeah, I saw your name on the buzzer at your apartment."

"You did?" My throat closes and I try my best to suck some air into my lungs even though it feels like a giant boulder sits on my chest. Why the hell didn't I figure out how I was going to handle this beforehand?

"Hart? Is that your last name?" he asks, leaning forward and steepling his hands.

I smile, as genuine and surprised as possible. "You have a knack for details," I joke and he chuckles, continuing to wait for me to answer the question. "Yes. Lennon Hart," I finally admit with a choked voice. It might just be Jacob's hands strangling me right now. You know, a twin thing.

Jasper's eyes light up with recognition and I wait for it. In the seconds I have to answer the question at the tip of his tongue, I weigh my options. Lie. I could definitely lie. Hart is not an uncommon name. If this was our only date would it matter? But the fact that he's been to my family's house for dinner continues to plague me.

"Do you know Jacob Hart?"

The question hangs in the air for an uncomfortable minute as I swallow down the wine I sipped at the last minute to buy me some time. He seems content to wait and lets me finish all while picking up his own drink. His eyes remain on mine over top of his wine glass.

"You know my brother?" I squeak out before I can change my mind about telling the truth.

He chokes on his sip of wine and coughs, beating his chest in an effort to catch his breath. Eventually, he swallows it and seems to recover.

"Brother?" he questions and that light in his eyes dims slightly. "You're Jacob's sister?" He takes another sip of his wine.

I nod. "Twin actually."

He doesn't choke this time, but it looks like he's having a hard time swallowing the liquid. After a big gulp he places his glass down on the table and leans back in his chair, a safe distance away from choking hazards. Quick learner.

"Twins? Wow. How did I not know that Jacob was a twin?" he says. I'm a little put off over the fact that Jacob hasn't at least mentioned that I exist. "I've met your parents." He cringes, like he's a little put off by that.

"Sorry," I respond, not knowing what to say.

He waves me off. "Your family is great, they remind me a lot of my own. When I took Jacob under my wing . . ." He pauses. "Did you know I was his mentor?"

"Oh, you're *that* Jasper?" My voice is about three octaves too high as I try to sell the idea that I'm surprised.

He nods, and the pit of my stomach weighs heavy with the lie. Jasper is the first man who's piqued my interest for more than his cock in years. Somewhere in the back of my mind, I realize this could blow up in my face, but I push the thought away.

"The one and only," he says. I smile. "Jacob's been great. He's a natural and his drive is exceptional."

"Have you ever heard of twin competition?" I ask.

"No." He laughs like it's not a real thing.

"Well, I don't want to hear how great my brother is unless

you want to compliment me equally." I pretend to flick my hair over my shoulder—pretend because I don't have hair long enough to manage it.

"Where do I begin?" His eyes twinkle and I'm glad to see that he understands my sense of humor.

"Usually at the beginning." We both chuckle.

He picks up his wine glass by the stem and tips it to his lips. "I can't believe you're Jacob Hart's sister." He shakes his head.

"Neither can I most days," I say and he laughs again but looks a little preoccupied, obviously still processing the information.

"Listen . . . now that I know Jacob's your brother I feel a little weird being out on a date with you." His face has an apology written all over it.

"Gee, thanks," I deadpan.

He reaches across the table and squeezes my hand. "Sorry, that came out wrong. What I meant is, I feel weird that he doesn't know. Depending on how things go . . ."

I see what he's getting at. "I'd prefer to tell my brother, if you don't mind. If it becomes necessary."

Jasper's shoulders relax and he smiles across the table. "That's all I'm asking. I don't want to feel like I'm sneaking around behind his back, that's all."

"No problem." Seems Jasper's a stand-up guy. Even more surprising is the fact that I kinda dig it. "But please don't mention anything to him before I have a chance to talk to him." And I will tell him . . . eventually.

He does a mock zipper motion with his mouth. "My lips are sealed."

Now that that's out of the way I want nothing more than to move this conversation along. "What about you?" I ask. "Family?"

"Well, I'm originally from Nebraska. My parents were farmers, but they live out here now. Outside of the city, but close."

I nod. "That's a big change."

"Yeah, they replaced corn stalks with vineyards, but they've embraced it. I'm an only child, so once they knew I wasn't going to take over the farm, they sold it to my uncle."

"Ah, so you didn't want any part in the family business either," I say. I lift my wine glass to take a sip.

"Yeah, your other brothers followed your dad into the police force, right?"

He knows way too much about my family.

"Mark and Kurt did. The fact that I'm female kept most of the pressure from coming my way, but I know Jacob struggled with that for awhile. My tits might not be huge, but they did the trick." I wink at him.

His gaze dips to my chest for a second before it returns to my face. "They look perfect if you ask me. The perfect handful." I suck my bottom lip into my mouth because the look he's giving me makes me want to slink under the table and do some seriously inappropriate stuff to him below waist level.

"Maybe you'll get to find out some time," I say in a breathy voice that gives me away.

"A man can dare to dream." He tips his wine glass at me and then takes a sip himself.

"Anyway . . ." I need to move this conversation back into a PG rating otherwise I will end up on my knees under the table no matter how fancy a place this is. A girl can only take so much. "Like I said, I had no interest, nor do I think I would've made a very good cop."

"I don't know, I bet you'd be a tough cop." His eyes swim with lust as though he's picturing me in one of those risqué police lingerie sets. I make a mental note to invest in one.

"Are you kidding? I'd be the worst cop. I'd probably let all the kids off with a warning if they agreed to give me their pot," I joke and he laughs but it rings hollow.

Okay . . . moving on. "So, are you still a banker?" I shouldn't have asked because I'm forcing myself to pretend like I don't already know his office address, the name of his company and his web address, but it was the first thing I could think of after the strange look he gave me with my last response.

"No. I started my own company shortly after Jacob worked for me at the bank. I partnered with someone I went to Harvard with and now invest in emerging companies trying to bring products to market."

I nod. "Do you enjoy it?" I ask.

"I do." Jasper sits up straighter in his seat like he's brimming with energy now. "It's kind of a high to take something in its infancy and nurture it into a success. It's always interesting to see which companies rise and become more than you imagined they could be. My partner and I are way too competitive. And we're not even twins." He winks.

I smile. "So you like living on the edge? You enjoy risk?"

"I straddle the line in my business life, but in my personal life I prefer both feet on solid ground." There's no smirk or humoured smile on his lips and thankfully, Leon brings our entrées to distract me from having to pry about the meaning of his last statement. I'm far from solid ground—more like quicksand, which would mean there's no room for me in his life.

I already knew I wasn't getting the business deal. Does this mean I won't get the man either?

chapter ELEVEN

THE FIRST PART OF the play was amazing. Jasper selected She Loves Me, a romantic comedy that's an adaptation of the original play that was once made into the movie You've Got Mail.

I walk out from the bathroom during intermission to find Jasper perched by the bar with a wine glass in one hand, a highball in the other. The playhouse must have the air on full blast because I'm freezing, but I'm guessing Jasper enjoys seeing my skin because I've caught him sneaking a few peeks at my ink tonight.

"The only time I wish I were a man . . . when it comes to public bathrooms." I roll my eyes, taking the wine glass he's offering.

He smiles then sips his drink and places his hand on the small of my back, right where the fabric dips down above my ass. His fingers skim along my bare skin and I squirm. His touch is like lighter fluid he's dousing me with before the match is struck. My radar has been off lately, but I'd place good money on the fact that Jasper knows exactly what to do to drive a woman crazy.

"Are you enjoying the play?" he asks, his gaze tracking every one of my movements.

"I am. My friend Tahlia will be so jealous when I tell her about it. She has this obsession with romantic movies." Talking about my friends feels natural with Jasper and I wonder about the company he keeps. Just as the thought sparks, a couple walks over.

"Jasper," the woman coos, offering her hand to him.

He accepts the hand, shaking it between both of his.

"Sabrina, where's Gavin?" he asks the redhead who's now appraising me and clearly finds me lacking. Her eyes skid along my body, almost faltering at each tattoo as though she can't believe it.

It's the same look I got every time Tahlia invited me to her family's country club. I'm way too awesome to let a bunch of uptight assholes make me feel bad about myself so I stopped going when she asked.

Sabrina glances over my shoulder and I turn to see a tall male walking over with two glasses of wine. Sabrina only graces him with a fleeting look because she's too busy sweeping her gaze between Jasper and me.

"Sabrina, this is my date, Lennon Hart." Jasper's hand finds the spot on the small of my back and gives me a soft rub.

She takes my extended hand but her hand is limp in mine, as if I don't deserve the effort of a handshake. I smile like the polite Catholic girl my mom tried to raise me as and then take a step closer to Jasper, wanting as far away from this woman's toxic energy as possible.

"Nice to meet you," she says, her eyes doing that sweeping motion again.

"Jasper, what the hell? It's been a while." The guy—Gavin, I presume—sets down the two wine glasses on the bar so he can shake his hand.

"Never thought I'd see you at a play." Jasper laughs and Gavin picks up both glasses, handing one to Sabrina. She sips it, but continues to study me as the men chat for a minute.

Gavin glances my way and I don't miss the way his eyes flare with I'm not sure what . . . surprise?

"Who's this?" he asks and Jasper's hand slides to my hip, his fingers digging into my flesh, pulling me flush against his side.

"This is Lennon Hart," he says, not giving me any breathing room so that I can shake Gavin's hand.

Gavin nods at me. "Nice to meet one of Jasper's many ladies."

Well, fuck a duck. I was expecting the first jab to come from Sabrina, not him. Two can play at that game.

"Well, tonight is my turn." I place my hand on Jasper's chest and weave his tie through my fingers. "I do only get him twice a week, but he's so worth it." My tone is sultry and sexual and Jasper's chest rumbles with laughter.

Sabrina's lips contort into a sneer of disgust and Gavin shoots me a half smile.

"I'm sure you keep his hands full," Gavin continues and Jasper wraps my hand in his and brings it up to his lips.

"You have no idea." Jasper looks down at me and my breath catches. I lose myself in the green and gold mix in his eyes and the rest of the room fades away. For a brief moment, it's only the two of us and the plethora of possibilities that exist between us.

The lights flicker, jarring us both back to the present.

"Well, we better go," Jasper says, taking my hand.

"Good to meet you." Gavin leans in and kisses my cheek. When he pulls back his gaze rakes over my body. Jasper's entire body stiffens beside me.

"Um, yeah, you as well," I stammer.

Jasper doesn't exchange handshakes or hugs with either of them. Instead he gives them a quick wave and then we're heading back into the theater, down to the front row.

Once we're settled in our seats, I look around to see where Sabrina and Gavin are sitting. Not finding them anywhere, I lean into Jasper. The question I'm dying to ask is like acid burning a hole through my tongue the longer I hold it inside.

"Can I ask you something?" I whisper and he leans into me as the curtain comes up. "My tattoos? They don't embarrass you? I mean, I saw the way your friends looked at me."

He chuckles. "First, they aren't my friends. I went to school with both of them. Second of all"—this time he turns to look me in the eyes—"do you really have no idea that every man in this room is jealous of me because I'm the one who gets to take you home?"

My face heats and his hand rises to my cheek as the spotlight zeroes in on the stage. Still, I can't look away from him.

"I would never hide you," he whispers and my eyes close as he seals that promise with a chaste kiss that leaves me wanting more.

He really does play to win. I can't wait to shine up his trophy later.

chapter TWELVE

THE TAXI DROPS US off at South Beach Harbor Marina. Jasper climbs out and pays the driver through the passenger window while I slide across the backseat.

"Why are we here?" I ask, allowing him to entwine his fingers with mine and lead me down the plank walkway through the boats.

"I hope I'm not being too presumptuous." He stops us and grabs my other hand with his. "I don't expect you to do anything. I just didn't want the night to end."

A foreign giddiness washes through my body like the ripples of the ocean surrounding us.

I eye the marina, figuring he owns one of the boats. "Which one is yours?" I ask, my gaze scouring all the boats, trying to guess which one is Jasper's based on what I know of his taste. Unless the flag is a one-hundred-dollar bill I might not be able to figure it out because they all look kind of the same from here.

He points to the far end, at a sailboat that's not as big as many, but not as small as the majority of boats lined up. Midsized and currently swaying a bit on the water.

"When the boats are a-rockin'," I say, a smile teasing my lips. I kick off my heels, hang them from my fingers as I step in front of him, eager to see what Jasper's packing and to get on the boat. I can't remember the last time I was on a boat.

He follows a few steps behind me, his dress shoes scuffing on the worn wood. In my mind, he's watching my ass sway back and forth. He's admiring the way my dress dips all the way down to right above my ass, remembering what my skin felt like when he rested his hand there. My imagination has him adjusting the chubby that's growing in his pants.

I stop at the edge of his boat, jumping up and down on my toes.

"You're like a kid on Christmas." He looks at me from the corner of his eye as he slips his own shoes off.

"I've never been on a sailboat before."

He steps up onto the boat, stopping and holding his hand out for me. When I step on, the boat sways and he grips my hand harder to keep me steady, but I fall right into his chest.

"You arranged that," I joke and his hand moves up to my cheek, his thumb caressing my skin.

"Let me show you around." He ignores my comment, his hand sliding down my arm until my hand is in his again.

I'm not usually a hand-holder, more of an ass-grabber. Anyone who knows me knows I don't like being led anywhere. I'm in charge of my own life. But with Jasper, it somehow feels right that he leads me.

He walks me around, and when we get to the wheel I pretend like I'm on the high seas. When we reach the front of the boat I sit down and let my legs hang off the edge before striking a pose like I'm a celebrity bathing in the sun. Jasper laughs, but when we reach the door to the cabin, all my amusement vanishes because this is where I'm going to fuck his brains out.

The entire date, I didn't waver about whether I was going

to sleep with him or not. That'd be like giving me a lottery ticket and expecting me not to scratch it. How the hell would you know if you're a millionaire otherwise? Tonight, I'm hoping for a lot of zeros after Jasper's performance.

He goes down the ladder first so he can steady me from below. As my foot hits the second rung, his hands slide up my hips.

"You aren't peeking, are you?" I joke and his fingers tighten on my waist.

"I don't spoil my surprises," he says in a low voice that I feel in all the right places.

My feet reach the bottom and he turns me around, stepping forward to crowd me into the ladder. My breathing hitches in my throat, but he continues his prowl, leaving my ass perched on a step of the ladder and him between my open legs. Smooth move that I didn't anticipate. I'm impressed.

"I haven't seen the bed yet," I pretend to whine.

His gaze stays on mine, fierce and predatory. "If I'm lucky you'll see every inch of this place. Repeatedly."

"Do you have any neighbors?" I ask, my hand sliding down the front of his slacks, gripping his hard length in my hand.

Not a chubby, girls, a full-on, hard-as-granite cock. I give myself a mental high five because unlike the last dick that was trying to make an impression on me, Jasper is rockin' cock. At least nine inches by my estimation and though I don't want to call myself an expert in such things . . . I kinda am.

The thought that I've turned Jasper on makes me throb between my legs. I'm going to rock this guy's world and pray he doesn't ruin me for others.

"There aren't houseboats. So you can scream as loud as you want." Moving closer, he kisses my collarbone, moving up my neck, until he pauses. "I promise to send you home with throat lozenges tomorrow."

"Who says I'll be the one screaming?" I giggle, my head

falling back until it hits the ladder. "Ouch," I say, still laughing.

He grips my ass, and I lock my legs around his waist. Swinging us around, he walks me back until I'm against a counter.

I jump down when he gives me some space and my hand moves to my back to unzip my dress.

Jasper steps forward, his hand landing on mine. "Allow me," he says, his hand on my hip, swiveling me around. He shrugs off his jacket and I watch it fall on the couch to our left. He cages me in, his hands grazing over mine and placing them on the counter in front of me. "Hands stay," he whispers, kissing where my neck meets my shoulder.

My skin scorches under the softness of his lips. He slowly unzips my dress, his finger gliding down my spine.

A strangled groan escapes his throat. He pushes the dress off each shoulder and I unglue my hands from the counter just long enough to allow the dress to fall to the ground, leaving me in my black thong and my heels.

"I'm such a lucky bastard," he says, his voice strained and filled with lust.

I shake my ass a few times, impatient to have his hands on me, and he grips my ass, squeezing. When I move to turn around, he steps into me, pinning me there, my front half falling to the counter top.

"You're used to control, aren't you?" he whispers against the skin on my back. When I don't answer he nudges my legs apart and I feel his thick, hard cock through his slacks. What I wouldn't do for him to take those pants off right now.

I nod.

"Tonight, I'm in charge," he says and a jolt of adrenaline courses through my body before I relax under his gentle touch.

"I don't take directions very well," I reply and he chuckles, a deep low sound that I feel between my legs.

"There will be consequences if you don't," he promises me.

I suck in a breath. God, I'm practically dripping between my legs for this man.

"Tell me you'll spank me," I say with a breathy voice, turning my head to the side so I can see him.

"I have a feeling there's no punishment you wouldn't enjoy." He squeezes my ass cheek.

I shake my head, my teeth digging into my bottom lip. "I'm open to most things." I rise from the counter and this time he allows me, taking my shoulder and swinging me around to look into his eyes.

"Undress me," he orders with a devilish tone that ignites a tremble through my body.

I fiddle with the buttons of his shirt as he stands there and lets me unclothe him.

I almost always call the shots in the bedroom, but I'm usually dealing with guys in their twenties like me. Jasper's in his early thirties though and he's all man. He owns his sexuality like I do and doesn't seem to make any apologies for it. I have a feeling he could rock not only this boat, but any surface he fucks me on.

His shirt opens and as I push it off his shoulders, my mouth drops open.

"That's hot." My hands run over the tribal tattoo on one of his shoulders that leads across to his muscular back. I push his inked shoulder and he turns like a fashion model and lets his shirt join my dress on the floor. A tattoo runs along the top of his shoulder blades across his entire back. Circling back around, he ignores the fact that I'm admiring his tattoos and eyes his slacks.

"Mr. Banks, would you like me to take care of these pants for you?" My hand snakes down his muscular chest until I cup his balls in my palm, squeezing and massaging.

"I'd like you to do that on your knees, Miss Hart." He cocks his eyebrow as though he's daring me.

Does he not get me at all? A dare pretty much guarantees I'm going to do whatever it is. I enjoy a challenge.

I sink to my knees, staring up at him as I swiftly unbutton his charcoal slacks.

They thud to the floor, pooling at his feet and he cocks that eyebrow again. His black boxer briefs tent with his throbbing erection and my mouth waters. Teasing has always been my forte and since he's informed me that I'm only in control until he's naked, I figure it's time to play a little.

My hand slides up his muscular leg. He's statue still, not even a flicker of an eyelid as he stares down at me, his gaze impassive. His hard length stops my hand and I squeeze, rubbing up and down.

I inch closer, arching my back and bringing his cock to my lips through his boxers. With the fabric barrier, I allow my teeth to scrape up his erection until the tip is in my mouth, where I let my tongue wet the cotton fabric. My hand continues to pump him up and down and his hands move toward my hair.

We both know what he wants, and I'm curious if he'll stick to his word that I lose control once I take off his boxers.

Unable to resist the burning question in my mind, I pull back and my mouth leaves his fabric-covered cock and my fingers hook on the sides of his boxers. I drag them down and his cock springs out, hard as a rock, straining toward his navel.

And what a beautiful cock it is. Holy shit. A spotlight with a chorus of 'ahs' should be ringing out around us in this moment. A chorus of angels should be singing hallelujah because this man is perfection personified.

I grab him, sliding his length through my hand before covering his mushroom tip with my mouth. I exhale in relief through my nose, but before I can get a good taste, Jasper bends down and picks me up under my arms, propping me on the counter. Though I'm disappointed, I can't help but be impressed by his strength.

"I told you, I'm in control now." He steps out of his slacks and kicks all our clothing out of our way. He pushes my legs to the sides, opening me to him, and he runs his finger along the underside of my thong, teasing my clit and making me grow even wetter.

I lean back on my elbows and his other hand comes up to slide my panties down my legs, tossing them over his head. Then his hands are on my inner thighs, pressing them down on the counter. I'm completely bared to him.

My eyes flutter closed in preparation to feel his breath or his tongue on me. A moan practically rests in my throat, waiting to be unleashed. But I feel nothing and when I open my eyes, he's watching me. His eyes are the flint and I'm the spark to ignite him.

He opens the drawer to his left and pulls out a condom. While his gaze stays on me, he tears it open with his teeth and spits out the wrapper.

Now, I've been in this position a few times—more than a few if I'm being honest—but no one has ever done that maneuver like he should be in a porno. Never as flawless as Jasper. No one has been able to keep me wet and panting while I'm waiting for his cock to take me.

He sets the package on the counter and his hands slide under my thighs to pull me forward. I'm perched on the edge and he directs my legs to his sides. I tighten them behind his thighs and he grabs the base of his cock with his hand, gliding the head up and down my wetness. A muffled groan echoes in the small space when the tip slides over my swollen clit and I scoot closer, needing him inside of me.

"You want it?" he asks and my breathing staggers, watching the movement of his dick, and for a second I think to hell with precautions. I just want him to slide it in me.

"Yes," I answer in a breathy voice that betrays how lost I am in him.

A slow smirk tips up the corner of his lips. Reaching over, he places the condom on and less than a second later, he's buried inside of me. He growls and his fingers dig so far into my hips, I know there'll be marks in the morning.

There's nothing slow about Jasper. He thrusts in and out of me like he's finishing instead of starting. Normally, a little primer would be necessary, but I feel like we've been doing the slow grind all night and it's time to unleash the animals we've been keeping at bay.

The desperation with which Jasper wants me right now is a bigger turn-on than his cut abs, his intelligence or his perfect dick. Nothing turns me on more than when I know a guy wants me just as bad as I want him.

Jasper pumps into me over and over again and the need to get closer to him builds, so I inch up, wrapping my arms round his neck and using my legs to draw him in deeper.

His hands direct the movement of my hips, forcefully pulling them toward him and then pushing them away. Before I have a chance to react, he hoists me up, walks a few steps and slams me down on something soft. He continues to ram into me the entire time and then draws my legs up so my ankles are at either side of my face.

Thank God for yoga.

"I wish I had a camera," he says, his gaze focused on our joined bodies.

"Next time," I remark and his sexy as sin smile appears and I'm pretty sure he thinks I'm kidding.

He thrusts into me a few more times and then his cock leaves me. I long for it immediately, but before I can complain he's lying in the bed beside me and directing me to get on top of him.

I don't miss a beat, rolling over on top of him and lowering down on his length.

He feels so much bigger in this position and I'm sure my eyes roll back into my head out of sheer bliss. Our movements are frantic as I slide up and down on him and he crashes his lips to mine. My fingernails dig into his shoulders as I grind my pelvis back and forth, my clit throbbing with the friction. Our tongues mix and mingle, our teeth knocking, our lips swollen. When he takes his teeth to my bottom lip, the explosion I was holding at bay floods out of me and I cry out. Every part of my body feels electrified, as if I've just been hit with a bolt of lightning. When I'm done riding out my orgasm I let my trembling body fall onto his chest.

Never, ever in my sexual conquests have I become a shaking mess after an orgasm. I'm always ready to give as good as I receive, but for some reason I feel weak-limbed and completely spent.

Jasper refuses to let me stop though. His lips continue to devour mine and as exhausted as I am, the tingling between my legs ignites again.

With his hands on my hips, he brings them up and down on his hard length until he stills inside of me. His head falls back to the pillow, the muscles in his neck strain and his mouth falls open as he groans through his orgasm.

I study his eyes as they flutter from open to closed and I swear I could watch him come every second of every day. He's even more beautiful with just-fucked hair, red lips and sweat glistening on his hard body.

A full minute later, he opens his eyes and I collapse on his chest. His fingers graze my bare skin, up and down my back.

"Shh . . . sleep now," he whispers and as much as I want to repeat what we just did, my eyelids close.

chapter THIRTEEN

I WAKE UP AND the slow sway underneath me reminds me that I'm on Jasper's boat. I'm not even sure of the last time I slept over at a guy's place unless I passed out after because I was drunk.

Last night, I never stirred and we didn't even have sex again. What the hell? There's a good chance he thinks I'm a stage-five clinger now and I've completely blown my chance with a fine specimen like Jasper Banks. One and done. I could kick myself.

He never even ate me out. Fuck.

I roll over, sitting up on the edge of the bed, narrowing my eyes while I glance around the small room. I'd like to investigate further since I didn't really get the tour last night. Unless demonstrating what the counter and the bed feel like under my ass counts. Unfortunately though, my bladder is screaming at me so I stand in search of a bathroom.

Bingo. The small door to my right holds my salvation. Thank goodness, because in about thirty seconds I'd be peeing in his sink or hanging my ass overboard.

I do my business and notice there's no toiletries. No shaving cream, not even a toothbrush or toothpaste. I cover my mouth, testing my breath. Oh, God, I need toothpaste. I scour under the cabinet, but other than some Band-Aids, sunblock and a brush, nothing. What the hell?

Giving up, I open the door and promptly scream.

"Jasper!" My hand covers my frantically beating heart as he stands there in his slacks and shirt from last night. He's a wrinkled mess and I smile inside at the fact that he didn't think to lay his clothes out neatly before we went at it.

"Coffee?" he asks, holding out a Starbucks cup.

I smile. "Thank you." I take it from his hands and see 'Bella' scribbled on the outside. "And you are?" I ask with a smile.

He circles his cup in his hand and I laugh at 'Edward' written on his.

Twilight.

"I love that you play my game," I say, inching up my toes to give him a quick, closed-mouth kiss on his lips.

He steps closer, prolonging the kiss a second. "What are you doing today?" he asks me, walking me backward until my ass falls to the bed.

"Um . . ." I rack my brain. I don't have any plans and the tattoo shop is closed today. "Shouldn't you ask who I'm doing?" I ask and he chuckles.

"Good answer." He sets his coffee down and leaves the small room, returning a second later with a Target bag. "I got you some sailing clothes."

I quirk an eyebrow. "Are there special clothes for sailing?"

"Well, there are, but they don't sell them at Target. I got you some shorts and a shirt. Along with a toothbrush and toothpaste." He passes me the bag and I set it in my lap.

I run a hand through my hair, knowing I could really use a shower.

"I also bought you a bathing suit," he continues. "There's a spot we can anchor and swim." His eyes light up so I root through the bag and pull out the skimpiest bikini. Seriously, almost all string. Now I'm all for working what your mama gave you, but I'm not auditioning to work the pole right now.

He holds up his hands in a placating gesture when I hold it up in front of me. "In my defense, it was either that or a one-piece and I just couldn't picture you in a mom bathing suit."

I chuckle. "Yeah, me and Mom probably shouldn't go in the same sentence." I glance away from the small amount of fabric in my hand and something flashes across Jasper's expression, but it's too fast for me to figure out what it's about. "At this point you might as well tie me up naked. It might cover more of me." I toss the bikini on the bed and he laughs. "If I ever have to buy you clothes, I'm buying you a Speedo." I eye him and he chuckles again. "A thong Speedo."

Still smiling, he moves into the bathroom with his toothbrush and toothpaste. "Do they make such a thing?" he asks.

"I'll have one shipped over from Europe." I sit on the bed, waiting for him to finish before I intrude.

"I look forward to it." He comes out a couple minutes later, grabbing my hand for me to get up and when I do he wraps his arms around my middle. "Now, go get dressed. I can't wait to have you alone on the water." He kisses my nose and pats my ass to get moving.

He leaves the room and I stare after him, wondering what the hell I'm doing spending the day with a man after I slept with him the night before.

Where are you, Lennon Hart? Are you still in there somewhere?

Pretty soon I'll be giggling, batting my eyelashes and pretending to like things I hate just to impress him.

I sigh and pick up the Target bag and lock myself in the bathroom to get changed. Somehow it just feels safer at the moment.

AN HOUR LATER, WE'RE out on the water. Jasper is behind the wheel and I have no idea what I'm doing, but I'm helping him as much as I can. Of course every task he gives me somehow means I need to bend over. I don't mind though. I enjoy the way I catch him watching me. Like he's the fisherman and I'm the prized catch.

Okay, maybe that's a bad analogy because I suppose after the fisherman hooks the fish he ends up gutting it or mounting its dead body on the wall, but you catch my drift.

I'm wearing the shorts and too-tight t-shirt he bought over my almost non-existent bikini. I sit back and grab one of the coconut water bottles he put in a cooler. I'm not sure what time he got up, but he was a busy beaver because we have drinks, snacks, wine, and he's making us lunch whenever we anchor.

"So, why a sailboat?" I ask, propping my feet up on the ledge, making myself comfortable.

He glances over to me. "When I went to Harvard my best buddy's family owned one. Much larger than this, but I don't know . . . I loved it. His dad showed me how to sail. Just took a liking to it, I guess."

Good answer. I pop a piece of cheese in my mouth from the plate he put out. I've never spent time with a guy who catered to me like this.

"What about you?" he asks.

I look up, thinking I must've missed something while daydreaming. "What?"

"Why tattooing?" The sun shines on his own inked skin. Wherever he went, they did an awesome job. Not as good as me, but not so bad that I'd suggest a redo.

"I love to draw. I went to Berkeley."

"Good school," he comments.

"It's no Harvard, but I'm proud. Anyway, I quickly realized I might be a good artist, but I'd need something more to make a living, so I changed my art major to business. Tattooing lets me mix the two, so I had a guy who showed me the ropes. Eventually, he wanted to move to San Diego, so I took over his shop."

He nods. "So you own the shop?"

"I manage it and we're on a buy program, but I'm not sure that's what I want to do with my life."

He leaves the wheel for a minute to join me, reaches down, grabbing a slice of cheese and a cracker, then returns to his spot.

"Your dream isn't tattooing?" he asks and my stomach clenches.

Do I tell him? No, because he'll really think I'm a loon. "It's fine for now, but the hours are exhausting. Especially on the weekend. When I'm working, I can be there until all hours of the morning. The only good thing is my younger employees usually want those hours. It tends to be more entertaining." I smile, thinking about all the drunken guys I've hooked up with who have come in there, and then cringe, thinking Jasper wouldn't much like to hear that. Of course, he has his own drawer full of condoms at the ready, so who am I to say?

"I can imagine you meet some pretty interesting people." He smiles as though he truly does believe that and there's zero judgment.

"Yeah," I say, looking out to the horizon. "It's beautiful out here. Peaceful." I raise my hand, letting the wind blow through my fingers.

"I think that's why it's so addicting. Come here."

I stand up to join him and he puts me between him and the wheel. "I didn't like you so far away." He kisses my shoulder and I fall back into his strong chest. "We'll be docking soon," he says. "Take the wheel." He holds both my hands and places them on the wheel.

"I have no idea what I'm doing," I tell him, but he shoos me off.

"I'll instruct you," he says before his fingers slide down the front of me. He unbuttons my shorts and shimmies them down my hips until they fall at my feet.

I suck in a breath.

"You have no idea how hard I was when I bought that bikini. Just from imagining you in it." His hands slide around me again and he cups my mound.

I let one hand drop from the wheel in anticipation of touching him, but he has other ideas.

"Hands on the wheel," he scolds me and I return my hand to where it was, all of my knuckles white as I grip the wheel.

"I think all I have to do is this." He pulls the string on one side of my bottoms and they flop open. "Ah," he says, his hand moving to the other side. "This is the view I really want to see." He undoes the tie on the other side and the bottoms fall to the wooden floor of the boat.

Then his hands are gone, his chest no longer warming my back. I glance over my shoulder to find him sitting on the bench behind me, admiring me while he rubs his hard-on over his shorts.

"Now this, this is a beautiful view," he says, and then glances up to see my gaze on him. "Tsk, tsk. Hands on the wheel, beautiful." His finger circles around in the air and I do as I'm told.

His hands splay my ass and he squeezes. "I love your ass," he says. "The jeans you were wearing that time I first saw you in Starbucks . . . I beat off to that vision that night."

I feel the wetness pooling between my legs.

"Why don't we do this when we anchor so I can touch you?" I ask softly.

He chuckles, his finger moving through my wetness and back. "Because I like control." He smacks my ass with one hand and I jump.

"I've figured that out," I say dryly and he chuckles again.

"You can act like you don't like it, but I know you do." He eases my thighs further apart. "Your body doesn't lie."

I say nothing because I'm not going to agree, and I can't deny that this alpha domineering shit turns me on more than a teenage boy looking at his first *Playboy*.

"So wet." He slides his finger back and forth over my slit until he mercifully plunges one finger into me. I rise on my tiptoes, surprised and elated.

He stands up while another finger massages my clit. "Tell me, Lennon, would you prefer my tongue or my fingers?" he whispers and sucks my earlobe into his mouth.

His other hand rubs my ass, and I should be expecting it but I startle anyway.

Slap.

I yelp and grip the wheel tighter, the boat weaving slightly.

Jasper takes one hand and steadies the wheel until we're going straight again. "Now, now, don't crash my boat." He nibbles on my neck. "Answer the question, beautiful. Fingers or tongue?"

He's asking me whether I want cake or ice cream. They're equally delicious and I want them both. Together. At the same time. I want the ice cream to melt a little on the cake until I can't tell where one ends and one begins.

"Both." I inhale a deep breath and I feel his head shaking no in the crook of my neck.

"One or the other," he says, his teeth lightly scraping along my skin.

"Please," I whisper.

Smack.

Now my right ass cheek is red.

"Tongue," I pant.

His lips move up my neck and his finger leaves my clit, much to my dismay. A second later, his mouth replaces his finger and

I arch my back—the way every man loves when they're doing you doggy style—giving him as much access as I can.

He swipes his tongue the entire length of my opening and my hands fall from the wheel.

"Hands on the wheel, beautiful."

And I do as he says because I never want him to stop. He plants his hands firmly on my ass and spreads me apart while his thumbs trace lazy circles on the inside of my thighs as he devours my pussy.

My hands ache from clutching the wheel in an iron grip.

"I'm so hard," he mumbles.

I let my head drop back and stare up at the blue sky, dotted with wisps of clouds as my orgasm teeters at the edge, ready to dive into bliss.

I pant and squirm, my hips rocking, needing the friction on my clit that he's expertly denying me. His thumbs stop and he grips my thighs tighter, the tip of his tongue moving faster.

"Jasper," I sigh, trying to squeeze my thighs shut from the throbbing, but he holds them open and continues to worship me, never rushing the job.

Small inaudible moans escape him and just when I'm about ready to beg, he pushes two fingers into me and I fall forward over the steering wheel.

What starts as slow and rhythmic quickly turns fast and deep and I whizz past the teetering stage and dive right into an earth-shattering orgasm.

Damn, either those Kegel exercises are really helping, or Jasper is a Jedi when it comes to sex. I'd put money on the latter.

Jasper places a light kiss on my pussy and then rises from the deck, taking the wheel from behind me. His chest accepts the weight of my body as I collapse into his strength. He kisses the top of my head as I let my eyes drift closed.

"I hope you know I'm already planning my payback," I

mumble, still falling back to Earth from the shooting star that was my orgasm.

"I would expect nothing less." He chuckles and kisses my head one more time. "You have about two minutes to regain your strength."

I turn around and he glances down at my bare pussy. "I so love that you want me like this, but I don't think I can orgasm again. I need to eat something first."

He kisses the tip of my nose and I feel my cheeks heat. Why do I love that small, non-sexual gesture?

"I need you to help me with the sails so we can anchor."

My face heats further. "Oh," I say and he chuckles again.

"You have a reprieve for now," he says and winks.

Just like that my embarrassment disappears because I know deep down that our attraction is mutual. I'd always wondered if I'd ever find anyone who could make me speechless and sated after sex. Someone call Guinness, because Jasper's the world record holder and I think he'll be holding that spot for a long time.

Why is that so scary?

chapter FOURTEEN

WE SWIM, WE EAT, we sail back to the marina. By the time the sun is setting on the city, every limb hurts. Maybe it's from Jasper taking me on the beach of the small island he anchored near. Or maybe it's from when he thought he could eat sushi off my body after I told him I worked at a naked sushi place for a bit and he took a break to suck on my tits. His drawer of condoms is almost depleted and although I would love to have him once more before coming back to the real world, my body is not going to survive.

Holy shit. Jasper has out-sexed me.

We're docked and my back is to his chest, each of us with a glass of wine, watching the sun disappear in the sky. The hand he has slung around my stomach tightens and he kisses my temple.

"Thank you for spending the day with me," he says and I crane my neck to look at him.

"Thank you for inviting me. I think if I owned this boat, I'd be on here every day." I place my hand on the seat and graze it along the soft leather.

"Well, I hope it won't be your last time here," he says,

sounding a little unsure of himself.

I twist around, up on my knees to face him. "Anytime you invite me, I'm here."

I mean it too. Jasper might not be mine. Hell, he might not want me for more than a few dalliances, but I'll take him while I can have him.

"Let's lock this up and we'll get you home." He pats my ass and I move to stand up.

A surprising rush of disappointment floods my veins and it feels like a boulder rests in my stomach. I wish I didn't have to say goodbye to Jasper. I push the thought away because there's no way I would ever consider monogamy. Too boring.

I climb down the ladder and grab my dress that Jasper so nicely put on a hanger in the small closet. A minute or so later, Jasper comes downstairs, grabbing flip-flops he must have bought, and throws his other clothes in the Target bag.

"Do you get sad when you leave it?" I ask him and he chuckles but nods.

"I do. I'd live on it if it was bigger," he remarks. From what I saw he could totally live on it, but men like Jasper Banks probably like to live a lusher lifestyle.

On the taxi ride home, my cell rings and I press ignore, not wanting to interrupt my last minutes with Jasper. It rings again and he looks over, releasing my hand from his.

"Go ahead." He nods and I slide the phone to my ear.

"Yes?" I answer, already knowing it's Whitney.

"Oh, my God!" she screams. "Oh, my God! Oh. My. God!"

I hang up.

"Who was that?" Jasper asked with a wrinkle in his forehead.

"I think my friend just butt-dialed me while fucking her boyfriend. I'm pretty sure I heard her orgasm."

Most friends would find it disgusting, but Whitney and I

went camping together a time or two in college and tents aren't exactly known for their noise-deafening properties. Let's just say I was woken up in the middle of the night thinking a bear was outside our tent.

His eyebrows crinkle. Yeah, welcome to my life.

My phone rings again and I look down to see it's Whitney again.

I answer.

"Whitney!" I scream into the phone and the taxi driver slams on the brakes.

"Oh, it's okay, she's on the phone," Jasper tells the taxi driver and he hits the gas again.

"Why are you yelling?" Whitney says.

Thankfully, her orgasm is over.

"You butt-dialed me while Cole's cock was inside of you," I say dryly.

"Oh, my God, that's so embarrassing." She laughs.

"Please don't repeat those words. I'll never be able to keep a straight face in church the next time my mom drags me there if you keep reminding me."

She laughs again. "Well, you should know that it wasn't Cole's cock. I was raving about Cheap Thrill."

Cheap Thrill is my newest creation and I just passed along the vibrators to her and Tahlia to try out.

I sit up straighter in my seat and my melancholy about leaving Jasper is replaced with a high over the success of my latest product.

"You like it?" I ask.

"Um, yeah." She lowers her voice. "That swirly thing it does? Cole has some competition." She giggles.

"The hell I do. I'm her unicorn cock," Cole screams behind her and I laugh that the two of them might have enjoyed Cheap

Thrill together.

"I'm glad you like it," I say softly because Jasper's studying me.

"I do. I hope Tahlia tries it out. This is going to be a *huge* seller, Len. Great job," she raves and I blush, slightly embarrassed at the compliment.

"I'm glad," I repeat because I can't very well ask her any specifics about the product right now.

"Why are you so quiet?" Whitney picks up on my uncharacteristic demureness.

"I'm just in a taxi," I remark, offering Jasper a small smile.

He seems appeased and looks out the window.

"That's never stopped you before. Ask me the questions. Cole was here so you can ask him too," she offers and I cringe.

"How about I stop by tomorrow sometime?"

"I'm not sure if he'll be around. Come on, you want our honest thoughts while it's fresh in our minds. Now or never," she singsongs.

I should tell her I'm with Jasper, but then she'd ask questions about why I'm still with him when the date should've been over last night. I'm not in the mood to try to define my feelings about him or what the hell it is I want from him. I'm in shambles as it is.

"Okay, well, I'll call you when I get to my apartment," I mumble into the phone, covering the receiver with my hand.

"Have you been abducted?" she asks, actually sounding concerned that that's a possibility.

"No. Are you a crazy person? No."

"Where's my Lennon? Is this someone with a voice changer? Give me back my friend," she jokes and I roll my eyes.

"You're taking that investigative reporter thing a little too seriously. I'm here. I'm fine. I'll call you when I get home." I click the phone off and thankfully she doesn't call back.

I turn to Jasper. "Just my friend," I say and he nods.

"She's very loud," he remarks and I nod several times.

"Tourette's."

He laughs and I smile that I was able to make him laugh.

A second later my phone lights up with a text. It's a picture of Cheap Thrill next to Whitney's head with a thumbs up. I fumble my hand from Jasper's to grab it, but he's faster, reaching across with his free hand.

"Is that what I think it is?" he says, lifting the phone to inspect it. "Is that the reporter from the WHFI Station?"

A rush of heat floods my face and I grab the phone back. "Whitney Knight, yep. She's one of my best friends."

"Is that a vibrator?" he asks, leaning over for another glimpse. "Are you bisexual?" he asks with a straight face. I almost want to say yes to see his reaction and if it were anyone else, I would've.

"Yes and no."

"Should I be upset that my buddies don't send me pictures of anal beads?" he asks and now I'm laughing, the uncontrollable kind that has tears streaming down my face. "Seriously, I know there's a lot of things the genders do differently, but do girls send pictures of sex toys to one another on the regular?" I can tell he's joking from the impish grin on his face, but I have no idea how to get out of this conversation.

Telling someone you want to start a sex toy company is hard. Even more so when this is the one topic of conversation I want to avoid having with him.

"No, not really." I shake my head.

"Care to explain?" He accents his voice like Ricky Ricardo and I'm about ready for him to scream "Lennon" with the same accent. Who knew a strait-laced guy like Jasper Banks had a humorous bone in that amazing body?

Not wanting to pile another lie on top of my lie-by-omission when we met, I take a deep breath and shift in my seat, flipping the pictures up on my phone.

"This is what I want to do." I hand him the phone and he scrolls through the pictures fast and then flicks back slower.

"You want to be a sex toy tester?" he asks, still focused on the pictures.

I take the phone away from him. "No, I created these."

The taxi slows and pulls up to the curb near my apartment and I catch the driver looking at me through the rearview mirror. He looks interested and if Jasper weren't here I might see if he wanted to purchase one of the samples I have in my apartment.

"Created?" he questions, completely oblivious to the fact that the taxi has stopped.

"I've designed a bunch of different toys and I have a guy who's been making some molds to produce the products and helping me through the testing process."

His fingers stop swiping and he stares up at me, eyes boring into me. "Mold? Helps you to test them?" His eyebrows crinkle and it's the most adorable thing watching his mind whirl with assumptions.

"We don't try them out together. He makes me a few samples of each and I give them to my friends." I move my hand in front of us to insinuate he should slide out of the vehicle.

"So it's platonic?"

I laugh. "Yes, it's platonic."

"Phew." His rigid shoulders relax and he falls back into the seat of the cab. "I was about to volunteer to be a mold." He grins.

I inch closer, my lips coming to his ear. "I'd take you up on that offer, but I don't think I'd want millions of women to know what you're packing. I'd never get you for myself again."

This time it's his cheeks flushing red. "Oh, shit. We're here." He fiddles with the door handle for a second, then he opens it and I file out behind him.

After he pays the cab driver, he joins me on the walk up

to my apartment. I'm surprised. I would've thought he'd had enough of me and would just say goodbye in the backseat of the cab—especially after what I just divulged to him.

He's quiet until we hop off the elevator and I can't help but wonder what he's thinking, which is new for me. Usually I could give two shits what a guy thinks about me. Take me or leave me as I am.

Is Jasper thinking I'm way more insane than he thought? That someone who wants to invent sex toys cannot be part of his strait-laced and organized life?

I insert my key into the lock and open my door. Before I can enter he cages me against the hinge of the door, gripping the top.

"So, you have samples?" he asks and I see the devilish gleam in his gold-flecked eyes.

"I do." I slip under his arm and he follows me in.

"I take it you've tried them?" he asks, his hands on my hips as he kicks the door shut.

"Well, well, Mr. Banks, your sexual appetite seems to have returned," I joke, batting my eyelashes at him.

"My appetite for you never wanes, beautiful." His lips descend on mine, mingling and mixing until the back of my knees hits the edge of the mattress. Sometimes it's good to live in a small space. Less time spent getting into bed.

I fall down onto the mattress and he looks around.

"Let's try some out," he suggests.

A slow smile creeps across my face. I get on my knees and scramble to the top of the mattress to grab my bag from the floor near my dresser. Bringing it onto the bed, I allow him to open it.

"Looks like I'm going to be exhausted tomorrow morning," he says, digging through the bag like a pirate who just found buried treasure.

"Promise?" I ask coyly.

He pulls out Tickled Pink, a hot pink vibrating dildo and

one of the first creations. His gaze locks with mine. "Absolutely."

After giving Jasper a strip tease while I undressed—at his insistence—I lay in front of him on the bed. He's still fully clothed, which hardly seems fair, but he says he wants this to be all about me. Who am I to argue?

The hum of the vibrator fills the room when he turns it on. My insides clench in anticipation. He trails the tip up and down my pussy a few times and I gasp every time it comes into contact with my clit.

Jasper's lids are heavy when he pushes the tip into me, just enough to get it wet and then pulls it out. I groan with displeasure and one corner of his lip lifts in a smirk. I watch as he brings the glistening pink toy to my nipple and presses it there, spreading my wetness around the puckered tip. The vibrations jolt through my nipple and straight to my swollen clit. He pulls the toy away and wets it inside me again before doing the same thing to my other nipple.

"I'm going to enjoy licking you clean," he says and bends forward to pull my nipple into his mouth. He sucks hard and settles the vibrator between my spread legs. I arch my back up off the mattress as the buzzing toy leaves me breathless.

Once he's driven me near the edge and I'm a panting mess, he bites my nipple lightly and sits back on his knees, keeping the vibrator in place between my legs.

"Are you ready to come all over my face?" he asks in a rough voice.

His erection strains the confines of his pants and though I'd give anything to get my hands on his perfect cock right now, I don't want this to end.

Jasper adjusts his position so that he's laying between my legs, my thighs spread over his shoulders. I watch, unable to breathe, as he slowly pushes the vibrator inside of me, his heated eyes not missing any of it.

I moan and cup my tit in my hand, tweaking my nipple.

Jasper's mouth clamps onto my clit and sucks, then flicks, then sucks again. He eats my pussy like a pro while he drags the vibrator in and out of me. It's only a couple of minutes before I'm ready to explode.

"Jasper . . . Oh, God. I'm going to come!" I scream out as he sucks hard on my swollen bud and my pussy clamps down around the toy while my orgasm rips through me. He pulls the vibrator from me and moves down to lap up every last bit of my pleasure.

"Fuck. You taste amazing."

I glance down at him between my legs while I try to catch my breathe and give him a small smile. It's all I can manage at the moment.

He tosses Tickled Pink to the other side of the mattress and reaches down beside the bed, pulling up the bag with all my creations. "So, which one do you want to try out next?" he asks with a grin.

I've officially met my match.

WITH THE SUN COMES morning. With morning comes Jasper's departure, though at the moment he's still in my apartment getting dressed.

He pulls his t-shirt over his head. "So, where are you in the process of trying to get all this off the ground?" he asks, nodding toward the bag of treats at the end of my bed.

I stare blankly at him, unsure how to respond. This is a do-or-die moment. My business needs him, but I fear losing him personally. Whatever. I can maintain my honesty with him and if for any reason he did offer to invest, I'll just turn him down.

"I had an inheritance from my grandmother that I've used

to get this far, but that's pretty well gone now. I tried to get a loan from a bank, but—"

"Jacob?" he asks and then shakes his head. "Nah, a bank would never take that loan anyway. That's a hard line." His comment shows how well he understands this business. "You need a private investor," he says, more as a statement of fact than a question. His eyebrows rise and his lips curve. "I think I know one."

I shake my head. "I could never let you do that." What a one-eighty. Two weeks ago and I would've been jumping for joy that I was having this conversation, not turning him down.

"Not me." His hand moves to caress my cheek. "I'd love to be your investor, but I never mix business with pleasure. And you are definitely pleasure, Lennon. Maybe I'm blinded, but I think you have a good thing here. Your entire approach is different than anything that's on the market as far as I know and you're definitely on trend with the female sexual empowerment angle." He eyes the slew of sex toys we tried out last night. "But as good as an investment opportunity as I think this might be, I don't want us to end because of it."

I nod, because unbeknownst to him, I'd already made that decision for us when I agreed to go on a date with him.

"Listen, my partner and I do a lot of deals together, but we've both invested in things independent of our business. Why don't you meet with him? I can't promise anything, but—"

I jump in his arms. "Seriously?"

He catches me, swinging my legs around his torso. "I can give you a personal reference on the products." A smile teases his lips. "I'll talk to him and set something up for this week?"

He poses it as a question, like I'd say no. The perfect solution to my problem just presented itself. This way I get Jasper and a way to help my business.

"Thank you." I kiss him on the lips and he deepens it, his

tongue diving into my mouth with such ownership that it feels like he's branding me as his.

Once he tears his mouth from mine, he lightly smacks my ass to get off of him so I slide to the floor.

"Now, can we talk about a second date for us?" he asks.

"Since our first date lasted thirty-six hours, I might need you to be more specific."

He laughs. "How about tomorrow evening?"

I nod. "I'd love to."

He kisses my nose again and I melt a little more for him. "Come on. I'll buy you some coffee."

I follow him out, not having the first clue where this thing between us is going. I'm usually fine not having all the answers and just seeing where life takes me, so I ignore the voice in my head telling me I'm already way too invested in Jasper and me.

chapter

FIFTEEN

THE FOLLOWING WEEK, MY palms are damp and I swear the skin behind my knees is sweating as I sit in a chair in the fancy waiting area of Jasper and his partner's business. The phone hasn't rung once since I've walked in. No one else has gotten off the elevator and no one looks like they've poured a cup of coffee from the area set up with a mini-fridge in the waiting room. It's a virtual ghost town.

I glance at my portfolio, wanting to open it up to make sure I have everything I need, but I must have done that ten times before I left my apartment this morning. Besides, I'd probably open it up just as Mr. Ashland walks out. So, in the meantime, my toes tap on the hardwood floors while the receptionist, Brittany, keeps peeking her head over the edge of the desk, clearly annoyed by my tapping.

I don't stop. Because the alternative is to allow all the pent-up nerves to amass in my system, resulting in me throwing up in this lovely reception area. So even though she doesn't know it, I'm saving Brittany from having the shittiest day cleaning up my vomit.

Jasper walks out from down the hall with two Starbucks coffee cups in his hands. "Why didn't you page me?" he asks Brittany and then smiles at me.

She twists her blonde strands around her fingers and shrugs her shoulders. "She asked for Drew."

"Mr. Ashland," he corrects, with authority in his voice. It reminds me of the way he likes to boss me around in bed and I press my thighs together. "I told you that when Lennon came in, you were to page me." He stops on the other side of her desk so he can look at her while he's talking to her.

"I'm sorry, Mr. Banks." She turns her gaze down to the desk in front of her and pushes out her bottom lip.

Jasper turns and walks toward me, rolling his eyes. "Hey, beautiful," he says, taking the seat next to me. He hands me one of the coffees and I turn it around in my hand until I see the handwriting.

Joy Mangano.

I laugh and he knocks his cup with mine.

After our dinner Tuesday night, he came over to watch a movie on Wednesday. He picked the movie *Joy* with Jennifer Lawrence because it's a true story about a woman named Joy Mangano who created the Wonder Mop and over one hundred other products. I see why he picked that now, especially since I offered to watch *The Magnificent Seven*. I'm a little relieved. I was worried he was a bit on the pussy side with his movie selection.

"Aren't you a sweetie." I lean over and kiss him on the cheek.

He smiles and rests his ankle on his knee. "I have moments. I'd take you to my office and let you thank me with a proper kiss, but I might lock the door and you'll miss your meeting." He winks.

"I can thank you in my own special way later." I flutter my eyelashes and he shifts in his seat.

"Stop doing that." He eyes Brittany, who is now typing on

her cell phone.

"Doing what?" I lower my voice, but make it high-pitched, like an innocent schoolgirl.

"That." His eyes widen and I giggle, turning my attention to his Starbucks cup.

"Who are you today?" I ask him, and a sly smile tilts his lips.

Gordon Gekko.

I arch an eyebrow and he shakes his head and presses his lips together in mock disappointment.

"I've stumped you already?" When I say nothing, he shakes his head. "I can see I need to educate you in fine cinema from the past. It's from *Wall Street*. Michael Douglas' character."

"Ohhhh," I exaggerate, knowing almost nothing about the movie except that all the guys wore suits. Much like Jasper. "Nice suit." I wink and he leans in closer to my ear.

"I'm freeballing today," he whispers and I smack his arm.

I press my thighs together even harder this time. "Seriously?" I smack his arm again so he knows how unfair he's being.

"What?" He holds his hands up in the air with an innocent expression on his face.

"How am I supposed to be in the meeting, knowing that if I unzipped your pants, your cock would pop out?" I run my tongue along my bottom lip.

"Shh." He chuckles and looks in Brittany's direction.

I glance at her, too, but she's doing nothing but typing on her phone still. "She's a real employee of the year, that one."

He rolls his eyes again. "She's Drew's cousin."

I nod my head back in understanding.

"Miss Hart." A nice older lady comes out from the hallway and then eyes Jasper beside me. "Oh, Mr. Banks. I was just calling your office. Mr. Ashland would like you to sit in on the meeting."

Jasper stands, taking my portfolio from where it rests. "I was already planning on it." He looks down at me and smiles in a cocky smirk because he knows I'm going to have trouble talking about sex toys when I know he's going commando beside me.

Jackass.

I take my portfolio from him and set my coffee on the side table. "Hello. I'm Miss Hart," I say and the lady nods.

"Sue. Please follow me." She walks a little ahead of me and I hear Jasper's deep breaths behind me. I know what he's looking at and to say I didn't think about him when I got dressed this morning would be a lie.

Sue stops us at a door and throws out her hand for me to walk through.

"Thank you."

"Thanks, Sue." Jasper trails behind me and I inwardly cringe that this is not the professional meeting I had anticipated.

"Jasper," she says and nods.

Drew sits behind a desk placed in his corner office with a view. Windows make up every inch of the exterior wall. When he sees us he stands, buttoning his suit jacket and rounding the desk.

Holy shit. He's hot.

Bad Lennon. He's . . . nope, no other word. He's hot. What can I say? Old habits die hard.

His black hair is gelled to perfection and he's wearing a dark green suit with matching tie. The man oozes confidence and sophistication.

"Miss Hart, I've heard a lot about you this past week." He holds out his hand and I shake it. Hoping I'm firm enough but not too hard. You know, professional.

He eyes Jasper over my shoulder. "Did you bring me a coffee?" Drew tilts his head and bats his eyes and I turn my head to see Jasper holding the coffee I left in the waiting room.

"Hell, no. Have Brittany fetch you one. Not like she's busy doing anything else." Jasper sits down on the sofa and I wonder if he's going to sit behind us the entire time.

"And here I thought your ornery personality would disappear the moment the lovely Lennon arrived." Drew purses his lips and I wonder if they had some kind of conversation before I got here. "Come and sit down." Drew waves his hand toward the couch.

I do what he says and, not wanting to take the chair and leave the two guys to sit by one another, I sit next to Jasper, throwing him a look, warning him not touch me. He slides over a bit, giving me room, understanding my non-verbal communication.

Look at me, I already have him trained somewhat. Oh, relax, I'm kidding.

Drew sits down on the chair opposite me and unbuttons his jacket and I eye his pocket watch that's connected by a chain from his vest button to a pocket—very old-school sexy. He rubs his hands together. "Tell me. What do you have?"

He's like one of those sharks on *Shark Tank*, the way he's so casual about it. Jasper sits up, granting me his undivided attention as well.

I open my portfolio and pull out the spec sheets of the products I've already had made and the drawings I've sketched out that remain only in my imagination—for now.

Drew takes my drawings, flipping through them while I tell him a bit about my ideas for the company and what makes my products different than every other sex toy out there. After he's done going through all my designs he looks up at me.

"Please don't take this the wrong way, but I'm not sure if I can work with you while you're dating Jasper. I mean, I can't help but wonder—"

"Stop it, Drew." Jasper's voice is low and his tone is filled with warning.

Drew laughs and looks at me. "Sorry, I just love messing with him." He leans in closer. "He's very protective of you. Interesting." He winks and my stomach rolls over on itself because

I'm not sure how to take his comment.

"Business," Jasper warns him again and is only rewarded with Drew's teasing laugh.

"I mean, he must really want you to succeed because I know he'd probably rather eat broccoli than have me be your investor."

I glance back to Jasper and his eyes rolling to the back of his head.

"Do you not like broccoli?" I ask and Jasper throws his hands up in the air.

"Hates it. Spits it out like a child." Drew laughs again and Jasper throws his cup at Drew, hitting him square on the head.

Luckily, it's empty.

"What the hell, man?" Drew stands up, looking over his suit.

My guess is it's expensive, God knows why. I do appreciate vintage, but he looks like a giant leprechaun. Of course, he does have a pot of gold he's willing to share. I'll be quiet now.

"Relax, it was empty." Jasper blows out some air. "Get serious or I'll take on her business and you'll be pissing and moaning about how much money you lost out on."

Drew sits back down, his humorous expression turning serious. "All right, let's get this pitch over with and then we can all go to lunch."

I can't help but feel offended that he doesn't seem to be treating this meeting professionally. I have no plans to rush through the pitch, not to mention the only plans I have for lunch consist of Jasper's cock.

"I assume you have samples?" Drew asks and as quick as the snap of a whip on my back, the meeting's tone changes into all business. Now I can see how this man makes all his money.

"I do." I open the bag I have, setting them on the table between us. I go through each one explaining what they're used for and what makes them unique.

For the remaining twenty minutes, Drew is the epitome

of an assured investor. Jasper sits quietly next to me, his elbows resting on his knees, facing forward to hear my explanations. Once I'm done, Drew asks me questions—the production cost of each unit, how much I've already invested in the company, how much inventory I'll need, how I plan to ship them out and finally how I'm going to sell them to women. I answer all the questions and hand him a copy of my business plan.

He sits back in his chair and crosses his leg so that his ankle rests on his knee. That's when I notice little pots of gold on his socks as he studies my business plan. I purse my lips and divert my eyes before I start singing the *Lucky Charms* song. Instead I admire all the degrees he has framed and posted above the couch.

Harvard for undergraduate and graduate. Figures. Mr. Smarty Pants. Show off.

"'Magically delicious,'" Drew sings, placing my business plan on the table next to him. I glance over to him with wide eyes and he cocks an eyebrow. "You were humming," he says by way of explanation.

I was not.

Jasper starts laughing next to me and I so desperately want to elbow him in the ribcage.

Here's my shot and this guy is going to put two and two together and think I was mocking him. "I'm sorry. I have no idea why," I lie.

"Now, Lennon. You don't mind me calling you Lennon, do you?" Drew asks.

I shake my head. He could call me a C U Next Tuesday right now and I'd just nod my head.

"I don't like doing business with liars." His face is stone-cold serious.

My heartbeat picks up pace, my face heats and those palms that had dried off are now sweating again.

"Well, I noticed your socks and the song just kind of got

stuck in my head." I nod toward the damn socks that might just cost me this deal.

He glances down and Jasper stands from the couch. "You moron. You purposely dressed like you're ready to slide down a rainbow into a pot of gold." Jasper holds his hand out to me, but I don't take it.

Drew looks down at his socks, like he doesn't remember putting them on this morning.

"I really meant no offense. I swear. It had nothing to do with your suit." I backpedal as best I can, but I'm making a bigger mess of this. The meeting was going great until my damn subconscious had to hum a theme song I probably haven't heard since I was ten.

"Come on, Lennon." Jasper offers me his hand once more. "I razz him all the time about how he dresses, he'll get over it."

"No." I shake my head and lean forward. "I'm really sorry." My voice is small, but it earns me his attention as Drew raises his head to look at me. His lips hold a coy smile and he looks like he's trying not to laugh. "Seriously?" I ask.

He falls back into his chair laughing, and Jasper blows out an exasperated breath.

"You're a fucking baby," Jasper says, but all I can do is release the tensed-up breath that was locked in my lungs.

"I'm brilliant." He puts his hand out in front of him for me to take. "I think you have something here. I'll need my team to do some due diligence to make sure there are no surprises, but from everything we've discussed I don't anticipate any issues. I look forward to working with you." He has a genuine smile on his face now.

"Really?" I ask.

"Yes. Now if you ever want to ditch jackass and show me how you use them, I'm open."

Jasper growls from where he stands behind Drew.

"I'm kidding. Of course." He leans toward me. "Like I said . . . protective. It's better not to poke the bear." He winks and I realize that his emerald eyes match his suit.

"Thank you so much," I say, realizing my hand is still in his, shaking it up and down.

"You can let go now, Lennon," Jasper mumbles.

"Maybe she likes my hand," Drew challenges and turns to look behind him where Jasper's eyes lock with his and he gives him a short shake of his head. "Oh, this is going to be so much fun." He lets go of my hand and heads back to behind his desk. "Sue will email you some papers and she'll include a list of what we need. The first thing we need to get to work on is the patents." He sits down and just like that he's all business again.

"Thank you for taking a chance with me, Mr. Ashland."

"Please, call me Drew," he says and I nod, picking up my portfolio. While I try to put the toys back in the bag, Jasper and he start talking about another client. I find their relationship refreshing and it shows me an entirely different side of Jasper. "So you two go and I'll meet you by Brittany's desk in what? A half hour?"

I eye Jasper and we share a look of understanding, knowing exactly what the two of us will be doing during that half hour.

"Perfect." Jasper walks to the door to open it for me.

This time when he takes my portfolio, I don't object because I'll need both my hands for what I'm about to do.

We walk down the hallway like professionals, Jasper leading the way, his arm lazily swinging back and forth in a casual manner. He stops, introduces me to his secretary who thankfully, is friendlier than Sue but about the same age.

"Hold my calls, Lynn," he tells her and opens the door to his office.

I walk in and he shuts the door, then flicks the lock. I take a moment to look around his office. It's as big as Drew's but more contemporary. Jasper's hand skims down my arm, swiveling me around.

"Thank you," I say and he only stares down at me.

"I'm glad it worked out." He takes his hand and pulls me toward him and I feel his length pressed against my stomach.

"I think you knew it was going to work out before I even walked in." I raise an eyebrow.

"Believe me, I may have talked to him, but I never know what Drew is going to do." His hand slides through my hair and he starts to dip his head for a kiss, but I shake my head.

With my hand in the middle of his chest I push him backwards toward his desk until he falls back into his desk chair. A grin tugs one corner of his lips up as I fall to my knees in front of him. This time I'm in control.

"I want you to think of me every time you're sitting in this chair," I say.

Jasper stares down at me as I unbuckle his belt, undo the button, pull down the zipper and let his already hard cock spring free.

I lick my lips when I notice the bead of pre-cum glistening on the tip. "Seems someone's looking forward to this."

"I've been staring at that red lipstick on your mouth all morning waiting to see what it would look like wrapped around the base of my cock."

His dirty words always get me so hot. "Well, let's see if it's everything you imagined it'd be."

I lick the pre-cum off his mushroom tip and then spread my lips wide and drag my lips down his hardness until he's breaching the back of my throat.

"Fuuuck," he moans and pushes his hands into my hair.

I suction my cheeks in and move back up his length, sucking the whole way. A few more bobs on my part and Jasper reaches for his phone on the desk.

"Mind if I take a few shots? You have my word I won't ever share them with anyone."

I let his wet cock slip from my mouth with a pop. "Be my guest. Just make sure you send me a copy."

I slid my hand up and down his cock a few times, twisting when I reach the tip, and his hips start to piston up off the chair. "God, Lennon. I didn't know what I was missing before you."

I smirk and get back to work teasing him to the edge several times before backing off. I can hear the shutter on his camera phone go off and it turns me on so much to know he's documenting this that I think I might finish before he does.

I lap at his sac and suck one of his balls in my mouth—gentle enough that I won't hurt him, but with enough pressure to make him wild. And it does. He sets his phone back down on the desk and his hands return to my hair.

"I'm going to be beating off to those pictures after you leave, I can guarantee that. You're so fucking hot."

I continue to jerk him off while I switch to his other testicle and his hands tighten in my hair. Deciding he's close and that I'll put him out of his misery this time, I pull back and then swirl my tongue around his tip a few times before bringing almost all of him into my mouth.

My free hand plays with his balls while I deepthroat him and a minute later he's groaning and coming down the back of my throat. I swallow all of him and pump him a few times before I lean back on my heels.

His hands fall from my hair and he lies back in his chair, his legs wide apart, his pants open, looking spent. Right or wrong, it brings a smile to my face that it was courtesy of me.

"You are . . ." He's shaking his head as he trails off.

I stand up and dust off my knees. "I'll take that as a compliment," I say and wink.

He laughs, but stops abruptly, his expression turning

determined and serious. "Now get your ass up on that desk and spread for me. I'm going to make you come on my tongue—twice."

Thank God Jasper is a man of his word.

chapter SIXTEEN

JASPER HAS WHISKED ME away for a two-day trip up in God knows where, like he expects me to hike or some shit. My only stipulation was a bathroom with running water and flushable toilet. I gave Tahlia so much shit a few months ago about how not outdoorsy she is, but truth is, I've never camped, nor do I plan to.

"Close your eyes," Jasper says, coming up from behind me and covering my eyes.

"I swear if you're planning to murder me, there are people who will search for me."

He chuckles and I smell the cologne on his shirt. It's been two weeks and I'm still in shock that I haven't gotten sick of him yet. Quite the opposite. I can't seem to get enough of him and the more time I spend with Jasper the more I want him.

"I'm not going to murder you. Okay, now walk forward." My foot hits something and he catches me before I fall face forward. "Sorry."

"Okay, when do I get to open my eyes?" I have my hands outstretched in front of me to make sure I don't walk into anything.

"In a second." From his tone, I can tell he's getting way too much enjoyment from this. "Step up," he instructs.

I hear a creak and then he takes his hands off my eyes. I open them and stare at the log cabin in front of me.

"I'm sorry, who do you think you brought up here?" I ask, turning around to find his Range Rover parked outside in front of the cabin and no other human being in sight. "Oh, my God, you're going to murder me. Either that or you want me to join some polygamist cult where I'll have to grow my hair long and wear those ugly dresses."

He laughs. "It's just us for two days. The fridge is stocked, movies are supplied, and we get two sunsets and two sunrises for us to watch from the bedroom upstairs." He casts small kisses up my neck and shoulder. He does that a lot and though I haven't asked I think it might be his favorite area of my body. At least his favorite that he can give attention to in public.

I turn to face the cabin. "Hmm . . . sounds nice." Now, it isn't the Ritz with room service, but a whole weekend away with no distractions except for Jasper? Pretty close to perfect.

"That's why we're here." He unhooks his arms from around my stomach. "Let's go check it out."

On the way to the door, I stop before he opens it.

"How close is the next breathing person?" I ask and he chuckles, inserting the key into the lock, disregarding my question.

But I'd really like an answer. Truth is, I've only known the guy for three weeks. Pulling out my phone, I send a quick text to Whitney and Tahlia.

Me: Jasper took me to the woods for two days. If I don't return, make sure the police question him.

Three dots appear next to Tahlia's name.

Tahlia: On it, although I'm pretty sure you'd be the smart girl in the murder movie. Just make sure if you hear something in the woods you don't go investigate it.

Oh, it warms my heart that she thinks so highly of me.

Whitney: Did you bring enough lube?

Seriously, she and Cole need to calm down because that would have been my line if the roles were reversed.

A deep throat-clearing interrupts my fingers, poised to fire back another text, and I look up to find Jasper standing in the middle of a beautiful living room.

"Sorry," I say, pocketing my phone. "Just letting my friends know where to look for my body."

He chuckles, holding his hand out for me to meet him in the middle of the huge room.

The couches are big brown leather, worn in with lacquered tables and a big screen television anchored to the wall. To my right is a kitchen, small, with a breakfast bar stretching along the front. An open staircase leads to a second level.

"This is nice," I say.

His arms slide around my stomach, anchoring on my lower back. "You're nice." He kisses my nose.

"Thank you." I mean it. In the past two weeks, Jasper has treated me like a princess and not just some girl he's fooling around with. He's taken me to so many nice places and shown me so many things I would have never seen otherwise.

Ugh, did I really just reference princesses? What's happening to me?

There have been limited nights that we've spent apart, living in our own little bubble, not inviting others to interfere. Drew wanted to get a move on quickly so he has their lawyer starting to work on the patents and according to Jasper, he's found a love for sex toys in his own personal life. Thankfully,

Jasper spares me the details.

Jasper has fucked me on every surface of his boat, my apartment, his office and my tattoo parlor. My hands feel empty if they aren't on him and since every time we're within a foot of one another, I'm usually on his lap, he must feel the same way.

"Come on." He grabs my hand, pulling me toward the staircase.

"We should get our bags," I mention, but he shakes his head.

"In a second." He pulls and I oblige, following him up the stairs to where I assume the bedrooms are.

See? All of our conversations happen naked and in bed where we do our best bonding.

We enter the bedroom through a set of double doors and there sits a king-size bed. I jump on it, throwing my body on top of the mattress.

"I'm going to miss you tonight," I mention and he jumps on to join me. "This bed is so big."

He snuggles into me, his hands cupping both my breasts. Our usual sleeping positions.

"I don't care if we have the biggest bed ever invented, this is how I sleep when you're with me." His thumbs move over my nipples and they peak in response. My tits are always ready to come out and be played with.

"Maybe I don't want to share my space." I grind my ass against him and he grinds me back, letting me know he's ready.

Last week I made us get tested. I'm already on the pill, and though it'd be a first for me, I don't want to worry about condoms with Jasper. He didn't seem thrilled about the idea, but he agreed to have the test and said we can discuss it later. Our tests came back four days ago and he's continued to use condoms, but this is something I want to share with him.

"Don't worry, I brought a lot of condoms," he says in that low voice I love.

I roll over and place my hands on his cheeks. "How about we forego anything between us? We're both clean."

His hands move to my hips and he throws his head back, blowing out a long breath. "I don't know . . ." he says, like it's taking every ounce of his restraint not to say anything more.

I lie on top of him, my hand massaging his cock though his worn jeans. "I'm sorry. I want to experience that with you. It's one of the rare firsts I can give to you."

He looks at me with eyes full of lust and yearning, but I can tell that the answer is still no. "Lenno—"

"It's fine, Jasper. One day you'll trust me enough."

He kisses my nose in thanks and grinds his erection against that perfect spot that has me moaning.

I'm not sure what his hang-up is. I mean, he does get BBBJs. That's 'bareback blow job' for those of you not down with the slang. So I know it's not that he's hyper-protective about safe sex.

Jasper's phone rings and now I blow out an exasperated breath. Lately, that thing hasn't stopped. The entire car ride up, I had to listen to his conversation about some key fob invention thing and blah, blah, blah.

"How about we lock the phone in the car?" I ask, kissing his neck.

He glances to the phone and holds his finger up.

One minute my ass.

He stays in the bed, and answers the phone.

"Banks," he says and I prop up, straddling his waist. My fingers unhook the button of his jeans and he shakes his head, holding up that damn finger again.

I take his finger and bring it to my breast so he's slowly circling my nipple. My tight tank top doesn't leave a ton to the imagination.

"Listen, I have some emails out and I'm waiting for calls back," he says, and I open his fist, moving his hand back to my tit, rubbing it around in circles. Pretty soon, he's doing it on his own.

I grind my center along his dick, and then slide down to his thighs, my fingers sliding down his zipper.

"I have to go, but I'll call you when I get news." He pauses, trying to move me off his body, but with one hand I'm stronger right now.

I strip off my tank top and he closes his eyes.

"Yes, I understand," he says in a strained voice.

Reaching behind, I unhook my bra, letting it fall forward to lie on his chest. His eyes bug out and he reaches out, but I slide away.

"Victor, I do understand, but not much will happen until Monday."

His eyes are on me and I wonder if Victor can hear the trembling in his voice.

I pull at his jeans and he helps me by rocking his hips back and forth. Once I get them off his legs, I find red boxer briefs below and wetness pools between my legs.

Maybe it's because we've been in San Francisco after workdays mostly, but Jasper has an overabundance of black boxer briefs, so the fact he's wearing something different excites me. Shows me a different side of him. Is this how men are with lingerie?

"I have to go, Victor. I promise to be in touch." He clicks off his phone. Fiddling with it, he holds it up. "I'm putting this thing on 'do not disturb.'" He drops it on the nightstand and I climb up his body. "Take off the shorts," he orders.

"Such a bossy pants," I say and he cocks his eyebrow.

"I am and you like it that way."

True, but he doesn't need to know that.

"I like control." I unbutton my shorts and push them down my legs, leaving me in a purple see-through thong.

"Believe me, you have more control than you think." He

sits up on the headboard, holding his hands out for me.

I crawl up, purposely grinding my tits around his dick.

"I like the red," I say and he smiles, reaching down to push my tits together around his dick.

"I like the purple." His thumbs rub my nipples. "Come here," he says and he slides up and I straddle him.

His hands massage my ass and I circle my arms around his neck.

"I'm going to try to be a good boy," he says, inching forward to kiss me.

The kiss is gentle and slow, similar to the one he gives me when he says goodbye to me. It's the sweet kiss. He has many kisses. The demanding kiss, the I'm-going-to-come kiss, the hello kiss, and each one of those is enough to make me crumple to the floor.

His goodbye kiss is always super-slow, super-gentle and his hands never leave the sides of my face. Usually he seals it with one more short kiss and then says something like, "See you soon," or, "Thank you." It's the one that tells me I'm more than just a great fuck, that I might just mean more to him.

I lose myself in this kiss, his fingers gliding down my spine, up and down. He's not grinding his cock to my center, his hand hasn't dipped down between my legs to feel how wet I am. In my mind, I realize this time is going to be different.

He pushes his weight up and places my back on the bed.

"So beautiful," he whispers, his lips trailing a path down the center of my breasts to my belly button. Hooking his fingers under the strings of my thong, he pulls them down my legs, painfully slow. "I'll never grow tired of your pussy," he says in a low voice, still sliding the small amount of fabric off me.

A rush of goose bumps rise to the surface of my skin. He rises to stand at the edge of the bed, looking down at me, bare to him. Most times I'm okay with men looking at me naked. I have no issue with my looks, no shame about the imperfections of my body, but this time is different.

Jasper isn't looking at me with the lust and animalistic need in his eyes like he usually does. This time his eyes glow with something else. Admiration. Satisfaction. Wonder. As I lie here I can't help but feel like I'm baring not only my body, but my soul.

I lie still, my eyes locked with his, craving more of him. His eyes don't waver and I hold out my hands for him to come to me.

He shakes his head and the reverence in his gaze makes me feel undeserving. "I have no idea what I ever did to deserve you," he whispers, stripping off his vintage beer logo t-shirt I bought him two days ago.

He lowers his red boxer briefs and his cock springs out in its full glory. I'll never tire of seeing it. My mouth salivates and I want to crawl on my knees and suck him off, but even though there's no romantic music playing or rose petals on the bed, our afternoon delight feels much different than the quickies we've been having at lunch. So instead, I stay lying down, anticipating the weight of him on top of me.

As always, he doesn't disappoint, crawling up the bed, licking his way from the tip of my toes, up my thigh, circling right above my mound. By the time his tongue is between my breasts, I feel his hard length running along my legs. I throw my head back, giving him access to my neck. His fingers thread through my short black hair right before his lips take mine.

My legs widen, allowing him space between my thighs, and the tip of his cock pushes into my center, teasing my wetness.

"You're so beautiful," he whispers and my heart pitter-patters, my hands moving to his back, running along his muscles.

"Jasper," I sigh, loving this slow dance we're doing. Our bodies slide and if I wrapped my legs around his torso, he'd be able to push inside me.

He finishes our kiss and draws back to stare into my eyes.

"I need you," I say softly, and he tucks his head into the crook of my neck.

His open-mouthed kisses ignite a shiver up my spine. Circling his hips, he continues the teasing and I know there's a condom in his jeans.

"Your skin is so soft," he says, his hands sliding over every part of my torso.

"Please," I beg him, opening wider and wrapping my legs over his so that my heels press into his calves.

He looks up to me. "I changed my mind. I don't want anything between us," he whispers, kissing my nose.

I lock my legs and he stops, a heart-stopping smile on his face. He pushes a stray hair out of the way and gazes down at me with reverence.

"I trust you, Lennon, but are you sure?" he whispers.

I nod. "We're not virgins," I joke, having to ease the heaviness of this moment, for me at least. My lungs constrict and you'd think that I just stepped out on a tightrope five hundred feet in the air, with no net below. But that's exactly how I feel. Like I'm operating without a safety net because everything that I'm feeling for Jasper is foreign territory.

That wickedly naughty smile I love emerges on his lips and he circles his hips then reaches down to direct his cock into me. Inch by glorious inch he pushes inside of me—my breathing hitches, my fingers digging into his back.

"Oh, God," I say from the overwhelming feeling of taking him bare inside me. I've never had sex with no barrier and though I made the joke a minute ago, in some ways I feel like a virgin. A teenage boy virgin because this is about to be over before it really begins, I'm so close.

Jasper rises to his elbows, staring down at me as he glides in and out in a slow, but glorious pace. He never breaks eye contact and I'm not sure how long it lasts, but I can tell you, I'll never forget this moment or the emotions swirling inside me.

"I never imagined you'd feel this fucking perfect," he says in a raspy voice.

At a pace that would challenge a tortoise, we enjoy each other's bodies until we collapse—not from exhaustion, but because we're physically unable to hold our orgasms at bay. We reach our climaxes together, tumbling toward ecstasy, gripping one another tight and feeling not only in a physical sense, but an emotional one, everything between us.

Jasper drops to the side of me, his hands on my side, his lips moving to mine with a satisfied smile. Our arms entwine and he brings me to him, our sweat-soaked bodies sticking together. I realize, in the woods, in a cabin with no one as a witness, Jasper Banks has ruined me for anyone else.

I gaze at him with dreamy eyes I swore I'd never have for some guy and soak in the contentment and peace inside of me. Jasper allows me to be something I never thought I *could* be—still.

Then his phone rings and the sound rips through the moment as sure as if it was a knife on a tapestry.

I smack his chest. "You told me you put your 'do not disturb' on." I crawl from his hold, because one thing I'm not used to with not using a condom is the clean-up required afterward. Seriously, it feels way better in the moment but this mess is a real bitch to deal with.

"I did, but . . ." He stops abruptly.

I rush into the bathroom anyway because all I can feel is Jasper dripping down the inside of my legs. Definitely a point in the con column for not using protection. "I think I'm going to have to shower," I call out. "You want to join me?" I wipe myself off the best I can and walk to the doorway, but Jasper is now out on the balcony, naked.

I'm guessing that means there really isn't anyone around. Good thing he just made love to me. I'd say murder isn't on the menu tonight.

As the word 'love' rings out in my mind, Jasper comes back in the room, his forehead crinkled in deep set lines, his entire body tense. He quickly grabs his underwear from the floor and starts putting it on.

"Is something wrong?" I ask.

He stops what he's doing and stares at me for second before bending to grab his jeans. "I have to tell you something." I can see him swallow past the lump in his throat from here.

My heart trips over itself as if it's saying, *you fool, you trusted him.*

I'll give Jasper some props. Somehow, he convinces me to get dressed and get in the car with him without any explanation of what's going on. Even with my heart screaming that something's not right here, something is about to change everything, I do what he says.

Now I sit in the passenger seat of his Range Rover as he speeds down the highway to some address he plugged into his GPS. A hospital about fifty miles away.

"Was one of your parents in an accident?" I ask, since he's yet to speak since we got in the vehicle.

He's pushed his hands through his hair no less than twenty times. I know this because I began to count after roughly the fifth time. When his hands aren't in his hair, he's white-knuckling the steering wheel.

He glances over to me. "No."

But something is definitely wrong. The worry radiates off him in waves and it's like he can't get to the hospital fast enough. "Okay, is someone you know at the hospital we're going to?" I ask slowly, as though somewhere between the bed and the car he lost his ability to understand English.

"Yeah."

"And who would that be?" I ask in a cajoling voice because

it's like drawing information out of a two-year-old.

He glances over to me, apology written all over his face. "My son."

chapter SEVENTEEN

MY EYES WIDEN AND I forget to breathe for a beat. "Oh," is all I can manage before I sink into my seat.

I wait for the anger to come. I should be up in arms, screaming about how he lied. Or lied by omission at the very least. I should be ramming him with a million questions.

His gaze veers over once more and his fingers thread through his hair. "Say something," he says.

For the first time in all my life, I can't. I'm stunned speechless.

My mind is whirling with no one thought landing for more than a second before it pings to the next one. I don't want to say the wrong thing, though I have no idea why because he lied. Who cares if I offend him? A war is being waged inside and victory wavers between my head and my heart.

"He's in the hospital?" I ask.

He nods. "He's at camp. That was the director who called. They think he broke his arm." The distress evident in his words has me wanting to reach out and soothe him, but I keep my hands to myself.

"How old is he?" I ask, still not understanding how I can sit here and not be losing my ever-loving mind on him. Maybe it's because I care about Jasper and seeing him in pain makes me want to help him. Maybe it's because if it was my niece or nephew, I would be as concerned as he is.

"He's six. Brady is his name."

I glance at the GPS and see we still have forty minutes until we arrive. Since he's preoccupied and doesn't seem like he's really into answering questions, I face forward, crossing my legs and staring out the windshield.

Eventually I grab my phone and text the girls to inform them of this latest development. Now their reactions? They seem much more in line with what I *should* be feeling right now. At least two out the three of us are thinking clearly.

"You have nothing else to say?" Jasper asks after some time.

I shift to face him. "No. We can talk later. Once you know that Brady is okay."

A strangled moan escapes his throat and I assume it has to do with his son. "Talk to me," he says, pressing on the gas as we reach a long stretch with no cars in front of us.

"What do you want me to say?" I ask, dropping my phone in the cup holder.

"Tell me you don't hate me," he says and I realize that strangled moan moments ago wasn't about his son, it was about us. Why does that warm my heart to him?

"I don't hate you," I say with little emotion.

A long stream of breath releases from his mouth. "I'm sorry, I know I should have told you, it's just . . . I didn't know how you'd react. In truth, not many people know about him. It's safer for him."

"Are you in the Mob or something?" I ask because my imagination is beginning to run away from me with the way he's talking. At this point I feel like anything is possible.

"No." He chuckles but there's no humor behind it. "Brady attaches easily. I've never introduced him to a woman I was dating. He's clingy with his teachers, clingy with my mom. He's always seeking out female attention because he's never known his mom."

Now my curiosity is piqued, but before I can ask him anything his phone rings through the speakers in his car.

"Hold on," he says, pressing a button on the steering wheel to accept the call. "I'm on my way," he says by way of an answer. I look at the screen on his dash and see the word 'Mom.'

"Thank goodness. I called the hospital and it's a break according to the doctor. Your father and I will start the drive in a few minutes." I hear mumbling and crinkling of paper in the background.

"No need. The camp leader called me and said they're casting it. I was away for the weekend, so I'm not that far. I'll pick him up and we'll stay up here until Sunday." His thumb hovers over the call end button like a sniper on surveillance.

"Your father and I will come up there then and watch him while you work." I hear a car door slam shut and an engine roar.

"Mom, I'm not working," he informs her.

"Then what are you doing?" she asks and covers the receiver, though not very well because I can hear her relay the information to who I assume is his dad.

Jasper looks over at me, a pained look on his face. "I'm with someone," he says in a defeated voice, like she has him locked up in an interrogation room with a spotlight over his head.

"Oh." Her voice is low and unsure. Again, she relays this information to his dad. "He's with someone," she says, and his dad says, "What? Who?"

"Who?" she repeats his dad's question and Jasper blows out an exaggerated breath.

"Listen, I'll call you after I get Brady. I might need your help because I doubt if he's going to be able to go back to camp."

"We don't mind meeting your special friend," she says.

A laugh bursts from my throat before I can stop it and I try to cover it up with a cough.

Jasper gives me the death glare, but his lips tip up after a second, too.

"I'm sorry," I mouth.

"Can she hear me?" his mother asks and I cringe.

"Well, I'm driving, Mom."

"Oh."

This whole scenario is so uncomfortable.

"Hello, Mrs. Banks," I say and Jasper's head swivels in my direction so fast, I'm surprised it doesn't continue all the way around in a move from *The Exorcist*. I wave off his frantic look. "My name is Lennon Hart." I figure it's best to just introduce myself rather than pretending I'm a mute.

"Hello," she says. "Lennon Hart," she repeats quietly to his dad.

"Oh," he says and I can imagine the conversation at their dinner table must be stellar if this phone call is any indication.

"Okay, there you go, Mom. I gotta go," Jasper says, sounding like he can't get off the line fast enough.

"Well, why don't we have Lennon over for dinner?" she asks, ignoring his last statement.

We? Does Jasper live with his parents? The fact is, he's only ever taken me to his boat, then to my apartment, and now this cabin. I've never actually seen his condo.

"We'll see. Let's focus on Brady right now." His thumb hovers over the end call button.

"Yes, please call me once you have him," she says.

"I will."

"So, we shouldn't come?" she asks again and I press my lips together to keep from laughing.

"No, you shouldn't. I'll call," Jasper repeats.

"Okay," his mom says. "Lennon?" she asks and Jasper sighs, his head falling back onto the headrest.

"Yes, Mrs. Banks?"

"Dinner. Monday night at five o'clock," she says in what's an authoritative tone now. "You can get the address from Jasper." I look over to Jasper who rolls his eyes and shakes his head.

"How about a 'would you like,' or a 'please?'" Jasper says, his voice laced with annoyance.

"I'd love to," I say, not really sure if I mean it.

"Bye, Mom," he says and disconnects before she can get another word out.

After his mom is finally off the line, I laugh. Probably not the best reaction, but whatever. "I don't know if I can be with you," I deadpan.

He glances over for a second before looking back at the road. "What? Why?"

"You just hung up on your mother." I tsk him, lightening the mood. This kid thing definitely changes things, but for once I control myself and avoid a rash outburst, figuring we'll talk after.

"Oh, just wait. You'll be hanging up on her too." He pauses for a second before adding, "I can get you out of the dinner."

I pat his leg. His thigh is rock hard and I really look at him for the first time since he got the phone call. He's like a guitar string wound too tight and close to snapping.

"Who said I wanted to get out of it?" Blood rushes through my ears and bile rises up my throat. I've never met any guy's parents except for in high school. I hate the whole meet-and-greet with the 'rents and having to pretend I'm someone I'm not.

He shakes his head. "You're something else."

I've heard that a lot in my life, but this is the first time I think it's a compliment.

chapter EIGHTEEN

WE CROSS OVER THE state line into Oregon a short time later and a while after that we pull into the hospital entrance.

"Just stop by the emergency and I'll park the truck," I say.

Jasper does exactly that. He's out of the car in a flash, running through the emergency room doors. I park the truck and then walk through the doors a little reluctantly. Mostly because I'm not sure what my place is here. The closer we got to the hospital, the more real the situation became. The more I wished I was on the brown leather couch back at the cabin, or hell, maybe back in San Francisco.

There's no chance this kid will like me, I think as I look around. But my brother's kids love me. *Yeah, that's because you're the irresponsible aunt,* my subconscious says and I shake my head to clear my thoughts.

Needing a coffee to curb my anxiety, I buy the horrible vending machine one. I'm sure this remote mountain town probably doesn't have a Starbucks anywhere in the vicinity.

I take a seat in the waiting room, figuring that when Jasper's done, he'll find me and introduce me to Brady. Thank God this is going to go down in a hospital because there's a chance I might actually pass out.

While I sip on the disgusting brew they're calling coffee, I spot some college-aged kids in Camp Tall Pines t-shirts. The two of them have worried looks on their faces and keep checking their phones.

"Why did you let him climb that?" one girl asks the other.

"You were supposed to be watching him," the other girl says.

They're passing blame. Surely, he can't be the first kid to break a bone at camp?

"Are you here for Brady Banks?" I ask them and for the first time I put his name together. Brady Banks. Makes me think about Richie Rich. I laugh inside.

The girls turn to me with wide eyes, neither one wanting to say anything.

I point to their shirts. "Or is there another kid here with a broken arm?"

The blonde girl smiles. "Yes, we brought him in with our leader," she says. "Are you his mother? I'm so sorry."

"Do I look old enough to be a mom?" I ask, a little offended. I can't be more than five years older than this girl.

"Well," the redhead says.

"How old are you?" I ask, still upset they think I could be someone's mother.

"Twenty," blondie says.

Okay, so six years. Whatever.

"I'm only a little older than you. Definitely not old enough to have a six-year-old."

Then I calculate the math in my head. Fuck me. I am old enough to be his mother. When the hell did that happen?

"Oh, sorry," the redhead says, hitting the blonde's arm.

I finish my coffee, place it on the table and turn my attention to the TV in the waiting area. Ah, good ol' Maury Povich.

"I can't believe this is still on." I chuckle to myself. "'You are *not* the father,'" I say in a deep voice.

The two young girls stare over at me like I'm a crazy person and yes, I've just confirmed to them that I am in fact old. At least to them.

So I remain quiet. A few minutes later, a tall woman with a ponytail and camp t-shirt walks in the room.

"Robin, Carrie. Let's go. Brady's dad will take it from here." She exits the waiting area without waiting for them.

The blonde stops beside me before she leaves. "We're really sorry. Brady is so great and we never wanted to see him hurt. I hope he's okay." She puts her head down and walks out of the hospital.

"Thanks," I call out, unsure if she heard me.

Poor girl, but at least she's escaping before she has to face Brady's father.

Father.

Dad.

Jasper is someone's daddy.

I still can't believe it.

By the time Jasper comes into the waiting area my ass is numb, my back aches and my legs are stiff. I'm cracking my neck and back, stretching out, trying to relieve some of the tension in my muscles.

"Man, what a view. Is this what I was missing?" he says, right as I arch my back, sticking my tits out.

It's nice to see a smile on his face again.

I stand and he grabs my hand. "How is he?" I ask.

He squeezes my hand. "Good. Broken arm, but thankfully

no surgery or resetting is needed. He's in the cast for six weeks, though." He huffs out a breath. "Here I thought he'd be at camp for a few more weeks enjoying himself, but he's coming home with me."

"Well, I'm glad he's okay." I hug Jasper to my body.

"Thanks for being understanding," he says, running a hand along my back and kissing my neck. Shivers shouldn't race up my neck in this setting, but they do.

He draws back and he's back to serious Jasper. "So it's time you meet him. They're putting together his discharge papers. We can stay at the cabin tonight and then talk. If you want to go back to the city tomorrow, I understand."

I nod, not giving him an answer because I have no idea what I want to do. I still need a lot of answers and truthfully, I don't even know what he expects from me. He said himself he's never introduced Brady to someone he's seeing. For all I know he's dreading this meeting as much if not more than I am.

"Let's go. He's excited." He smiles and it seems genuine.

My tummy twists into a million tiny knots before combining into one giant ball that sits in the pit of my stomach.

I follow him down the hallway and I take the last breath I have before his son becomes a real live person to me. One who can and will judge me. Usually that's not something I give much thought to, but I find myself wanting to make a good impression on Jasper's son.

I step in to find a smiling boy with Jasper's hazel eyes and a head of moppy brown hair. His arm cast is green. Go figure.

"Hi, I'm Brady," he introduces himself, sliding over the bed as though he's making room for me. "Will you be the first to sign my cast?" he asks and my gaze darts to Jasper for a second. He shoots me a look of apology and that only endears Brady to me more.

"Well, yeah, that means I'm number one, right?"

Brady smiles at me like I hung the moon in the sky and I know I'm in deep trouble with this little boy, the same as when I first met his father—if not more.

chapter NINETEEN

SOMETHING JASPER FORGOT TO mention was that Brady never shuts up. Okay, I should've put that more nicely. Let's just say he's expressive and he has a lot to talk about. Is that more appropriate?

Luckily, he's fast asleep in the guest room and I'm sitting with Jasper on the steps of the cabin.

"I was just finishing up my master's when Gina got pregnant."

Jasper and Gina. Damn, those two names sound good together. Way better than Jasper and Lennon.

I say nothing and wrap my arms around my legs, then rest my cheek on my knees, watching him and waiting for him to continue.

"She wasn't ready to be a mom. Truthfully, I don't even know if she'd have ever been ready." He looks away from me and out to the forest in front of us.

I remain quiet and he slides closer to me. The heat from his thigh seeping through his jeans warms my bare leg. I want to place my hand on his thigh but I don't.

"She wanted to abort and at first I did the whole 'it's your body' thing, but the closer it got to the day, the more I wasn't okay with it. The night before she was supposed to have the abortion, I had a law student friend draw up some papers for her to sign. I paid her throughout the pregnancy, and paid her to sign over her parental rights." He turns his head and stares up at the window that houses his sleeping child. "That stays between us. I'd prefer it if Brady never found that out."

I nod. "Of course."

"So I ended up marrying her for a short time so insurance would cover the pregnancy, because although I was making decent money, I couldn't afford medical bills like that."

"Oh." Now I sound like his father.

"We divorced right after her post-care was done. She left town and I send her pictures and letters giving her updates, but half the time they get returned. Sometimes it's months before she gets in touch and tells me she's moved to a different state again. She has no desire to see him or know him." His voice cracks and I put my arm around his shoulder.

"I'm sorry."

He shakes off my apology. "It's her loss." He turns to face me, my arm falling off his shoulders. "I know you just met him today, but he's so caring and funny. I'm sure every father thinks his kid is the best. I'd hate to meet a bastard who didn't."

I divert my eyes because I'm not sure my parents ever thought that of me. Maybe Jacob, but Lennon was the crazy one who wouldn't sit still and was always causing them trouble.

"He does seem great. Talkative, but adorable." I laugh and he nods, knowing, I think, that Brady would never be able to chew gum because he'd never shut his mouth long enough to taste the flavor. I realize that he reminds me of myself in that way, even now.

"I never meant to put you in this situation. You've been

thrust into it without warning and now we have to make a decision."

My heart plummets to the depth of my stomach. Decision?

He takes my hands in his and I mentally prepare myself that this is it. He's going to break up with me and choose his kid. Which I could never fault him for.

"I've enjoyed our time together." His voice is so low I almost can't hear him over the leaves rustling in the wind.

I pull my hands from his and slide over. His forehead wrinkles. "It's okay, Jasper. You owe me no explanation. It's been a great three weeks and I'll always remember them, but I understand. Really." I move to stand, but Jasper cages me between him and a giant log post holding up the porch.

"What do you mean?" he asks.

"I get it, okay? We were having fun and you don't like to mix the two, but now that Brady met me, you're kind of stuck. I'm giving you the out you're looking for." I say the words out loud even though they're making me feel physically sick. I guess I didn't realize how much I wanted to stick around until Jasper was letting me go.

He stares at me long and hard, while my heart hammers against my chest so loud it could be part of a drum line.

"Lennon." He says my name slowly. "Do you remember this afternoon? Before I got the call?" His voice is low and holds that confidence I've admired from the first moment I met him.

I nod.

"Did I rip off your clothes?"

"No."

"Did I bend you over a table, pull my cock out and fuck you until you couldn't take anymore?"

"No."

"Did I push you against the glass window, spread-eagle, demanding you tell me how much you want me?"

"No."

All those scenarios sound nice though and now wetness pools between my legs.

"Was I gentle and loving? Did I caress your skin and tell you how beautiful you are?"

A rush of heat rises to my cheeks thinking about our time together this afternoon.

He cocks an eyebrow.

"Yes," I whisper.

"Do you think I would do that if I was 'just having fun with you?'" He uses air quotes for my phrase.

I look away, but he places his forefinger under my chin, forcing me to look at him.

"Maybe," I say and a small smile plays on his lips.

"Lennon?"

I blow out a breath. "No, I suppose not."

A full-wattage smile emerges and his hand moves up and pushes back the hair from my eyes. "So I think we can agree, I'm in this."

I shrug.

"Lennon." Again with the stern voice. Must be a dad thing.

"Yes?"

He kisses the tip of my nose. Damn him, why does that always get to me? "I need to know if you're in this. I need to forge a plan."

"A plan?"

"I'm in uncharted territory. Brady's never had to compete for my attention. He's never known what it's like for me to have a woman around. And you don't really seem like the kid type. No offense."

"Okay," I say, slightly offended that he thinks I can't handle a child even if I've been questioning my own ability all day.

"I just meant tha—"

I hold my hand up in the air. I get what he means—I'm irresponsible, I have my head in the clouds, I'm never serious about anything. Whereas he has a mouth to feed, a roof to put over that little guy's head. He *has* to be responsible. He has someone relying on him. I don't even have a fish to feed.

If I don't go grocery shopping, it's only me who will starve to death. I don't have to make sure I eat from all sections of the food pyramid to ensure I'm healthy. The only time I drink milk is in my coffee. I'm way out of my league here.

I realize all this and then I look at Jasper and the thought of us breaking up turns the fissures around my heart into full-on cracks. "I don't want to break up, Jasper, but like you said, I have no idea what to do with a six-year-old."

"I'm not looking for a mother for Brady, but I need you to commit somewhat." He looks at me and I can't help but feel he's offended that I haven't hopped on board the happy family train yet.

"What if I lose him? Or what if I say a bad word? I mean I do have the mouth of a truck driver." I stand to get away from the fears pushing their way into my psyche.

"I don't expect you to pick him up from school, or feed him. And believe me, Brady knows all the bad words. He has me as a father." He says that like he's not the most perfect dad when I know he is. He must be. Just look what he's doing here. Vetting me to make sure I won't put his son's heart at risk.

I look back at him on the stairs of the cabin, his elbows resting on his knees, his hair a dishevelled mess, eyeing me and waiting for my decision.

I look through one of the cracks in my heart searching for the answer. I'm quiet for a long time before the answer comes from within and it feels right. It feels right in my gut and I've always been the kind of girl who goes with her gut and I've never regretted it. I'm not about to change that now.

"Okay," I say softly.

Jasper arches his eyebrows. "Are you sure, Lennon? You have to be sure."

"Yeah." I stare up at the star-filled sky. "I mean, I was a kid once. I'm sure I can channel that energy." I nod my head a couple times, convincing myself. "I'm a good aunt . . . I think." I shrug.

"I don't think you have too far to go," he jokes and pushes himself off the steps and walks toward me. His footsteps crumble the gravel under his weight and his arms wrap around me.

"Positive?" he clarifies.

I smile, becoming more convinced that I got this. People might doubt me, but I'm an adult and surely I can act like one and be a good influence.

"Positive."

He smiles and dips his head, giving me his goodbye kiss, except this time I'm not going anywhere. I guess I need to change the name of this kiss.

But to what?

It comes to me as Jasper's hands leave my cheeks. This kiss doesn't feel like a goodbye. It feels like a beginning.

A beginning kiss.

The beginning of what? I can't be sure.

chapter TWENTY

I WAKE UP TO a small lump next to me in bed.

"Ah!" I scream, sliding out from under the covers and onto the floor. "Jasper!" I whisper-yell, but he doesn't come.

Prepared for an animal of some kind that's joined me from the great outdoors ten feet away from the cabin, I look around the room for something to protect myself with. But there's nothing, so I try to tiptoe out of the room.

One of the floorboards creaks under my foot when I'm almost at the door and I whip my head around. The lump in the bed moves side to side and a scratching sound echoes throughout the quiet room.

My eyes widen and I stay focused on the lump while I walk slowly backwards until I reach the door frame. I turn the knob and slide through the opening, carefully closing it behind me. Then I dart down the stairs to find Jasper.

He insisted we sleep separately last night since he wasn't sure how Brady would react to the two of us in bed together. He wants to take things slow between the two of us. And that was fine—last night. Before some wild animal decided to take a catnap in my bed.

I find him sleeping on the couch and I hop on top of him.

"What?" he yells and I cover his mouth, but he sits up straight anyway.

A dreamy lust-filled look enters his eyes and his hands slide up my nightshirt, squeezing my ass. The blanket between us does nothing to hide his morning wood and he grinds into me.

Now usually I'm a morning girl. Hell, that's a lie. I'm a morning, noon and night girl—who am I kidding? But as great as that feels, there's an animal upstairs.

He moves his face and my hand slides off his mouth.

"What do you say we go to the bathroom for a quickie before Brady gets up?" he whispers and I crawl off him.

"There's an animal in my bed," I say and his eyes widen.

"Animal?" he asks.

I nod. "Yes. And I heard scratching so it must have claws. I almost woke it up."

Jasper's eyes narrow and he looks toward the stairs leading to the bedrooms with an 'are you serious' expression.

"I'm serious. Come on." I wave my hand in the air and he stands up, his red boxers tenting from his erection.

I cover my eyes. "Put your pants on," I say, shaking my head.

He walks over to me and removes my hands from my eyes. "You've seen my cock before. In fact, if memory serves you quite like seeing it," he reminds me.

I shake my head. "Well, Brady doesn't need to see it."

"Sorry, babe, he's seen it."

I glance down at it again. "Really?"

He nods, sliding on his pants. "Never like this though. I'm not ready for that conversation." He chuckles and begins walking toward the stairs.

"You can't go empty-handed," I squeal and he stops, turning back around.

I glance around. Bingo. I grab the poker from the fireplace and run it over to Jasper like it's a hot potato, letting go and backing away from it the instant he has it in his hands.

He rolls his eyes and climbs the stairs as I tiptoe behind him, hanging onto the waistband of his pants.

"You have to be quiet, it could be on the other side of the door," I whisper when we reach the landing and he nods, but I can tell he's not taking this situation as seriously as I am.

He throws the door open, the knob hitting the wall behind it, and I scream and jump on his back.

"It's gone!" I yell, my legs around his waist, my arms probably strangling him.

Jasper steps into the room, ignoring the fact that I'm acting like a koala bear on his back. A koala bear on crack. He flips open the covers and—there's nothing there.

For some reason my response is to try to climb higher up on his back.

"Quit kicking me." He stops my foot from kicking his stomach.

"It could be under the bed," I whisper-yell.

He stalks toward the bathroom instead.

"What are you doing? Look under the bed. I bet it's under there." I smack his bare shoulder and he shakes his head.

The bathroom door is open and I hear water on and then the scratching sound again, so I tense on his back. "Oh. My. God," I say, my flight response seconds from kicking in.

He steps into the doorway of the bathroom and there's Brady, standing in front of the toilet, peeing with his Spiderman boxers at his ankles, all the while scratching his cast.

I hop off Jasper's back then turn around and cover my eyes. Two penis sightings in one morning. What have I gotten myself into?

Jasper laughs as a very sleepy Brady flushes the toilet and

then walks past him. "Morning, Dad," he says and crawls into bed.

He throws the covers over himself, burrowing himself in my bed.

I run out of the room and Jasper follows, shutting the door behind him.

"Sorry," I say, cringing.

He hands me the poker and walks down the stairs.

"How was I to know?" I follow him and he gets back on the couch while I put the poker back near the fireplace.

"I missed you," he says, completely ignoring the situation upstairs, as if it didn't happen. He pulls the blanket open. "Join me?"

I look over at the stairs and back to him. "What if . . ."

"A half hour," he says and I trust that he knows his kid well enough to know that he'll sleep a little longer.

But sometime shortly after, I'm awoken by the blaring of a cartoon on the television. I peer over to find Brady sitting in a chair, still in boxers, but instead of watching the TV his eyes are wide open, staring directly at me.

Oh, boy. Literally.

chapter TWENTY-ONE

MY FINGER SHAKES AS I press the buzzer button of Jasper's condo. "Banks," I murmur to myself. How did I ever end up here? I have a Toys "R" Us bag and a bag of groceries to cook dinner, and I'm perching a tray of Starbucks coffee precariously in my other hand. What I should have is a drug store bag filled with condoms and a case of beer, and dinner shouldn't even be on my mind.

"Lennon!" Brady screams through the speaker and the door buzzes and unlocks.

The smile that seems automatic when it comes to that little guy emerges and I remember exactly why I'm doing all this. I press the elevator for the top floor because where else would Jasper Banks live but on the top floor?

When the doors open Brady's already there, jumping up and down.

"You're late," he says and his eyes widen when he sees the Toys "R" Us bag. He calms down, clasps his hands behind his back and looks up to me. "Do you need help?" he asks, but I know what he's really asking me.

I chuckle and switch the coffees to my other hand, then hold out my bag with his new board game in it. "Here, you can take this."

One of the smiles I'm slowly becoming addicted to brightens his face and he slides it off my arm.

"What is it?" he asks, peeking through the plastic. "A game?" he asks.

"Yep, I thought we'd play it after dinner."

We walk next to one another on the way to the condo, him looking skeptically into the bag and me wondering what kid doesn't love games.

"Okay," he says, walking through the door and holding it open for me.

"Brady, go wash your hands," Jasper dictates as soon as we're inside, pointing to where I'm assuming the bathroom is. He grabs the coffees from my hands, placing them on the counter before helping me with the bags.

"Dinner's not even ready," he whines, but Jasper gives him a long stern look and his head falls and his shoulders slump as he walks down the hall.

Once he's out of sight, Jasper pulls me to his body, his lips quickly finding mine. His tongue parts my lips and he lifts me by my waist, but moments later the water down the hall turns off so we separate and start unpacking the groceries.

I've learned this is what happens when you have kids. I'm trying to look at it as a form of tantric sex. Maybe I can fool myself into thinking I'm down with delayed gratification.

Brady's feet barrel into the kitchen seconds later, and he props himself on the breakfast stool.

"Man, that cast is slowing you down," I comment and Jasper carries some of the food to the fridge, his hand slyly brushing along my ass when he passes me.

I smirk, but don't let on.

"Look how many signatures I have." Brady holds his arm out to me and I nod.

"Where'd you get all those?" I ask.

Jasper walks back to the counter. "He went to the community center with my parents," he says.

"Oh, I still need to meet your grandma and grandpa," I remark, side-glancing Jasper. He was able to get us out of the dinner with his parents, feeling that Brady was enough newness for us to deal with for the moment.

"Grandma asks a lot of questions," Brady says, staring down at his cast in admiration.

"Really?" I ask, folding the empty plastic bags on the counter.

Jasper's body stiffens and I have this feeling that he's delayed the meeting between his parents and me because he's concerned it won't go well, not out of concern for how I'm coping with all the changes.

"Yeah, she asked what you look like. Oh, and she wanted to know if you're nice to me."

"She can be inquisitive," Jasper says and when I look up I catch him non-verbally telling Brady to quit it.

I move over to Jasper, and place my hand on his arm. "It's okay. I'm used to people judging me and not liking me right away," I whisper so Brady doesn't hear but apparently, the kid's got bat ears.

"She'll like you," Brady says and Jasper's eyebrows shoot up to the sky.

"Now you know . . . there's no secrets with kids in the house." He smiles and I slide by him, purposely brushing my breasts against his chest. He sucks in a breath.

Since this is my first time in Jasper's condo, he pulls everything out for me and a half hour later, the pizza roll-ups are on a plate with Brady looking at it like I'm asking him to eat a pig's foot. Or broccoli.

"What's the matter, Brady?" I ask.

"Brady, eat," Jasper says.

I bend down to look into Brady's eyes.

"What is it?" His voice is low and unsure.

I take my knife and cut it open, showing him that there's cheese, sauce and pepperoni like he asked. His eyes light up with recognition.

"It tastes just like pizza," I say, cutting a small piece and placing it on a fork to hold it out in front of him.

His lips touch it and he pushes back. "It's hot," he whines.

"Brady," Jasper warns and I have to say his fatherly tone does a little something for me between the legs.

I bring the food to my mouth and blow on it. Brady smiles and then I hold it out again. "Try again," I urge and he nibbles a bit first, until he slides the rest off his fork. While he chews, I continue to cut up his egg roll pizza.

"It's good," he says like he can't believe it.

I smile. "I'm glad you like it."

Sitting back up in my seat, I begin to cut my pizza roll-up, but I sense something and glance up to find Jasper's eyes on me. He smiles and I smile back, wondering why he's staring at me.

"Grandpa said you guys are bumping uglies," Brady says.

Both Jasper's and my eyes widen and our heads whip in Brady's direction. I try to hide the smile and swallow the laugh threatening to escape.

"I asked Grandma what it meant, but she told me Grandpa's losing it and not to pay any attention to him." Brady gobbles down a few more bites of his pizza roll up, blissfully unaware.

I swallow some of my water to keep from laughing, and eventually Jasper's face returns to normal coloring.

"I think I need to talk with my father," he mumbles, eating his pizza roll up.

Four hours later, a kid's Monopoly game is strewn on the coffee table, and the three of us are lined up on the couch watching the Teenage Mutant Ninja Turtles movie. I'm cozied up to Jasper and Brady is cozied up to me.

A head falls into my lap and Brady's moppy hair is strewn on my blanket, his eyes shut.

"Thank God," Jasper moans. "I love him, but damn, he has energy for days." He slides away from me, stands and picks Brady up in his arms like he weighs nothing. Brady's little body lies limp, one of his socks hanging from his toes.

"I'll be right back," Jasper says and heads down the hallway.

I've been on Brady lockdown since I arrived. The only time I've had a moment to myself was when I went to the bathroom. Even then when I opened the door he was there waiting for me. Clingy is an understatement. But rather than annoying, the reason behind his behavior makes my heart go out to him.

Watching Jasper as a dad has only made me fall harder for him—not something I could have anticipated. But he's so loving and patient with his little boy. And at the same time, he's stern and forthright when he needs to be. I had no idea single dads could be so hot but damn, they've got game.

I stand, stretching, and then lower the volume on the television. Moving to the open blinds, I look down at the streets of San Francisco and again the question plagues me. How did I get here? Worse is, do I belong?

Two arms wrap around me from behind, and Jasper rests his chin on my shoulder. I've missed him. I know that's such a girly and ridiculous statement. I've been with him all night, but not truly.

I close my eyes, inhaling his scent of musk and man.

"I thought I was never going to get you alone," he whispers, dipping his lips to my neck.

I turn in his arms, circling them around his neck. "He's

great," I say.

A proud smile forms on his lips. "I know." Then he kisses the tip of my nose. "I'm glad you think so, too."

He pulls me closer and my head falls to his chest. My hands skim up under his t-shirt and he inhales a deep breath.

Holding my head between his hands, he bends down and his lips meet mine. It's his sweet kiss and I love it, but I miss the animalistic ones. The ones that made my lips feel bruised and sore. I really miss the one where he's right on the edge the entire time until his cock sinks into me and a groan of pleasure releases from his throat. We had three weeks of that and this week, besides a quickie in the back of the tattoo parlor when he came to visit, there's been nothing.

He slows the kiss, obviously not going any further. Surely parents fuck? I mean, it's not something I've ever really thought of because the only parents in my life are my own and who wants to think about that? But I'm taking Jasper's lead on the physical part of our relationship and the fact that he ends our kiss says he's not ready for any sleepovers just yet.

"I guess I should go," I mumble and he stares down to my eyes, nodding.

"How about I get a sitter for this weekend?" he asks as I walk toward the coat rack with my purse hanging from it. Swinging it crosswise over my body, I shove my hands into the pockets of my jeans.

"Sure."

He takes me in his arms again, more forceful than before, and I clench my thighs to keep the pulsing to a minimum.

"Thank you for dinner," he softly says in my ear.

"You're welcome," I whisper.

With one last goodnight kiss, I'm walking down the hallway of Jasper's condo building feeling very alone and very horny. I suppose I should be thankful I create sex toys at a time like this.

By the time I step off the curb on the way to my van, the reason for my melancholy is clear to me. I miss him.

"Fuck!" I blurt out, a little too loud. A few couples and families walking along the sidewalk look at me and I lower my head. "The bastard owns me," I mumble.

chapter TWENTY-TWO

"OKAY, SO YOU'RE SURE. A kid?" Whitney asks, sipping her coffee.

"As in a little person?" Tahlia clarifies and I nod again.

"As in a six-year-old little boy. Yes," I say.

I sip my coffee and the two of them exchange looks. I know the look. It's the one that's silently agreeing with my subconscious that I'm in over my head. But it's been two weeks and Brady and I are getting along like best friends. It's Jasper and me who have somehow moved backwards into a platonic relationship. Other than quickies in his office or my place at lunch, we're in junior high hand-holding mode. I'd probably get more action if I challenged him to a game of spin the bottle or seven minutes in heaven.

"I don't know what to say." You know it's bad when quick-thinker Whitney, the reporter, is speechless.

"Is he nice? Or does Jasper have one of those nightmare hyperactive ones?" Tahlia's expression morphs into a disgusted look. Which is out of sorts because I'm fairly sure she'd be the best mother out of all of us. Nothing against Whitney. Or me.

"He's great. Clingy." I tilt my head. "But great. He really likes me. Sometimes I worry he's too attached."

Both their eyes bug out.

"You guys do realize that I'm a likable person?" I ask and they share that same damn look. I'm ready to throw my coffee in their faces.

Tahlia reaches over, patting my hand. "Of course," she singsongs, clearly lying.

Whatever. I know I'm likable.

"You guys probably behave similar," Whitney adds as though she didn't just insult me.

"Um, guys. Jasper isn't looking for Brady to have a friend to have play dates with. He's looking for a mother," I say. Although Jasper said the exact opposite, which makes me wonder what we're doing then. Every time we're together I can't help but feel like I have to prove myself to him.

"Did he say that?" Tahlia's mouth hangs open.

"No. He said he wasn't, but I'm so fucking confused. I mean how should things be? He has a kid and he's in a relationship with me. There have to be expectations. I mean we're not just dating into infinity now. There are expectations with monogamy. Hidden promises of happily ever after."

"Well, you're young still," Tahlia offers, trying to give me an out, I think.

"You don't get it." I shake my head, frustrated that no one gets where I'm coming from.

They both look at one another and shrug, not understanding me.

"I've never thought about my wedding. I never believed I would get married. Kids? Only if I was the last woman on the planet and Chris Hemsworth and I needed to repopulate the earth," I ramble, my blood pressure increasing the more I think about all the things I've never thought of before. "I mean, I'm starting a sex toy company. How is that going to work for career day? Can you see me strutting in with a tank top, my tats on full display, pulling out a dildo?"

I thump my forehead on the table and Tahlia smooths my hair. See, what'd I tell you? She's motherly.

"You could do the sex ed class," Whitney says, laughing, and Tahlia joins in.

I lift my head to narrow my eyes before I stare down at the table again.

"You're thinking too far in the future, Len. Calm down," Whitney offers. This is the same advice I repeat on an hourly basis to myself.

"If all these thoughts are surfacing. Do you think . . . I mean—" Tahlia hesitates. "Maybe you love him?"

I lift my head slowly, and stare her dead straight in the eyes. "No. I'm just saying when a kid is involved, there's more expectations."

"Not really," Whitney says in a soft tone.

I look over at her and she draws back. "I mean, a future is a future, Lennon, and if you don't think you'll be able to commit down the road, you shouldn't be in a relationship, let alone one with a man who has a child."

I lean back in my chair, focusing on the outside world past the window. I can't be upset because what Whitney is saying makes sense. Jasper and I were fooling each other that day at the cabin. There's no 'let's give it a try.' There's only 'all in and pray you make the right decision.' I've been teetering on that line the past couple weeks and it's time I fully step over it and embrace all that decision has to offer, if that's where I want to be.

A slow smile tilts the corners of both their lips because

they know. They knew before me.

"I don't love him," I bite out and they share a smile, shaking their heads.

"Only you would know," Tahlia says, raising her shoulders up and down in a condescending way.

"And I don't."

Whitney tips her cup to her lips. "Definitely not," she mumbles.

I stand up from my seat, eyeing the scribble on my coffee mug. "Annie Reed? Really?" Tahlia and her damn romance movies.

They both laugh and I roll my eyes.

"You know it's funny." Whitney practically spits out her coffee from her laughter.

"I'm not Annie, Jasper isn't Sam and Brady isn't Jonah. This isn't *Sleepless in Seattle*, it's my life." My frustration reaches a boiling point and it's clear in the tone of my voice.

Their laughter screeches to a halt like a car reaching the edge of a cliff.

"Lennon." Whitney sits up straighter, her eyes laced with sympathy.

"We didn't mean—" Tahlia begins but I hold up my hand.

How can I really fault them when I'd be doing the exact same thing if it was one of them? "It's fine. I gotta go, though." The two of them stand but I shoo them back down into their seats. "Really, I'm fine. I just need to figure this out." I toss my coffee cup in the trash, and I'm walking away when Whitney's voice pulls me back.

"It's okay, Lennon. You know that, right?"

I turn around, not understanding what she's saying.

She's nibbling on the inside of her cheek. "I mean . . . you can want more. It's okay to want more."

I nod, and swing open the door, making my exit into the warm summer night.

I know it's okay to want more in theory, but am I the girl who can handle more?

chapter TWENTY-THREE

I STEP OUT OF the elevator of Jasper's office, my heart in my throat, my stomach a churning mess. "Hi, Brittany, I'm here to see Drew."

She nods. "Mr. Banks, Lennon Hart is here." She's nice and polite, but she's an idiot because she called the wrong person.

"I'm here to see Drew Ashland," I clarify and she smiles.

"Mr. Banks informed me any time you come to the office, he's to be rung."

I stare blankly at her, my mind whirling. I have no chance to say anything else because Jasper rounds the corner, a giant smile on his face, his arms already outstretched for me.

"You want lunch?" he asks, and kisses my cheek.

"I have a meeting with Drew." My voice is void of the usual giddiness it bears when I'm in Jasper's arms.

"Oh." He draws back. "I didn't know." His lips turn down.

He doesn't know because we're apart more than together these days and that's not me blaming him or Brady. I'm starting to realize that maybe Jasper hasn't completely let me in. That maybe there's still doubt in him about us.

"It was last-minute. I guess he has some things to discuss regarding branding."

Just then Drew gets off the elevator. "Shit, Lennon. Give me a second and I'll be ready." He's in a brown suit today and he has a hat on. You'd think he just walked out of the forties and a swing song starts playing in my head.

"Nice hat," Jasper says, and it's clear from his tone it's not a compliment.

Drew tips it down, slightly bowing. "Thank you, sir." Then he snaps his heels together and holds out his arm for me. "Now, I'm going to steal your lady."

I giggle and take the offered arm.

"She's my lunch," Jasper calls out after us.

"That's not appropriate talk for the office," Drew says back, leading us forward.

I look over my shoulder and Jasper winks, the naughty minded grin back on his face. My stomach and my heart both flutter.

Sue stands with a stack of papers when Drew approaches.

"Good afternoon, Sue," he says and I'm wondering if he's just coming in today.

"Mr. Ashland. Miss Hart." She looks skeptically at me, but she follows us into the office.

"Do you want anything to drink?" Drew asks me, motioning for me to sit down.

"No, thank you," I say. She nods and focuses her attention on Drew.

"Nothing for me either. Thank you, Sue. Shut the door when you leave."

She leaves and the door clicks shut.

We discuss the branding for a half hour and surprisingly he's on board with my ideas. Drew's been a pleasure to work with. He made sure the due diligence portion was seen to right away and he's already got his patent lawyer drawing up the paperwork to file. I'm lucky to have him on my side.

I'm collecting my things when he leans back in his chair, smirking, and I can't resist.

"What?" I ask.

Drew and I have come to a casual friendship as of late, since he likes to joke as much as I do.

"So, what do you think of Brady?" he asks and I stare blankly at him because this isn't the first time I've seen him since I found out about Brady. "Jasper told me you guys are hitting it off."

"He's a great kid," I say.

"He is. He's also a kid looking for a mom." He raises his eyebrows in question.

"Jasper isn't," I say, still not sure if I believe it.

"I'm not so sure about that." He straightens, clasping his hands in front of him on the table, and stares at me for an uncomfortable minute. "He likes you."

"And I like him, so why are we having this conversation?" I ask.

"She tore him apart," he says softly as though Jasper's perched outside with a glass to the door. "I've known Jasper since freshman year at Harvard."

"And?"

"And I've seen him with a lot of women. They've come and gone, and he wouldn't return calls, or he'd dodge them at parties after they hooked up. Only two women have had a lasting affect on him. You and her." I can't help but hear the disdain in his voice when he refers to her.

"I don't think my relationship with Jasper is any of your business," I say and cross my arms in front of my chest.

"She didn't tear him up because he loved her. She tore him up because she didn't want anything to do with his son." Again, his eyebrows rise and my gut clenches into a knot.

"Well, Brady was hers. Of course it tore him up."

Drew leans back in his chair. "Is that how you think of it? Brady is Jasper's but not yours? But who gets hurt if the two of you don't work out?"

"Brady," I whisper. I know this, Jasper knows this, but for some reason we're risking a child's feelings.

"I don't say this for you to break it off, because you've met him and the kid wants a mom more than he wants to meet Iron Man. He's at the age where all the kids are talking about their families and he's realizing he doesn't have what most do."

"Shouldn't you be talking to Jasper about this?" I stiffen my back, narrowing my eyes on him. "It's not all on me."

He nods. "I think we both know it is." He knocks his knuckles on the desk in front of him and stands.

"Drew, with all due respect because I appreciate what you're doing for my business, but on a personal level, fuck you." I stand, too. "Do you think I don't think about that kid all the time? The carefree Lennon has disappeared because I'm so afraid of saying or doing the wrong thing and I'm freaked out that if Jasper and I don't work out, I'm screwing up an innocent kid."

"First lower your voice unless you want Jasper to run in here." He walks around his desk to meet me. "I don't mean to rile you up. I just wanted to make sure you know the stakes. They're my family and when emotions get in the way, sometimes it's the people on the outside who can see the train wreck about to happen."

I scoff. "So you think we're a train wreck?" I cock my hip to the side.

Drew dips his chin and looks at me from under his brows. "I think the two of you are in a bubble and I'm not sure either one of you truly will know what you'll do when someone pops it."

"Well, *I* think you're an asshole," I snap.

"Don't get upset, Lennon. I like you. I think you're great

for Jasper, but I also think the two of you have no idea how to navigate this relationship."

"What makes you think you know me so well?"

"Let's see . . . you're the party girl, you like your freedom, you're probably not in a hurry to settle down, you're used to doing what you want when you want." He checks each of these things off on his fingers as he says them.

"What makes you such a psychologist?" I ask, picking up my stuff, ready to bolt out the door.

"I'm just protecting my friend. He's done it for me in the past and now I'm going to do it for him." He sits back down in his chair, his face indifferent. "I like you, Lennon."

I stand at the edge of his desk, peering down at him, my veins burning hot with anger. "Do me a favor and let's keep this to business." I gesture between us and then spin on my heel and stomp over to the door.

"I like your fire. I'll take that to mean that you do love him," he says, laughing to himself.

I roll my eyes, swing the door open and run right into Jasper's chest. As hard as I try to push back my tears, I blink and they begin to run in a steady stream down my face.

chapter
TWENTY-FOUR

"WHOA," JASPER SAYS, SMOOTHING my hair, holding me to his chest. He tries to walk us backwards into Drew's office but I hold firm outside his door.

"Sue, will you excuse us," he says, that sweet gentle tone long gone now.

"Yes, Mr. Banks." I hear the sliding of her chair and Jasper pushes me back by my shoulders to look at my face.

I wipe the stupid tears and divert my gaze to anywhere but his face.

"Lennon, what happened?" he asks, and he eyes Drew from over my shoulder. "Drew?"

"It's nothing. I need to go." I attempt to slide by him, but he sidesteps, gripping my shoulders.

He points into the office at Drew. "I'll deal with you later." His voice is authoritative and demanding.

He pulls me into his side and we walk down the hall to his office. He shuffles me in and he locks the door behind us.

I can't believe this is happening. I'm Lennon Hart, I have

it all together. I'm not this emotional, weepy girl.

"What's going on?" he asks. I sit down on the couch and he joins me, wrapping his arm around my shoulders.

I glance over to him. He's in a sharp black suit with the faintest pinstripes. Classic and sophisticated like always.

"How come I can't spend the night?" I ask the question that's been niggling at my subconscious.

Jasper blows out a stream of air, and tips his head back to stare up at the ceiling. "I just, I'm not—"

For the first time, Jasper is speechless.

"What?" I turn to face him, and he leans forward, his elbows on his knees.

"I told you, I'm in uncharted territory, okay? I don't want to hurt Brady, I don't want to feel like I'm forcing him on you."

"I like him. You're not forcing me."

He blows out a breath and stands to start pacing. "If you spend the night, Brady will jump in our bed in the morning. I'll be taking a cold shower instead of burying myself into you to relieve my morning wood. We'll have breakfast and barely be able to have a conversation because he'll be there, clamoring for your attention." He leans back on his desk, crossing his ankles. "I'll admit, I'm not sure you're ready for it."

"You think I'm not terrified? I've never had a relationship, let alone one that if it doesn't work out an innocent boy is going to be hurt." I exhale a huge breath, the truth escaping from me.

"How do you think I feel? He's my son. Brady doesn't truly know what he's missing by not having a mom. He only hears the stories and sees his friends. I always thought my mom would fill that role for him, but it's something he's still searching for. Two years ago, he made a pin at school. It was a Mother's Day project and the teachers expected him to give it to my mom. You want to know where that pin is?"

I swallow past the lump forming in my throat. "Where?"

"It's in the top drawer of his dresser. He's waiting to give it to someone—to his mom. I want to give him everything, but I'm not even sure I can give him that. It's hard to allow someone to get close enough to him that they could hurt him if they decided to leave us." He pushes off the desk and begins pacing again.

"I don't want to hurt him. I don't want to hurt you," I whisper. Another tear slips from my eye and I quickly wipe it off.

Jasper stops pacing and stares down at his feet with his hands on his hips.

"I still remember the first time Brady asked me why he didn't have a mom." His voice cracks and I feel that crack spread across my heart. "I thought I'd prepared myself, but I thought it would happen when he was eight or nine. It happened when he was three. We were at a park and a little girl fell off the swings. She went crying to her mom and Brady looked up to me and asked who that was. I casually told him it was her mommy. I patted his head and told him to go up the slide again. On the way home, he asked me where his mommy was."

"Jasper," I sigh and clutch my chest, more tears falling from my eyes.

"I don't tell you this to make it harder, Lennon. I'm telling you because this is how deep and long he's wanted it. I see the way he looks at you and I worry that it will make you bolt. He's already had one mother who didn't want him. I don't know what would happen if another person he looked at like a mom left him." He comes back to the couch, but sits on the edge.

"I can't promise you," I whisper and he nods.

"I know."

"Neither can you," I remind him and he nods again, the corners of his lips tipping down.

"I know."

"I don't know what to do."

He turns to me and cups my cheek as his thumb swipes

away my tears. "I don't want to lose you," he says. "Sometimes I think I'm more scared about me hurting than Brady," he says softly and my heart flutters.

"What if you decide I'm not good enough?" I ask him and he slides forward, his other hand cupping my opposite cheek.

"Don't ever say that," he says. "I'd never think that." He shakes his head vehemently.

"You wouldn't be the only one." I tip my head down and he pulls it back up.

"If you take anything away from this conversation, know that if I didn't think you could, we wouldn't be here."

The determination in his eyes and the caress of his hands seal it for me.

"I'm all in, Jasper," I say and a slow smile crosses his lips.

"Me too," he whispers and he delivers another sweet kiss.

No, strike that, he delivers a loving kiss, and it melts every bone in my body.

chapter TWENTY-FIVE

JASPER TOOK THE REST of the day off and we picked up Brady from the local daycare and took him to the zoo. Well, we did all that after Jasper stormed into Drew's office and raised hell. Drew's response? He laughed and said he was happy it worked out.

"What's your favorite animal?" I ask Brady, walking hand in hand with him into the zoo.

"ROAR!"

"I take it you like the lions then?"

"Yep." He lets go of my hand and skips ahead a few steps.

"Then it's lions first," I say.

Jasper pulls out the map from his back pocket, locates the area and tells us which way to head. We arrive at the building a while later, after being distracted by the geese and food carts. Brady bounces up and down on his toes to see better and eventually, Jasper picks him up.

All the animals just lie there and I can't help but think how lonely they must be. "It's kind of sad," I say.

"Why?" Brady asks.

I shrug. "I don't know, I mean, I wouldn't make for a very good caged animal." I shrug again. Jasper laughs, knowing I'm right. "I definitely wouldn't be just lying around like that."

"Me either," Brady agrees and I can't help but think that's true. Me and Brady are cool like that.

"Here's to crazy, Brady." I put my fist out and he hits it.

"Crazy!" he screams and Jasper shushes him.

After we see the lions, I can tell Brady is getting excited—he's talking so fast that I'm barely understanding him while he's jumping and running. Jasper keeps telling him to slow down, quiet down, calm down and I can't help but smile to myself because I heard those same things so much when I was younger.

We head to the play area because Jasper thinks Brady needs to burn off some energy and the two of us sit on the picnic table watching him run around having fun.

"Are you always so strict?" I ask him, sipping my slushy. I got red, Brady got blue, Jasper got a water. Boring.

"What do you mean?" He eyes me like I'm crazy.

"You're so bossy."

He leans forward. "I thought you liked me bossy?" he asks in a seductive tone that has me pressing my thighs together. It's been so long.

"*I* like you bossy, but I bet Brady doesn't," I say, eyeing the child in question going up and down the slide.

"He has a hard time following rules. Plus, he can be a lot to handle if I don't consistently keep him in check." I see the questions in his head—how badly he probably wants to tell me to mind my own business, that Brady is his son—but he doesn't say anything.

I pat his hand. "I'm not telling you how to raise him."

"You're not?" he asks, not so sure.

I stand up, keeping my hand on his. "No. I just know what it's like to be a Brady. My entire family tried to keep me in check and tame my personality and the harder they tried to shove me into the box, the more I pushed and prodded until I broke free. You don't want to raise a kid who has tattoos on his entire body, invents sex toys and has a hard time with commitment, do you?" I raise my eyebrows, pat his hand one more time and then walk out to the playground to play with Brady.

The park is pretty busy, so I try to always keep my eye on him, but the little man can hide. I'm searching the area for him, but I follow Jasper's eyes because of course he has an eye on his son. I smile, seeing a giant rock on the far side.

Tiptoeing over there, I peer over the edge to find Brady.

"Gotcha!" I scream and he yelps to stand and run, but he trips over his shoelace and falls to the concrete.

"Ouch," he says, right before a wail of a cry rumbles out of him. He buckles over in pain.

"Brady!" Jasper yells and I crouch down to him, brushing his arm.

"Are you okay?" I ask.

Jasper reaches us and kneels down, ready to pick him up, but Brady sits up and then throws himself into my arms, crying.

Jasper falls back on his ass as I stare at him with wide eyes. He smiles and I know he's thinking about that day at the park three years ago. Even though my heart rate is at a record-setting pace, Brady's small body against mine feels natural somehow.

My hand slides up and down his back. "Are you okay, buddy? Let's take a look," I say. He inches back, letting us see that he has a scratch on his forehead.

"Oh, buddy." Jasper stands and walks to the table.

"Let's get it cleaned up," I say and Brady stands up and walks to the table with his two hands around my waist, his face pressed into my side.

Jasper gets a napkin from the churro vendor and pours water on it from his bottle. I guess he thinks ahead because I'd only have a red slushy to clean it up with.

He pats Brady's head and tells him it's okay, that it's small. "How does it feel?" he asks him.

Brady smiles, nodding his head. "Better."

I put my arm around his shoulders, handing him his blue slushy. "Best therapy," I say and he smiles, sucking it up the straw immediately.

The three of us sit there for a few minutes with our drinks, watching the other kids play.

"Where do you want to go now?" I ask Brady. "We could do the Little Puffer train, the carousel . . ."

"Let's see the kangaroos." He jumps up and his blue slushy falls from his hands, and it splatters to the ground.

I laugh and Brady cringes, looking over to Jasper, who rolls his eyes and looks none too pleased.

"Well, let's clean it up." I bend down, scooping the blue slushy in the cup, using the extra napkins to wipe it up. Brady helps me and throws away the napkins and cup. "Thanks, Brady," I say and he smiles, proud that he helped.

I look around for something to clean up the stickiness and spot the water. Jasper hands it over to me and I pour it over the mess and it washes away into the mulch.

Who knew a bottle of water could come in so handy? I always thought that was reserved for bottles of tequila.

While we're in the Australian Walkabout, Brady is hopping on fences, running from exhibit to exhibit. I notice Jasper says nothing to him.

I slide my arm through his. "I think I was wrong," I whisper close to him and he looks down at me. "I think that you do a great job with Brady. I shouldn't have given you advice. I mean, who am I to say anything? You were like MacGyver with your bottle of water to hydrate, clean cuts and wash away a spill."

He chuckles. "You're Lennon and you were right. I've been

afraid that he'll scare you off with how hyper he is, so I've been coming down a little hard on him. But at the park I realized you two will probably just keep each other busy." He laughs and I hip-check him.

"I was apologizing."

He glances down at me, that you love me smile on his lips. "Don't. You were right." His head dips and I prepare for a kiss when Brady jumps up to face level.

"I'm hungry," he screams.

My one eye shuts for a second from the pain in my ear. We share a smile and Jasper grips his upper arm, keeping him at ground level, and then kisses me. It was short and sweet but it meant a little more this time around because Brady was there.

"Come on," I say to Brady, finding a pretzel stand.

"Let's have lunch," Jasper offers and I share a look with Brady.

Turning around, I walk backwards. "There is no such thing as a balanced diet while we're at the zoo. Come on, MacGyver, I'll buy you a water." I wink and he laughs, then chases us until we're screaming and he's circling around us.

I guess my man can hang with us crazies.

chapter
TWENTY-SIX

AN IMPATIENT KNOCK RATTLES my apartment door. I scurry half dressed to answer it, because we're already late. I was late leaving the tattoo parlor and Brady was upset that his dad was leaving for the night to be with me. He truly wants to spend every waking moment with us. It's sweet in its own way.

I swing open the door and before I have a chance to see Jasper's face, I'm backed up into the apartment. The door slams shut, and the shirt I just put on is brought up over my head and tossed to the floor. My bra is unhooked as I hear two shoes thump to the ground.

His lips land on mine, my hands weaving through his hair. I unbutton his pants and he swings his hips side to side to let them fall to the ground.

"I need you once before we go and another five times after." He uses the weight of his body to push me back until I collapse on my bed. He comes down on top of me and presses his weight into my body.

"Sounds good," I say, moaning when his erection grinds

between my legs.

"Turn over," he demands.

I like bossy Jasper. Why the hell did I ever question his bossiness? "Feeling a little alpha tonight?" I joke and he smacks my ass as I wiggle it in front of his face.

"I always feel alpha with you," he says in a strained voice, his hand gliding down my spine. "No panties tonight." He rips them off me and his shirt lands on the bed. His hand slides between my legs, his fingers moving from front to back, spreading my excitement all over my pussy.

"Hurry," I say, my insides clenching.

"You're definitely wet enough," he says and my nipples harden into taut peaks.

"How bad do I need to beg?" I groan.

"Tell me how bad you want me," he orders while he leans over me and slides open the top drawer of my nightstand. My insides clench even before I see the lube and anal plug he's pulled from the drawer.

I'm not sure when his boxers left his body, but his cock presses against my slit and I try to push back into him. He grips my hips, directing the movement himself. Control freak.

"I ache."

His tip teases me, but he doesn't respond. Instead he drizzles lube down my ass crack. I arch my neck to look behind me. He's watching on in fascination as he spreads the liquid over my puckered hole.

"I've been wet all day waiting for you." I moan as he pushes the tip of the butt plug in then let my forehead drop to the mattress.

"You like that? Want me to put it all the way in?" he asks in a hoarse voice.

I'm too on edge to speak so in response I push back into him. The head of his cock teases my slit and the anal plug pushes in a little more.

"Jasper, I need you," I beg. I can't take it anymore. I need to move. I need him to fill me. I *need* to come.

"You're going to come all over me. Don't worry about that." He pushes the remaining length of the toy into me and I gasp in pleasure.

I wiggle my ass side to side, desperate to move. "More. I need you to fuck me."

"All in good time," he says, his voice a low rumble.

He pushes his cock in an inch and then backs out.

"I haven't masturbated for two days, waiting for you," I say, hoping he'll give me all of him.

Two inches in and then out.

"The sooner we get there, the sooner we get home and I can wrap my mouth around your cock until you come down the back of my throat."

He slams into me. I knew that'd do the trick.

I'm full. So full that I'm seeing stars. He drags himself out of me and in an instant I'm desperate to feel that fullness again.

He grabs my hair and pulls me up a bit so his other hand can grab my nipple. He licks my neck and I've never craved a man like I do Jasper.

As he moves in and out of me, my hand moves to my clit.

"Keep touching yourself," he whispers in my ear and my head falls back to his shoulder, my lips searching for his. He kisses me, his tongue deep, our mouths ravenous.

"Harder," I pant and he thrusts hard and deep, his balls smacking me right where I need them to. Every time he pushes into me, I'm in sensory overload. Pleasure rockets from deep within my pussy and my ass until I'm a writhing, panting mess.

"Like that?" he asks and his hand skims around my waist, keeping me in place while he drills into me over and over and over again.

Faster than ever before, he leads me up that rollercoaster track and I don't even have time to gasp for another breath before he rounds me right over top of that hill. My hand falls off my clit, my body weakening, but his firm arms hold me up. He pulls the butt plug from my ass mid-orgasm and I scream in pleasure—what I have no idea.

I'm a trembling mess and Jasper must notice because he lets me fall to all fours, his hands on my hips, bringing me to him over and over again.

"Jesus, you feel so fucking great," he yells and I moan, a second orgasm quickly rising to the surface. Seems this roller-coaster has more than one peak.

He thrusts into me, rocking my hips into his pelvis more, and a couple minutes later, we're both on the bed, sweaty and spent. He pulls out of me and I lie there making a mess of my sheets, but uncaring.

"Let's stay in," he says. "Give me five and I'll be ready again." He smiles and I shake my head, sitting up.

Grabbing my towel from my shower, I clean myself up. "We promised. Plus, my friends want to meet you."

I move to the bathroom to use a wet washcloth. He follows me, washing himself at the sink.

"You can take a shower," I offer but he shakes his head.

"No way. I want to smell you all night," he says, bringing his hand to his nose, inhaling deeply.

And just like that I'm wet and ready again. I step up, rise to my tiptoes and plant a kiss to his lips. "God, I missed our loud fucking."

"Me, too. I forgot about that soft whimper you do right after you come."

"Let's get tonight over with." I fall down to my heels and go get dressed.

BY THE TIME WE arrive, Cole, Whitney, Lucas and Tahlia are waiting for us. From the ten texts I received I know they're annoyed, but that orgasm was worth it.

"Hey, guys," I say, barging into the lobby of the building we're meeting at. Jasper follows behind me, like always. His stride is confident. "So, this is Jasper." I put my hands out in the air like I'm introducing Brad Pitt. Well, he's my Brad Pitt.

They each smile at him and introduce each other. When Lucas steps up, Jasper tilts his head. "Lucas?"

Their handshake grips a little firmer. "How are you, Jasper?" Lucas asks.

"You guys know each other?" Cole asks and Whitney and Tahlia share a look. I remember Lucas telling me Jasper was an asshole back in the day and I might have purposely left out the fact that Jasper would know someone here tonight, in case it made him not want to come.

"We were at Harvard together," Jasper says, a genuine smile on his lips.

"Yeah," Lucas mumbles, that casual easy-going personality he's known for lacking at the moment.

"Okay, guys, I know there's like bad blood or whatever, but we're all adults now. So, kiss and make up," I say.

Tahlia laughs, although it's an uncomfortable laugh. Whit stares between the two guys and Cole looks utterly confused as to what's going on.

"Bad blood?" Jasper asks, apparently clueless about the fact that Lucas didn't like him. "I don't know about that. I was an asshole back in the day, granted, and I had a giant chip on my shoulder for the rich boy here." He gestures at Lucas. "I'm sorry if I ever offended you, man, but I'm not that guy anymore."

Lucas smiles. "Your best friend still Drew Ashland?"

Jasper nods.

"No kid richer than Drew." Lucas laughs and Jasper follows suit.

"That is true."

Look at my man being all mature and apologizing. Isn't he the sweetest?

Lucas shoves his hands in his pocket and rocks back on his heels, back to the guy with no worries I'm used to.

"Okay." I clap my hands and everyone looks at me. "Now that's settled. Let's go attack some zombies!" I raise my hands and head over to the check-in counter.

Yep, we're doing an Escape Room because how else should friends bond than by arguing with each other? With three alphas in our midst, this should be a huge bonding experience for them.

We all sign the release papers and watch the video. We have an hour to free a government spy before he's killed. Good times.

Once the employee has locked us in our room and started the timer we all scatter to separate areas to scour.

"Let's remember, I'm the investigative reporter." Whitney pushes her chest out and uses her thumb to point at herself.

"Hate to break it to you, but there's no Google Search available," Cole jokes and Whitney narrows her eyes, trying to get out of his hold, but he tightens his arms around her shoulders.

"No messing around, we need to find the key," I say, scrambling over to a bookcase.

Jasper goes to the desk. Lucas and Tahlia head over to the corner. Cole and Whitney start going through all the books.

"Why aren't you looking?" I ask Lucas and he laughs.

"I did this for one of the adventure dating nights." He shrugs and now it makes sense to me why Tahlia isn't bossing him around, telling him what to do.

"Is that how you two met?" Jasper asks, stopping his search for the moment.

"We can chitchat at dinner. Look!" I point to what he's supposed to be doing and he shakes his head.

"I think I can talk while I search." Jasper talks to me like a fifteen-year-old sassing back to his mom.

"Don't make me take you over my knee, Jasper," I say and laugh.

"Don't make me take you over mine," he snips back and everyone says, "Ohh."

He walks over to me and I roll my eyes in annoyance even though I'm anything but. "Get away." I squirm as he tries to take me in his arms, looking for somewhere to kiss.

"Oh, my God, I never thought I'd see the day. Lennon is a smitten kitten," Whitney says, her hands on her hips while she stares at me with amazement.

"I'm not a smitten kitten." I let Jasper put his arms around my waist and kiss me.

"You so are," she says back and laughs.

"Whatever." I kiss Jasper once more before smacking his ass. "Get to work."

He laughs and although I know he'd like nothing more than to smack my ass back, he heads to the desk, searching the drawers.

Cole finds the key and we all run over to the next door.

"Clues," Tahlia says.

"Puzzles," Lucas corrects.

"Okay, guys, I'm great at clues," Tahlia says, practically pushing people out of the way to find some huge puzzle only she can solve.

"It's puzzles," Lucas corrects her again.

"And this isn't *Survivor*. There are a bunch of puzzles we need to solve," Cole says.

Jasper stays quiet during the whole exchange, which makes me happy because then I don't have to worry about anyone's head being bitten off. I love Whit and Tahl, but Cole and Lucas are pretty new to our group, too, and we just patched Lucas and Jasper's relationship back together.

Four of us go from puzzle to puzzle, solving and cheering. There are only two of us who take a seat and chat about the good ole days—Jasper and Lucas.

Not that I'm paying too much attention, but I hear them recalling names back and forth between each other and laughing about this or that. Then as Cole and Whitney are arguing about how to solve one of the puzzles and Tahlia's trying to make sure we have everything in order, Lucas asks, "Whatever happened to Gina Freemont?"

My entire body freezes. I doubt there were two Ginas. Yeah, I know it's a common name, but something deep inside me says that's her. Brady's mom.

Jasper doesn't miss a beat. "Last I heard she was down in Miami," he says and for a second I think maybe I was wrong. It is a different Gina. "I'm sure you heard we had a child." He just throws it out there.

Trying to act like I'm paying more attention to the puzzle in front of me than to their conversation, I tip my head further down.

"Yeah, I heard something about that right before I left, but I'd forgotten until just now."

I turn around and shoot Lucas an annoyed look. He catches me and bites his lip. He forgot until now, my ass. Before Jasper can turn around, I move my attention back to Cole, Whitney and Tahlia.

"Well, she's out of the picture anyway. It's just me and Brady and now Lennon."

I think my heart just floated out of my body and right into Jasper's hands.

I turn around and Lucas has a cheesy smile on his face,

making Jasper turn around. He catches the sight of me and the smile on his face widens. He holds his arms out and I walk right into them.

It feels like home here, nestled into his hard chest. Home used to be a stranger's bed, a bottle of booze and a hangover the next day. This home is *so* much better.

My arms wrap around his waist and he kisses the top of my head. I peer up to his face, needing his lips on mine. Then our kiss gets a little PDA-inappropriate.

"Yeah, I think I'll join them," Lucas says, rising from the chair and leaving us.

Jasper walks us back into a corner and we make out like a pair of teenagers falling in love for the first time.

chapter TWENTY-SEVEN

I'M ON JASPER'S KITCHEN counter and he stands between my legs, his hands buried under the boxer shorts I borrowed from him last night, running along my ass. My lips are on his, our tongues gliding and sliding together while my hand ventures down to rub the hard erection tenting his pajama pants.

A door opens down the hall and little feet barrel toward us. I startle and Jasper turns to adjust himself.

"Brady!" I exclaim, hopping down from the counter. "You're awake," I say like I'm not pointing out the obvious.

"Yep." He climbs up on the breakfast stool. "Morning, Dad."

"Morning, bud." Jasper keeps his back to him, beating the eggs. I giggle inside because I'm sure he'd rather I was beating him at the moment.

I sit next to Brady. "What do you want for breakfast?"

"Chocolate-chip pancakes." He nods with confidence, the six-year-old's final answer.

"You got it." I walk around the counter and Jasper turns after finally getting his tonsil-tickler to relax.

"I'm making eggs," he says as though we have to make a choice.

"We'll have both," I say with a giant smile to appease him. I walk over and kiss his cheek.

"Not too close, I'm liable to rise to attention again," he murmurs and I glance at Brady, who's playing with his McDonald's toy from last night.

Who do you think got him that? Not Mr. Responsible, I can tell you that.

I peer into his pantry, finding the Bisquick, and since unlike my house I know he has eggs and milk, I figure all I need is chocolate chips.

"Well, color me surprised," I say, pulling out a bag of chocolate chips.

"Daddy makes the best," Brady says.

"The best what?" I ask, putting everything out on the counter.

"Cookies." Brady smiles and Jasper sneaks a look my way, pouring the eggs on the griddle.

"Your dad bakes?" I ask with an I-don't-believe-it tone and Jasper laughs, while Brady's head moves up and down with a huge grin.

"Dad, make them," Brady asks, but Jasper's already shaking his head.

"How about tonight? We'll watch a movie, and have cookies and milk?" Jasper offers, turning around and hitting Brady's nose with the end of the spatula.

"A fort. We need to build a fort for Lennon." Brady hops down from the stool, having already moved on to another thought. "I'll go get the blankets." His footsteps paddle down the hall again.

I measure and mix the pancakes, already knowing where everything is because as of this past week, I've been here more than my own place. I call that progress, ladies and gentlemen.

"Hmm . . . can I say, I'm surprised you're so handy in the kitchen?" Jasper comes up behind me, his hands slowly moving down the front of my boxers. "Still wet," he whispers.

I look down the hall to see blankets being thrown out of the closet.

"Well, that's probably all you," I deadpan.

His hand glides the wetness around my clit, making it swollen before that sweet ache sets in. It turns out you can have sex with kids in the house. You just have to wake up extra early. And by that, I mean I've been setting my alarm for an hour before Brady gets up. Seems an orgasm is just as effective as caffeine in the morning. Well, almost.

"There's something sexy about knowing a part of me is still swimming inside of you."

"Let's hope there's no egg for it to swim into," I joke and he kisses my neck.

"Would that be so bad?" he asks, and I don't turn around right away, but my whisk circles a little faster.

"What?" I ask in a squeaky voice.

"Never mind," he says and steps away.

Leaving the batter on the counter, I step back until I see his eyes. Staring into his eyes, I ask my question once more. "What did you mean by that?"

He shrugs. "I'm not going to lie, Lennon. The thought of you pregnant has crossed my mind." He shrugs again and I can tell he doesn't want this to be a big deal.

"But will it stretch out my tattoos?" I whine and he continues to stare at me, no smile present. I hit his shoulder. "I'm kidding. I know I'm not a traditional girl, but you'll have to marry me first. And of course, you'll have to ask my dad," I say, hoping that scares him off for the foreseeable future. I'd be lying if I said I hadn't pictured the three of us as one big happy family and what it might be like in the future, but it's too soon to be talking about kids. At least for me.

"Speaking of your family, your brother called me yesterday."

Uh-oh. The whisk sinks down into the batter as panic flares and all my muscles tense. "Jacob?" I clarify.

"Yeah, he called about a client he wants me to meet with. Funny, but he didn't mention anything about me dating his sister." He turns around with a plate full of scrambled eggs.

I switch places to make the pancakes, not wanting to stay on this topic. I've yet to tell my brother I'm dating Jasper and I've yet to tell Jasper that I knew who he was before I met him. Surely he won't care at this point.

"Um, my dad has a retirement party in a few weeks. Why don't you guys come?" I offer the invitation that should've been extended weeks ago.

He steps up beside me and dips his face in front of me. "You've told your brother about us?" he asks, though the tone with which he asks tells me he already knows I didn't.

"I will. I promise. Before the party." I put up my Girl Scout fingers like I did when I was five.

"You better. I didn't mention anything to him because you said you wanted to tell him, but I'm not comfortable keeping it from him."

I let my hand drop. "I know. I'm sorry."

"I don't know why you're keeping it a secret. I'll tell him if you'd like." He drops the chocolate chips on top of the pancakes.

"It's fine. I'll do it. I'm sure he'll have no problem with it," I say, not believing my own words. "I feel like you're hiding me." I turn the tables to get the heat off of me.

"What do you mean?" he asks.

"Your parents. I've yet to meet them." I pop one of the chocolate chips from the bag into my mouth.

As though I wiggled my nose like Samantha from *Bewitched*,

I hear a key insert in the lock and freeze in place. Jasper moves but before he can do anything, an older couple walk in and give Jasper and me the once-over.

"Mom," Jasper says, with a warning in his tone.

"Grandma!" Brady screams and runs into the room with stacks of blankets. "We're making a fort tonight for Lennon." He places them on the couch.

"It appears she already spent the night." Her eyes scan over my body slower than a CT scan, logging every tattoo, the fact I'm in Jasper's boxers and my tight tank top.

"Dad." Jasper shakes his dad's hand and then he rounds the corner back to me. "Mom and Dad, this is Lennon. Lennon, these are my parents, Natalie and John." He places his hand on the small of my back, as though he's presenting me to them.

John smiles, and I can see where Jasper gets all those smiles I love so much. Natalie's not so friendly, but I'll give her credit for at least trying to cover up her scowl.

"Hello." I step forward, offering my hand.

John shakes it like a man should shake a woman's hand, a little loose but enough that it still shows his strength. Natalie on the other hand barely grips my hand.

Finally, Brady joins us, interrupting the awkwardness.

"Why are you guys here?" he asks and Natalie mocks offense.

"We wanted to see you. It seems you never come visit us anymore," she says, her gaze veering over to me.

"I told you, we've been busy." Jasper's bitter tone can't be missed, but no one says anything.

"I think I should go change," I say quietly to Jasper, who nods in agreement.

"Don't change on our account. We've always loved looking at art." She smiles and I manage to keep my lips zippered shut, but this lady is going to challenge me.

I give a small smile and head around the breakfast bar and down the hall. I'm not sure I breathe until I'm behind Jasper's bedroom door.

I turn on the shower because if her judgmental eyes will be on me, I'm going to be squeaky clean. A minute later, Jasper enters the room, just as I'm taking off my shirt.

His pajama pants begin to tent.

"Nope. Nope. Nope. Your parents are right outside," I whisper-yell, pointing to the door.

He laughs and listens to me as well as a puppy would. "I'm sorry," he says, and steps up to me, his hand cupping my cheek.

I look up to him, his face serious, his hazel eyes missing their usual gleam.

"You don't have anything to be sorry for," I say. "Your mother seems very . . . conservative." I smile in a way that says, *See? I can play nice.*

"She's a farmer's wife. She grew up in a small town and judges those who are different."

Man, does this man know his mother.

"Well, I am definitely different."

The corner of his lips dip down when I say that.

I ignore his reaction and shimmy out of my shorts. He steps closer, his hands finding my ass before he pushes me against the glass wall of the shower, his erection throbbing against my pussy.

I can't deny that I want him inside me. I want to know he doesn't care that I'm not some farmer's daughter who goes to church every Sunday and that I wasn't a virgin until him. I'm in desperate need of the worship he grants me with his eyes and his body. I want the look that says he loves me, even if he doesn't say it himself. The guy who told me he'd never hide me.

So I have a lapse in judgment.

My legs tighten around his torso and my heels push his pajama pants down until they fall to the floor. He steps out of them and his cock pushes past my opening. Locking me to the wall, he takes one hand and glides into me.

"Oh," I moan and he covers my mouth, although the shower should help drown out our noises.

He plunges in and out of me fast and quick, and I'm surprised I'm still so wet, especially after the chill his mother brought in with her.

I hang onto his neck, my breasts smashed to his chest as he thrusts in and out of me. Faster and faster.

"You're so fucking tight. I love the way you squeeze my cock," he says, and that tingling between my legs burns hotter.

He fucks me like he'll never get enough, as if I sate him completely and yet never quite enough. The way he takes me makes me feel like I'm it for him.

"Jasper," I sigh, the arousal peaking around me. "God, fuck me," I whisper, the glass rattling behind me.

He continues and without any foreplay—no nipple tweaking or mouth around my clit—and even with the ice queen outside, I explode all over Jasper for the second time this morning.

A minute later, he follows me and my legs aren't even down on the ground when I catch sight of his mom staring at us from the opened bathroom door.

"Oh, my God." I cling to a very naked Jasper.

He looks up at me, that foggy, just-orgasmed gleam in his eyes until he registers the shock on my face. Turning his head, he must catch a glimpse of his mom.

"Mom!" he yells. "Get out!"

"I'm so sorry. We just heard glass banging and didn't know. The door was unlocked and—"

John peeks in and then throws his hand over his wife's eyes. "Natalie, what are you doing?" Then he turns his own head and says, "Son, a time and place."

"Just get OUT!" Jasper screams and the two of them leave.

I don't move until I hear the door shut.

"That about seals the deal," I mumble and we break apart. I open the shower door and step in.

Of course he follows me. Jasper isn't one for space.

"Hey," he says, pushing my hair under the stream of the water. "It's fine. I have a son. It's not like they didn't know I've had sex." He laughs, somehow thinking that his mother finding me pressed against a glass wall with her son's dick inside me isn't mortifying.

"She hates me," I say, allowing him to place shampoo in his hand and lather up my hair. I take the bottle from him and return the favor.

"No, she just doesn't adjust well to change." He steps closer, nudging me under his shower faucet head. The shampoo suds drip down our bodies.

"I might be too much change for her," I remark, grabbing my conditioner, but Jasper takes it from my hands and applies it like I told him to the last time we showered together.

"Don't say that. You're the best change. I know I'm happier than I've ever been and as much as it kills me to say it, Brady is too." His hands smooth through my hair, rinsing the conditioner.

He grabs the soap and my loofa, but my hands land on his. "Jasper, she could make you . . . I mean, she might not ever warm up."

How can I fault her? Some days I'm not sure my own mom even likes me that much. How can I expect someone else's to?

He grips my hands in his, staring down at my eyes.

"You're second in my life," he says. I smile, knowing I could never and never would want to top that place in his life.

"You're second in mine too," I say. "After my vibrator of course," I joke and he laughs.

"I can't lie to you. Brady will always be first, but he's the only one who will ever come before you."

I stare up at his determined and serious eyes, hoping to God his mom and I just got off to a bad start. Because feeling like I don't fit in in one family is enough, I'm not sure I can handle two. If that happened there's a chance it might not be Jasper who ends us. I could very well bolt.

chapter TWENTY-EIGHT

AFTER JASPER AND I dress we exit his bedroom. My hair is still a little wet, but I did my make up more conservative than usual. See? I'm flexible.

Brady's voice bounces off every wall in the condo, but when he sees us, he runs over.

"Grandma and Grandpa are going to take me to Dave and Buster's." He jumps up and down.

I look to Jasper, who looks at his parents.

"We have plans tonight to make a fort," he says, and then goes into the kitchen.

I'm not sure my face could match the color of Brady's Spiderman blanket more, as I try to follow Jasper without making direct eye contact with either of his parents.

His mom joins us while John plays with Brady. "Well, we just thought the two of you would like to be alone." Neither Jasper nor I miss her meaning.

Jasper turns around, plating food for Brady. "Brady, come and eat." His voice is short and curt.

I'd like to say, *Don't take it out on Brady,* but I sip my coffee, still hiding my eyes from her.

"Mom, we don't need alone time," Jasper says. "We've been managing fine."

"I was just trying to be nice, Jay," she says, taking the fork and knife to cut up Brady's pancakes.

He swivels around, eyeing Brady, still by his dad. He leans forward, his body stiff. "You ambushed us and you know it." He looks over at me and boy, do I wish I could be like Alice in Wonderland so I could be ten sizes too small and hidden behind my coffee cup. "You purposely surprised us by coming here today so you can check out Lennon." I realize now that he's seething.

"Well, what was I supposed to do? The two of you have been seeing each other and Brady told me during FaceTime that she spends the night."

Slam.

Jasper's open hand smacks the counter. Unsure if I should leave or stay, I bury my head in the fridge as though I'm looking for something. *Smooth, Lennon.*

"You should have waited until we reached out to set a date. I was going to call you this week to set up a dinner, but you had to push your way through."

"Jay, stop being like this," she whines and I'm thinking that voice usually gets her her way.

"How am I supposed to be? You're making the woman I love uncomfortable," he says in a harsh whisper.

I smile at the pickles because he hasn't really told me he loves me yet.

"Well, that wasn't my intention," his mom fires back.

Figuring I can't keep my head in the fridge the entire time, I back up and close the door, pretending to put more milk in my coffee.

"Don't force this," Jasper warns, similar to the way he does with Brady. I realize that my mom and his mom might be a lot alike.

She slides onto a chair at the breakfast bar. "You're right. I should have waited."

Except for that. I'm quite sure my mom has never told me I was right.

"I'm sorry, Lennon," she says and I look up for the first time.

"No apologies necessary." I'm polite and mean what I say. Who's to say I wouldn't do the same thing for my own son some day? I'm not exactly known for my boundaries.

We each force a smile and Jasper grabs a cup, filling it with orange juice.

"Brady!" he calls out. There's a specific tone Jasper has that tells Brady not to push that line and he recognizes it so he runs over, sliding up onto a breakfast stool.

"Would you like some coffee?" I ask Natalie.

"That would be lovely, Lennon." She clasps her hands on the counter in front of her and I catch John walking over.

I go to the cabinet and pull out two mugs. "You must be here a lot since you know your way around the kitchen," she comments. I don't stop my movements because I'm pretty sure Jasper must be giving her the evil eye right now.

For the rest of the morning, that's the way our conversation goes. She tries to dig for more information about how often I'm here, where we met, what stuff we've all done together, but I think what she's really trying to figure out is how close I am to Brady. She asks nothing about what I do for money, my family, or my education.

We're all seated on the couch and I glance to the clock to see it's almost noon.

"We should get going," John says, slapping his hands on his knees.

Jasper stands right away, ready to see them out. I'm thinking he's as eager as I am.

Natalie holds her arms open for Brady and he kind of leans in, offering her his head. She kisses it.

"So we'll have some time together next week," she says and my stomach twists. Jasper hasn't told her that he asked me to watch Brady next week while he has to go out of town for a night.

"Oh, about that, Mom. I'm going to have Lennon watch him." He opens the door as casual as can be and her eyes dart to me.

Even John's back stiffens, his gaze drifting between Jasper, his mom and me.

"Okay," she says with no enthusiasm in her voice. "Well, leave my number in case she has any questions," she says, offering me a tight smile.

"It was a pleasure meeting you, Lennon. Sorry for . . . well, sorry." John holds his hand out to me, his face matching my own shade of red.

"Pleasure to meet you," I say, my voice lower than normal.

Natalie waves from the doorway. "Bye, Lennon. We'll have to make official dinner plans at some point."

I put my hand up in the air to wave, but she's already out the door. Jasper shuts the door, walks over to the couch, and plops down. He pats the cushion next to him and I join him. His arm swings behind my head and he pulls me to him, kissing my forehead.

"Sorry," he mumbles, his tone truly apologetic.

"I'm going to get my sleeping bag." Brady runs down the hall, clearly oblivious to the awkwardness that was the past few hours. His head is one hundred percent in fort zone.

I sit up and look at Jasper. His eyes are filled with distress. "Just have her watch him," I say, because it's not worth his mother feeling slighted. I have a feeling that will only come back to bite me in the ass.

"No." His eyebrows crinkle. "She needs to get used to not being the only woman in his life."

From his tone, I should let the topic go. But we all know me better than that by now, don't we? "Just do it, it will make her happy."

"End of discussion, Lennon. You're watching Brady. Unless you don't want to?" he questions.

I rest my chin on his chest, looking up to him. "I've already made our plans."

A worried look crosses his face. "Nothing illegal?" he jokes.

"Nah, but do you think he's too young for a tat? He did ask me for a Superman one." I laugh and in one motion, I'm on my back and he's tickling me.

"What are your plans?" he asks.

"That's between us. We need to bond so it's a secret."

He tickles me more, okay that I'm not telling him what I'll be doing with his son. Brady runs in and stops to stare at us. Both our faces turn to him.

"Tickle monster," he screams and joins Jasper in the act of tickling as we all laugh.

I'm not sure how I got here, but I never want to leave.

chapter
TWENTY-NINE

"THIS IS THE BEST!" Brady screams, running down the pier with cotton candy in one hand and a churro in the other.

I'm pretty sure I'm the best babysitter, but the worst mom-in-training. Yes, I've decided to refer to myself as mom-in-training in my mind. It seems fitting.

His footsteps halt and he admires the Ferris wheel. "Can we, Lennon?" he asks.

"Like I'd say no." I lead him over to a bench. "But you'll have to finish your treats first."

"Okay." He chomps on the blue cotton candy, leaving a ring of sticky blue sugar around his lips. After he dumps it in the trashcan he takes a huge bite of churro and dumps that in the trashcan. "Ready," he mumbles.

"Um, no, you're not ready."

Taking my cue from Jasper, I bought myself a water. So I go over to the funnel cake stand. Man, those smell good.

"I want one of those." Brady's eyes bug out and he points to the one loaded with a scoop of ice cream, strawberry topping and a pile of whipped cream.

"Maybe later."

"You said you'd never say no." His lips turn down.

"Maybe isn't no," I correct him.

"When Daddy says maybe, he really means no." He stares into the window and I swear a dribble of drool drops from his mouth.

"Well, I'm not daddy." I pour water on the napkin and wipe his mouth. "Good as new!" I tap his nose with my finger and he smiles, looking at me with love in his eyes. Oh, boy, I hope he isn't getting a crush on me.

"Let's go!" This little man switches gears fast, grabbing my hand and pulling me to the Ferris wheel.

We wait in line, Brady staring up the entire time the wheel stops and goes, letting people on and off.

"It's high," he says, his voice shallow.

"Brady, we don't have to ride it." I place my hand on his shoulder, but he shakes his head, never looking over at me.

He says nothing, which is odd. Brady's like me, there's always something to say. We hardly ever run out of words.

I crouch down and I catch sight of the middle school kids behind me. "Brady, let's go on a different ride," I offer and he glances at me, ready to take the bait.

"Yeah, this ride is for older kids," one of the kids says, inserting himself into our conversation.

Brady's face turns red and he looks down at the concrete, littered with gum and trash.

"Why don't you mind your own business." I stand up, narrowing my eyes at the little shit.

"Whatever, lady," the punk says and I feel rage starting to boil in my veins. This kid with the spiky red hair and pig-shaped nose needs to learn a lesson.

Being the adult I pretend to be, I turn my attention back

to Brady.

"Come on." I grab the edge of his t-shirt sleeve and pull a little, but his feet stay glued to the ground.

He shakes his head. "No." He steps up in line and I hear the kids behind us huffing and puffing.

"Okay." I release a breath. If he wants to ride it, who am I not to teach him to face his fears?

A few minutes later, it's our turn. The carousel guy holds up the stick to Brady, and Brady's face pales slightly.

"Okay, hop on," the guy says.

I let Brady go first, but he doesn't step on.

"Come on," the punk kid behind us moans.

Very explicit words rest on the tip of my tongue, but Brady glances behind me to him and I know I need to maintain my adult status here.

"Lady?" The kid continues to be the porcupine needle up my ass, causing me to be about a millisecond from losing my shit.

I turn around, my eyes probably resembling the dark sky right before a wicked storm. "I'm handling it. I get that you have some hot date with your right hand later, but relax."

All his friends laugh and I regret my words immediately when his face turns red in embarrassment. Brady looks confused by my words for a second, then he goes back to looking at the Ferris wheel in fear.

The operator snickers his own laugh but raises his eyebrows to me, silently asking if Brady is riding.

"Yes or no, Brady?" I ask.

He stares up at me for the longest time and I'm about to step us to the side when he surprises me and steps into the cart. It rocks and he swallows hard.

"You okay?" I ask before stepping on.

He nods his head a few times and I feel like the worst mom-in-training at this point.

"Finally," the kid groans.

I disregard him, still wishing I hadn't said what I did. This mom-in-training gig is hard work.

The man brings down the bar and Brady slides his legs as close to the seat as he can.

"It's okay." I hold his hand tight with mine.

He nods, but says nothing. The strong and silent type.

The ride moves and the jackass kids behind us holler and rock their seat.

"Let your momma swing it, baby," the kid continues to razz us.

The ride moves us up a bit and Brady's entire body stiffens. Figuring the hand-holding isn't working, I place my arm around his shoulders and pull him close. His body loosens a little, but my idea is barely working.

"Lennon," he says and I dip my head to see he's crying.

"Oh, Brady," I say, rubbing his arms. "It's okay," I try to soothe him, but we're moving into advanced stages of mom-in-training and I'm still stuck in the orientation.

"I want to get off. I don't feel good."

Just then the ride starts going and there's no way we're getting off until it's over. We swing by and I raise my hand to grab the guy's attention, but he's busy flirting with a blonde bimbo. Just my luck.

"Just keep your head in my side. It will be over in a second."

We pass by again and I raise my hand, but he still doesn't look at me.

"Fuck," I mumble.

"What?" Brady asks.

Great, I swore in front of the kid.

"I told you this ride wasn't for babies," the kid says, like we're about to go over the hill on one of those crazy rollercoasters you see on Facebook that says, *Would you do this?*

I lean over, our cart tipping back a little, to finally shut this kid up. "Listen, right hand man—"

"Lennon," Brady groans, looking over the back with me. A second later, a stream of vomit leaves Brady's body, right onto the redhead's head.

I purse my lips to try to keep from laughing. *Nice work, buddy.*

"What the hell? I'm gonna kill you, kid!" He points to Brady, who is still throwing up.

Serves him right.

"You won't lay a hand on him," I warn and Brady looks up at me, the first smile crossing his face since the funnel cake.

Brady leans forward and finally the guy stops the ride after all the commotion.

"I'm sorry," I say to the guy and he looks at the cart and the kid behind him, snickering another laugh.

"Priceless," he says.

I dig into a purse, handing him a twenty.

"Not necessary." He hands it back to me.

I dig out my card instead. "Here, free tattoo on me." I eye his skin and that excites him.

"Thanks," he says and Brady hunches over again.

I get him off the ride, onto stable ground, and run him over by a trashcan, where he throws up again.

"Let's get you home, buddy."

We walk toward the car and once we're secure in the van, he looks over at me. "Thanks, Lennon." His head leans back on my seat cushion and his eyes drift closed. "I don't like unicorns," he mumbles.

I laugh to myself, driving down the street while sneaking looks at him. It's probably weird, but this is the first time I've felt like a *real* mom.

chapter THIRTY

WE PULL INTO JASPER'S designated parking spot, which he has informed me he's not thrilled about me using because though he doesn't want to change anything about me, he does want to change my car. I see his point a little. Were the unicorns a little drastic? Yes. Will Brady like it if I have to pull up to his school with unicorns shitting rainbows on the car that drops him off? Probably not.

I climb out of my car and then go around to the back passenger side to get Brady out. He's fast asleep already. I nudge him and he moves his head, blowing a stream of vomit breath right into my face.

A deep rumble flows up my throat and my breath is about to match his before I can swallow it back down. "Brady," I coo, nudging his shoulder again.

He sits up, looking around lost until his eyes focus on me. I smile and his shoulders fall.

"Let's go take a bath and get to bed," I say.

He holds his arms out to me and I stand there. Am I supposed to pick him up? Sure. I mean that's okay, right?

"My legs hurt," he whines and so I swing my purse over my shoulders and pick him up. He wraps himself around me like a koala bear and I struggle to make it to the elevator.

The occasional yoga class I take hasn't exactly prepared me to carry however many pounds this little guy is and my arms are aching by the time we reach the elevator. I press the button and my phone rings. There's no way I can answer it so I let it ring, figuring I'll catch it once I get inside.

The elevator doors open and after I struggle with the key in the lock, the door opens to a dark condo. Using my knee, I prop Brady up on me a little higher. This carrying a kid thing is really a dad's job. Sorry, feminists.

"Okay, we're home," I say to Brady, blindly making my way to the couch.

My phone starts going off again, but instead of answering, I go to the bathroom and start the bath.

"Do you want bubbles?" I holler out the door, but hear nothing.

I walk out, finding Brady curled in a ball with a blanket over himself, a corner of it still clasped to his hands.

A text message dings from my phone and since whoever it is is persistent I walk over to my purse near Brady and scramble to find my phone in the big bag. Pulling it out, I sit in the chair, seeing two missed calls from Jasper and a text message, asking me where we are. I poise my fingers ready to text him back, but my phone rings with his name flashing.

"We're fine," I deadpan.

"Where have you been? I've been trying to call." His voice is tense and scared.

"Sorry, Brady fell asleep on the way home and I was carrying him up."

"Where did you guys go?" he asks, his voice relaxing.

"The Pier. Remind me to tell you how your kid schooled

this older kid who was making fun of him." I laugh, thinking about that redheaded prick's face as Brady was puking on him.

"I'm not sure I want to know," he says, and I hear a smile on his lips.

"I'm going to get him into a bath if I can get him up." I place my hand on him.

"Okay, call me after he goes to bed. I'm horny and hoping you can instruct me on how to stroke my cock. In explicit detail."

A tingling begins between my legs and man, do I wish he was here. "Well, I am the best," I say in a singsong voice.

"The only one who gets me off."

"Don't forget it down there in Los Angeles," I say, my insecurities coming forth.

He chuckles. "No worries on that front."

"Good."

"Talk to you soon."

I hang up and Brady still refuses to roll over. Having no choice, I start taking off his shoes and socks, thinking that he'll start stirring once I make him uncomfortable.

By the time he's down to his boxers, he's only gotten up long enough for me to wiggle him out of his clothes. His forehead falls on my arm and it's hot.

Adjusting him so that he's sitting up, I place my hand on his forehead, thinking I must be wrong because he was fine an hour ago, but no, he's so hot.

"Brady?" I ask and his eyes float closed again.

I place his head back on the couch and run down the hall, scouring the bathroom for a thermometer. I should call Jasper. *And tell him what? That his kid is sick and you're panicking?* I listen to the devil on my shoulder and run into the ensuite.

Finally, I find a thermometer in the medicine cabinet with bottles of medication that all have the word 'children's' plastered all over them. I so have this. I look over the bottles, grab the acetaminophen and the thermometer.

At least I know how to use an ear thermometer. Thank you to Tahlia for getting the flu months ago.

I stick it in his ear and the seconds it takes for his temperature to register seem like forever. He hasn't moved an inch.

"103 degrees," I screech, clearing it and placing it in his other ear. As though that's going to have a different reading. A second later it beeps. "102.6 degrees. Same fucking difference."

I read the back of the bottle. Okay, apparently kids are dosed by weight. As if I know how much he weighs.

Jasper knows.

Weigh him, the devil on my shoulder urges.

So I run into Jasper's bathroom where I know there's a scale. I weigh myself and then run back out to grab Brady. Picking him up like I'm his mama bear, I walk us to the bathroom.

We step on the scale and I struggle to hold my balance. Bingo. *So, one hundred and fifty-two minus one hundred and twenty-five is, fuck, I hate math. Take one away from the five, making it twelve. Twelve minus five is seven. Four minus two is two. Twenty-seven pounds.*

"That can't be right. I can lift twenty-seven pounds." I put Brady on Jasper's bed and re-weigh myself.

Nope, one hundred and twenty-four. Maybe I lost weight with all this running.

Picking up a moaning and groaning Brady now, I clear the scale.

One hundred and seventy-one pounds. Here we go with the math again. *Take one away from the seven this time, making it eleven. Eleven minus five is six. Six minus two is four. Forty-six pounds. That makes sense.*

I carry Brady back to the living room and lean him up on the couch.

"We need to take some medicine, Brady," I coax him, after

pouring the right amount into the small shot glass.

He shakes his head.

"Come on, Brady, just a little."

He shakes his head again.

"Here comes the train, choo choo." I make the glass stutter along toward his mouth.

Hey, don't knock it, I'm desperate.

He shakes his head.

"Please," I beg and he opens his mouth. "Thank you." I pour it into his mouth and then he lies down on the couch again. I place the blanket over him and sit down in the chair to call Jasper.

As I dial his number, I wonder if I should keep the fact that Brady's sick to myself.

"I'm naked, and I'm fisting your favorite guy," he answers and I laugh, wishing every limb of my body wasn't depleted of energy.

"I do love that guy," I say.

"Talk me through it, baby," he says in a husky voice.

"Hold that thought for a second."

"What is it?" His panicked voice returns.

"Brady has a fever."

"How high?" The tension increases.

"103 degrees in one ear and 102.6 degrees in the other."

"Okay, there's some Tylenol in my bathroom. He takes a teaspoon."

I shouldn't be surprised that Jasper knows the exact amount. He's not in training. He's the real dad deal.

"Yeah, I weighed him and figured it out."

He laughs. "Weighed him? I'm surprised, usually when Brady has a fever, he's like dragging an elephant around on a leash."

"I weighed myself and then I held him and weighed us together."

His laughter bursts out and I'm sure if he was drinking it'd be spit out all over his room. "Seriously?" he asks after he's calmed down somewhat.

"Yes, seriously. I didn't know what to do."

"You could call me," he says.

"And make you think I can't handle it?" I lean back in the chair, my eyes on Brady.

"Baby, I wouldn't have left you with him if I didn't trust you could handle it."

His words calm me but I know deep down he's still on guard. "Do you mind if we wait until you get home tomorrow and I demonstrate the stroke for you?"

"You sound tired," he says and a yawn escapes me at the exact moment.

"Yeah."

"Parenting will do that to you. I'm sure I can find someone around here to stroke me." The teasing tone in his voice clear.

"Try it and you won't have anything to stroke," I warn and he chuckles.

"Man, that was scary. You made him turtle."

"Good night, Jasper," I say.

"Night, baby. See you tomorrow," he whispers and we hang up the phone.

I click on the television, turning on whatever will fill the noise of his quiet condo. I must doze off because when I wake up a few hours later, the television is going, Brady's still asleep.

Grabbing the thermometer, I take Brady's temperature to make sure it went down, but when my hand touches his forehead, he still feels hot.

"104 degrees," I say, my heartbeat picking up pace.

Clearing it, I take the other ear. "104.3 degrees."

No, no, no.

I look at the back of the bottle and sure enough, he can't

even take another dose.

Picking up my phone, I call the only person I know can help. The phone rings and I glance at the cable box, seeing it's after ten, which means she's asleep.

"Hello," her groggy voice answers.

"Mom!" I say.

"What is it?" Her voice clears quickly.

"So . . ." I realize I've told my mom nothing about Jasper. I haven't even talked to Jacob about Jasper. Fuck a duck. "I'm watching someone's kid and he has a fever of over 104 degrees. I gave him Tylenol a couple hours ago and it hasn't brought the fever down."

"You're babysitting," she clarifies.

"Kind of, yes."

"Okay, go get a cold cloth and put it on his forehead."

I scramble into the kitchen, run a washcloth under cold water and come back and place it on Brady's forehead. "What else?"

"You need to call the parents," she says. "They need to come home and care for their child."

My stomach plummets.

"Um. That can't happen."

"Lennon?" She uses the same tone she has my entire life. The one that suggests she already knows I'm in over my head. The one that says, *What crazy thing did you do this time?*

"It's my boyfriend's son and he's out of town." I ramble on as though she wouldn't clue in.

"Boyfriend?"

Of course that's the one word she pulls from my sentence. "Yes, and he's in LA, so he can't come back." I glance down to Brady, my worry deepening. "Mom, my gut says this isn't good."

"How long ago did you give him the medicine?"

We start from the beginning and I even tell her how I let him gorge on sweets all night, for which I receive the disappointed sigh I'm so familiar with.

"I'm going to tell you to do something but don't panic, okay?" she says, which makes me, guess what . . . panic. "Go to the emergency room."

"Emergency room? Surely this can be handled at home."

She sighs. "It's a high fever and honey, I'm out of practice. You could call the paediatrician if your boyfriend left the number, but if the medicine isn't working, I don't think you have any other option."

"Okay. Okay." I straighten my back as though my inner mom-in-training is armed and ready. "I'm going."

"Lennon," she says before I have time to click her off. "I'll meet you at Memorial. And call his dad." She says the last part because she knows me well.

"Okay, see you at Memorial," I say and as I'm hanging up, I hear her repeat.

"Call the dad . . ."

chapter
THIRTY-ONE

I SWING MY PURSE crossways over my body, pick up Brady and we head out of the condo, down the elevator and into my van. I'll never have to do another biceps curl in my life. My adrenaline must be pumping because Brady hardly even feels heavy now. I feel like I could compete in the world's strongest woman competition.

I hit Jasper's number on my phone and put it on speaker as I turn the corner on his block, heading toward the hospital.

"Did you get a second wind?" he says when he picks up and I so wish I could be in his bed right now, ready to seduce him with my dirty words.

"Jasper." The panic can't be missed from my voice. Tears prick my eyes because I'm a horrible mom-in-training.

"What is it?" His own tone matches mine now.

"Brady's fever hasn't gone down. I'm taking him to Memorial." My foot presses on the gas.

"How high?"

"104 degrees and 104.3 degrees."

"You gave him Tylenol how many hours ago?"

"Like two hours ago, maybe a little less."

He pauses for a while.

"Jasper?"

"Yeah, I'm just thinking. Go ahead. I'm going to see if I can catch a flight. If need be, I'll rent a car."

"I can handle it." Though it's not how I'm feeling right now.

A long breath flows across the receiver. This is the do-or-die moment. Does he trust me enough? Hell, should he?

"As hard as this is, call me when you get word. I'm going to call his paediatrician. I'm hoping this is viral."

Viral? I rack my brain for any medical jargon I know. I think there's viral and bacterial. Damn Whitney for always distracting me in Biology. Actually, it was the other way around.

"I'll call you as soon as I get him in."

"Okay," he says, and I can tell he's distracted by his thoughts.

We hang up and I pull up to the emergency entrance, stop and round the car, pluck Brady out and walk through the sliding door.

"Ma'am," someone calls out but I ignore them.

Walking up to the nurses' station, I see the waiting room is packed. Well, I'm going all *Terms of Endearment* on their asses if they don't get Brady in ASAP.

"Hello," the exhausted nurse says to me. I'm assuming that based on the bags under her eyes and stench of irritation and impatience wafting off of her.

"He has a fever of 104 degrees," I say, placing him on the counter so he can lean on my chest.

"Fill out the paperwork." She plops a clipboard down on the counter beside us.

I glance down at the paperwork and slide it over. "I don't think you're listening. He's six and has a high fever. I gave him medicine—"

"Lady, look at the room." She points to the waiting area.

"All those people are sick, too."

I grit my teeth. "I don't care about them. I only care about this boy."

"Lennon," my mom says, coming alongside me, surprise in her face when she sees me clutching Brady to my chest.

"Fill out the forms and we'll get him in."

My mom grabs the clipboard. "What's his name?"

I tell her and we go through any of the information I do know. I don't know the insurance information or even their paediatrician's name.

"I'm a horrible mom-in-training," I say, tears falling down my cheeks as Brady's head rests on my shoulder.

"Mom-in-training?" my mom questions.

"Yeah. I mean he shouldn't trust me with his kid. I took him to the Pier and let him eat all that bad stuff, he threw up and now he probably has some kind of virus because of me. I ruined his son. He's going to hate me." My chest racks with sobs and my mom places her arm around my shoulders.

"You were having a fun time with him. Relax. This is completely unrelated." My mom walks the clipboard back up to Nurse Jackie and then returns to her seat.

"Mrs. Banks," the lady calls out and I look around to see who the other Banks here is.

"I think she assumes you're the mom." My mom nudges me with her elbow.

"Not if this little guy is lucky." I stand, my mom follows. The nurse heads us back to a room where someone else takes his temperature. They nod and soon we're being taken into another room. I place Brady on the bed. His body looks so small and helpless.

"Hi, I'm Marie. I'm your nurse." She looks to Brady. "What's up, little guy?" she asks and Brady stares up at her, the bright lights rousing him a bit when I laid him down.

She asks me to tell her what happened and I do. I sit on the bed next to Brady, holding his hand and comforting him. She takes the same vitals the other person did, confirming yes, his fever is high.

He looks over at me after she leaves saying the doctor will be in. "I'm tired," he says and my hand moves to his hair, smoothing it out.

"I know, but we're going to get you better." Then I spot my mom staring at the two of us. I've been so wrapped up in Brady that I almost forgot she was here. "I have someone I want you to meet," I say to Brady and his eyes scan the room. My mom rises to stand at the edge of the bed. "This is my mom, Mrs. Hart," I say. "Mom, this is Brady."

"Hi, Brady. It's good to meet you. Now don't you worry, you're going to be okay," my mom assures him. Brady nods and insecurity makes me think he almost believes the words from her mouth more than my own.

The nurse comes in a few minutes later and I see the concern in her eyes. "The doctor has asked that I put an IV in Brady to give him some fever-reducing drugs." She gives me a small smile and we both know this isn't going to be a cakewalk.

"What's an IV?" he asks and my eyes shoot to my mom, who cringes.

"It's going to make you feel better," I say, disregarding the question.

The nurse washes her hands, puts some gloves on and sits on the edge of the bed. "Brady, did you want to watch something on television? Your mom can turn it on for you."

Brady looks at me and I'm waiting for him to tell her I'm not his mom. But he just nods.

I click on the television and scan through the channels until I find some Disney show that seems appropriate and I leave it there.

"Mom, why don't you come up on the bed and hold him up to you," the nurse offers and again I glance to my mom, but I do as the nurse directs.

I climb on the bed and Brady has no problem cuddling up into me. In fact, he seems soothed by my close proximity.

She grabs his arm and he looks down at the needle that's about to go in and starts crying.

"No, no, no!" he says, trying to get his arm back, but the nurse is too strong, which I think freaks him out.

"It's okay, Brady," I repeat over and over again as his tears wet my t-shirt.

"Done," the nurse says a painful minute later.

Brady looks down at his arm and up to me in confusion.

"You know how you sip your medicine out of a cup usually?" I say. He nods. "She's going to give them to you through there."

He nods, before his eyes find the television again.

"The doctor will be in soon to evaluate him," the nurse, who I swear is younger than me, says.

"Thank you."

Brady watches television and my mom sits in silence while I'm sure a million questions are floating through her mind. Not long after, she turns to me.

"So who is his father?" she whispers.

I glance down at Brady, who's totally engrossed in the TV show. Now that's something I have learned . . . TV and kids equal tunnel vision. "If I tell you, it stays between us for right now."

Her head draws back and her eyes narrow on me as if to say, *Oh, no, Lennon. Not again.* "Fine," she says in a voice that says she's not sure if she can promise that.

"Jasper," I answer.

A wide smile crosses her lips. "Jacob's Jasper?"

My Jasper.

"Yeah, Jacob's mentor, Jasper," I clarify and her smile widens.

"Oh, my gosh. He's the little boy." A surprised look crosses over her face.

"How many times has Jasper been over for dinner?" I ask, curious how well she knows him and also upset that no one ever called me to join them.

"Not for a while. Mostly when Jacob was working under him. It was only a few times and I think Brady might have been two or so at that time." She smiles, as if this is a fond remembrance.

"How come I was never invited?" I'm upset because this entire time I was prancing around San Francisco a single woman and I could have met Jasper earlier.

"Well, Lennon, you were always so busy." She shrugs and rolls her eyes. I nod, not wanting to get into drama. "So, if he's trusting you to watch Brady, I'm guessing you guys are close?" she asks, prodding me for more details.

I eye her and then Brady. "Yeah," I answer, not giving anything else away.

"Monogamous?" She continues sticking that shovel in the ground, digging for the worms.

"Yes." I look down and Brady's eyes beginning to drift closed. "I think I may even l—"

Her eyes widen and the corners of her mouth start to rise.

"Here you go." The nurse from earlier enters the room and behind her walks in none other than Natalie Banks.

"Thank you." She nods to the nurse and rushes over to Brady's side. She feels his forehead, grips his hands and then pulls the blanket down to inspect his body.

"Natalie," I say, rising to my feet and coming to the other side of the bed.

She looks up. "What did you do?" Her voice is venom and I almost fall back from surprise.

"Nothing."

My mom, sensing something isn't right, walks over to my side.

"I knew he couldn't trust you with him," Natalie says. I glance down to Brady, thankful his eyes are still shut. "You're just trouble. I knew it the minute I set eyes on you. All you care about is fun and there's not a responsible bone in your body."

I won't lie, her jabs hit their target and the pain comes swiftly.

"Why are you here?" I ask.

"Why do you think? Jasper called me because he knows you can't handle this. You might be some fun toy he likes to sleep around with, but don't fool yourself into thinking you'll ever be anything more."

I blink a few times and my mom's hand lands on mine, gripping it tightly.

"I'm guessing you're Jasper's mother?" she asks, while I try to push away the vertigo from being mentally slapped side to side by this woman.

"Yes. And you are?" Her voice is nothing but mean and spiteful.

"I'm Eva, Lennon's mother. Now, I understand you're upset that your grandchild is sick, but the way you're talking to my daughter is not nice nor will it be tolerated."

I look over to my mom. Color me surprised.

"You raised her?" Natalie questions, her gaze directed at my inked skin.

My mom's back straightens and she tightens her grip on my hand. "Her father and I did."

"You stand there looking like you're proud of her. Look at her." She wrinkles her nose in disgust.

"Who are you to throw daggers?" I ready myself for a fight, but my mom squeezes my hand.

"Proud of her? Did you know that she attended Berkeley on an art scholarship? Now, she switched that major to business because she had the guts to find what she loves. She paid off her school loans after she lost her scholarship by tattooing her friends. Figure out how many hours that is in your small brain. Now she's getting a business venture off the ground all by herself. And that's just her career. You want to talk personal life? Did you know she sometimes volunteers at shelters, or donates her time to tattoo over the scars of veterans, or how she gives almost every homeless person she passes money, food or a drink? Or maybe we should discuss how she never judges anyone because they're different or misunderstood. You'd be so lucky to have your son love her."

Natalie rolls her eyes and a long sigh flows out of her mouth.

"But let me tell you a little secret as a mom with three boys, two of whom I've already married off."

Natalie looks like she could care less.

My mom leans over the bed to double-check that Brady's sleeping.

"You can't control who your son loves. And I personally think if he chooses Lennon, he's one lucky guy. But no matter if it's Lennon or not, you better be ready to play nice because those women call the shots and if you want a relationship with your son, you sure as heck better not treat her the way you just did my daughter. Otherwise, you can kiss your son and your grandson goodbye."

My mom draws back over to my side and puts her arm around my shoulder.

Natalie eyes me. "I'm sorry, you just aren't responsible enough to take care of my grandson. One night and look, we're in the hospital."

A knock sounds from the door before I can respond.

"Greg," Natalie coos, walking over to shake his hand.

"Natalie," he says, shaking her hand and placing his free hand on her shoulder. "Jasper called."

Greg is about Jasper's age, maybe a few years older, with dark brown hair and a thin runner-style body. He's in slacks, a button-down and his doctor jacket.

My mom and I stand there and I can't help but feel like a third wheel.

"You must be Lennon Hart?" he asks me, holding his hand out. "I'm Dr. Bierdman, Brady's paediatrician. I happen to be filling in for a shift. Jasper had me paged."

"Yes. Nice to meet you." I step out of my mom's embrace and shake his hand. He gives a bright white-teeth smile. "This is my mom Eva Hart." I place my hand on my mom's back.

He extends his arm out to her. "Nice to meet you."

"Now that all the introductions have been made, what do you think is happening with Brady?" Natalie sits down and grabs Brady's hand.

Greg grabs the thermometer from the table and takes Brady's temperature. "His temperature has gone down. Jasper says you gave him Tylenol?" he asks, looking in my direction.

"Yes."

"Okay, I don't think this is anything serious, but I'm going to look at his eyes and do a few tests."

I step away from the bed, as does my mom, but Natalie stays put.

Greg coaxes Brady up and his eyes wander around the room.

"Right here, sweetheart," she says.

"Where's Lennon?" He sounds upset so I walk to the foot of the bed.

"I'm right here, buddy." I grip his foot and shake it a little.

He smiles and Natalie turns her head and gives me the death stare.

Dr. Bierdman does his exam and he definitely has a way

about him because Brady's sucking on a lollipop and laughing by the time he's done.

"He looks good. I think we just need to deal with the fever. Now, who should I give instructions to?" he asks, looking between me and Natalie.

Natalie stares me down, almost baiting me to dare step up. I look to Brady and realize it's his decision not ours. I want him wherever he's going to be most comfortable.

"Brady, do you want to go home with Grandma or me? Daddy won't be back until tomorrow afternoon," I tell him and this devilish gleam gets in his eye.

"Can't Grandma come home with us, Lennon?" he asks.

Damn it.

Mom-in-training note to self: Never let the kid have a say.

chapter
THIRTY-TWO

BRADY'S ASLEEP IN HIS bed. Natalie isn't letting him out of his room, even though after his fever broke he was ready to wrestle. She's washed his sheets, as well as Jasper's. Cleaned out the fridge, washed, dried, and folded every stitch of laundry. Disinfected every light switch, door handle and drawer pull. You'd think that's enough, right? Nope. She's even dusted and vacuumed—the floor and the furniture, I might add. I mean, who vacuums the kitchen chairs?

What have I been doing, you ask?

Nothing.

I'm done trying to prove my worth to her. It's Jasper and Brady I'm invested in.

So, I'm sitting on the newly vacuumed couch, clicking through Netflix.

"Don't you have a tattoo shop to manage?" she sneers.

I stare directly at the television, clicking the buttons on the remote. "Brady said he wanted me here, so here I will be."

She huffs like a thirteen-year-old girl who was told she can't get the brand-new jacket everyone else has and stomps down the hall. The sound of spraying bottles bounces back to me in the family room. I laugh to myself because I'm so over this woman even if she is Jasper's mom.

A half hour later and two clean bathrooms for Natalie, a door opens and small footsteps pad down the hall.

Brady rounds the corner, his smile appearing once he sees me. Grabbing the blanket swung over the chair, he snuggles into my side and I straighten the blanket over his legs.

"Did you sleep well?" I ask, touching his forehead. Lukewarm and a little clammy.

He nods, and I turn the station to the kids' movie I saw while I was channel-surfing.

"Brady." Natalie comes in and her shoulders slump before she rushes over, snatching up the thermometer on her way over. "Sit up," she demands.

Brady does and she takes his temperature. In both ears, I may add.

"Oh, good. Your temperature is down." Appeased, she goes to the kitchen. "I'll make you some soup," she says.

"I want chicken nuggets," he whines.

"No, you need soup."

"Shouldn't we just make sure we feed him?" I speak up and her eyes narrow on me from behind the breakfast bar.

"Let me handle this, Lennon," she says, so I turn around and shrug to Brady.

"I'd let you have chicken nuggets," I whisper.

Was this the right move? Probably not. But since when do I ever do the right thing?

"Grandma." He sits up on his knees and peers over the couch. "I want chicken nuggets and fries!" Jasper would probably have a fit if he heard the way Brady's raised his voice to an adult.

I cringe internally, thinking I shouldn't have talked to her like that. Respect and all that bullshit.

"Brady, chicken nuggets and fries are not what you need right now."

He plops down on the couch, crosses his arms and stares at the television.

"I should have just said you," he says, his voice angry.

This time I keep quiet, not wanting to rock the boat even more.

Minutes later, the bowl hits the counter and a spoon is being dug out of the drawer.

"Brady," she says. "Come eat."

Brady rolls his eyes, flings the blanket off him and stomps over to the counter.

"Gross," he mumbles, staring into the bowl.

"Oh, stop it. You've eaten this a million times." Natalie busies herself at the sink.

I walk over and sit down next to him. As much as I would hate to give Natalie a compliment, the soup looks good. And smells amazing. The ding of the oven goes off and she pulls out a fresh loaf of bread.

My mouth waters, but I pretend not to be interested as it sits on the counter, perfectly shaped, the aroma filling up every crevice of the condo.

"Would you like a bowl, Lennon?" she asks, her voice the epitome of niceness with that twang of, *Try it and I drop a large sack of poison in it.*

"That's okay," I say, staring off toward the door, wishing Jasper would walk in.

"Come on, Lennon," Brady whines, his spoon swirling around the broth, not scooping any of it up.

I look down at the little guy, run my hands through his thick hair that's just like his father's.

"For you . . . sure."

He smiles and I give serious thought to whether Natalie

would actually poison my soup.

Natalie begins to grab a bowl, but I rush over and take my own, ladling my soup up myself. She smiles, noticing Brady watching our interaction.

I sit down next to Brady again, while Natalie cleans as usual. I dip my spoon and bring the broth to my mouth. Okay, the woman's got skills in the kitchen.

Shit. This is what Jasper grew up with. I'm totally fucking screwed.

"Try it, Brady. Your grandma makes good soup." I nudge his arm and he rolls his eyes like I've seen his dad do more than a few times, but he scoops some up and brings it to his lips.

Natalie peeks over her shoulder and I want desperately to tell her I complimented her soup for the sake of the kid and not her, but I exercise self-control.

I cross my legs so I'm facing Brady while leaning over my bowl and eating small amounts of my soup in case I need to eat the whole bowl to actually keel over from Natalie's poison. I'm kidding. Sort of.

A better surprise happens. I hear a key jiggling in the lock from the other side. My eyes shoot to the microwave clock. It's only three. Jasper isn't due until eight. Brady's ears perk up hearing the same thing and we're like two dogs waiting by the door with our tails wagging at max speed for our master.

I'm not sure I've ever wanted to see Jasper more—well, except for the first time we met. Who am I kidding? I'd knock Brady over and stomp on him if I was that kind of girl. Thankfully, I'm not.

Jasper enters, his suit jacket open, his tie long gone, a suitcase rolling behind him.

Brady's off his stool in a second, running to his dad and throwing his arms around his dad's neck. Jasper's arms lock around his son's waist, bringing him up to hold him to his chest.

His large hand splays across the back of his son's head as though he can't get close enough.

The image is so tender and caring that I have to fight the tears welling in my eyes. I've always known that Brady and Jasper love each other, but I've never witnessed this level of adoration.

Brady draws back and Jasper looks him over once more before hugging him tight again.

"I was in the emergency room," Brady says like it's a source of pride and not one of the scariest moments of my life.

Jasper nods and mumbles something I can't hear. When I glance to Natalie expecting to find her washing dishes, her eyes are set on me. She arches her graying eyebrows and I move my gaze away from her.

Once they're done, Brady hangs off his dad's neck as he walks over to me.

"Hey," he says, kissing my forehead. "Thank you for taking care of him."

I nod.

"She didn't do it alone," Natalie says, trying to make a joke, I think, but we all understand her underlying meaning.

"Yeah, your mom cleaned," I deadpan.

Jasper's eyes move from me to his mom and back to me. I should've tried to hide my annoyance more.

"And Lennon watched television," Natalie says with a condescending smile.

"Thank you both," he says, giving me another kiss. This time on the lips.

A little tongue would have been awesome, but since Brady is literally millimeters away, probably not a good idea. See, I'm getting this whole having-a-kid-around thing.

Brady slides off Jasper and onto the breakfast stool.

Jasper walks back over to the door and opens his computer bag, pulling out a brown paper bag. Anyone can tell it's from

McDonalds and Brady's smile is bigger than when Jasper came home. Jasper places it on the counter and slides his bowl of soup over.

"Thanks, Dad. I asked but Grandma said no." He gives her the stink eye and although we shouldn't laugh, we do. He tears the bag open, pulling out the carton of chicken nuggets and fries out.

"Jasper." His mom sighs.

"It's been his go-to every time he gets sick. It's our thing." Jasper silences her and she listens, moving to the stove.

"Okay, but be prepared for him to get sick again." She shakes her head, wiping down the counter.

"So, Mom, we're good now. Go home to Dad." Jasper walks over to her, stealing a slice of bread from over her shoulder. Okay, if Jasper survives, that loaf is mine.

"It's okay, honey. I can stay for a while." She pats his shoulder.

Jasper's gaze shoots to me and I try to act indifferent, although I want to sneak him into his bedroom for at least a real kiss.

"I insist, Mom. Thanks for taking care of the insurance thing at the hospital. You didn't have to come back here."

She looks to me and then to Brady and back to Jasper. "Can I have a word?"

His head falls back and he shrugs off his coat, placing it on the back of a kitchen chair.

"How about tomorrow? I'll call you," he offers, dipping his bread into my soup.

Soup that's gone cold now. Like my heart for this woman.

"It will only take a moment. In the hall." She moves to grab her purse and overnight bag that she brought to the hospital.

Obviously, she isn't taking no for an answer.

"Fine."

"Bye, Brady." She comes over and kisses the top of his head.

"Bye, Grandma." He continues to play with the toy from his meal.

"Lennon," she says in her usual curt tone.

"Bye, Natalie. Safe trip back home." *To hell on your broomstick,* I don't add.

"I'll be right back." Jasper shoots up his eyebrows with a tight smile, obviously not looking forward to his mother's lecture.

"So, what did you get?" I ask Brady, trying not to think about what Natalie is saying to Jasper a few feet away behind a closed door.

Brady plays with his toy and my eyes stay glued to the door until the doorknob turns. Then I focus my attention solely on my soup as though I don't care what his mother had to say.

"Brady," he calls out, shutting the door behind him. "Lennon and I will be right back."

Brady doesn't really answer, his mind still on his meal and toy.

I climb off the stool, slowly following Jasper to his bedroom. He walks in, leaving his suitcase by the door and then shuts and locks his bedroom door.

"What did—"

His lips slam onto mine as his body cages me against the door. My hands circle his neck, and I arch my back, needing his hands on me. Shivers run up my skin as his hands slide under my shirt, moving up my back until he undoes my bra.

Once it's loosened, his hands slide forward, squeezing both my breasts at the same time. A small moan escapes my throat as one leg wraps around his muscular thigh.

He tears his lips from mine. "You have no idea how hot it makes me that you took care of Brady. I've had a raging hard-on since I walked through that door and saw the two of you in my house, at my breakfast counter."

I pull his mouth down to mine again, and his tongue wastes no time invading my mouth. His lips slide off mine, traveling down to my jaw and then my neck as he scoops me up in his arms and I wrap my legs around his waist.

He walks us toward the bed and then drops me on the mattress.

"Quickie?' I ask and he nods, unbuckling his belt and slacks until they fall to the floor.

I shimmy out of my pants and underwear, spreading my legs for him. He stares down at my pussy and his chest rises and falls with rapid breaths.

"Tonight, I'll take my time," he promises and then yanks his boxers down, steps out of them and he's inside of me within three minutes of shutting that door.

chapter
THIRTY-THREE

MONDAYS CAN SUCK IT.

As I walk into the office, with my three coffees on the tray perched in my hand, I glance at the names on the cups and laugh to myself.

Brittany's painting her nails when I place the coffees on the receptionist's desk. She looks up and, without saying anything, picks up the phone. "Mr. Banks," she says. "Miss Hart is here for Dr—Mr. Ashland." She catches herself.

At some point, hopefully, I'll be able to just walk past her and straight to Jasper's office so that I can spare myself the irritation of dealing with her.

"He said to go in, but wanted to be clear that you go to his office." She lifts her eyebrows, clearly insinuating that Jasper is going to have me bent over his desk.

Well, I'll show her—little does she know that it's me on my knees when it comes to Jasper's office.

"Thanks, Brittany." I walk down the hall, and catch Jasper on the phone when I reach his office. He waves me in and since his assistant isn't there, I walk through his door.

He holds up his hand so I place his coffee down in front of him and then grab mine, taking a seat on his couch. Circling the cup around, he laughs when he spots the words.

"Yeah, I understand. Okay, I said I'd handle it," he says, his tone about as irritated as I sound with his mom.

"Mom," he sighs.

Huh. I guess she has that effect on everyone.

"Yeah, if you could watch him overnight. It's Lennon's dad's retirement party." He rolls his eyes, and his head falls back in frustration. "I'll drop him off. He can spend the night with you guys." And almost a lifetime later—"Bye." He hangs up, stands with his coffee and walks around the desk. He shuts his door, flicking the lock, and I grow wet between my thighs.

"I have to meet Drew, or as his cup now refers to him, Sugar Daddy," I remind him but he pays no attention. Not even a raised eyebrow.

"He'll understand if you're late. I've had a rough day." He sits down, his hand threading through his hair.

Under normal circumstances, I'd probably fall to my knees and work that irritation out of him. But I have to meet Drew and that has to come first today.

"Why's your day been so bad?" I ask, afraid of the answer.

He looks at me and shakes his head. "Nothing. What are you and Drew going through today?" he asks, attempting to move the conversation along.

"Jasper?" I ask with a tone clear that I want an answer.

He shakes his head. "Nothing I can't handle."

"So, what does she want now? Me on a stake so she can set it on fire?"

He chuckles until he sees the seriousness on my face. "She doesn't hate you."

I cross my arms, similar to Brady when he doesn't get his way. "Really?"

Now I've never told Jasper what his mom said to me at the hospital. Nor did I tell him what my mom told her. I'm not going to put him in the middle. I'm a big girl and I fight my own battles.

"She's just protective."

I huff. "Protective? She thinks I'm scum and that I'm completely incapable."

He stares out this window, sipping his coffee. "I just got it from her. Can I not get it from you, too?" he asks, annoyance laced through his deep voice.

"Sure. I need to meet Drew anyway." I stand and grab Drew's coffee from the tray.

"Don't." He comes up behind me, his lips finding that magic spot halfway between the back of my neck and my ear. "I need you," he whispers. "I want to be buried deep inside of you right now."

"I want lots of things I can't have, too," I sneer and he chuckles, thinking I'm joking.

Don't do it, Lennon. Don't do it.

"You do know one day you'll have to choose?'

You idiot, you did it.

His hands fall from my stomach, his lips leave my skin. "What?"

Say forget it and go to Drew's office.

"Do you think I'm going to allow her to treat me like shit forever?"

He tilts his head and I'm guessing he's wondering where this is coming from.

Apologize and say you lost your mind.

"I understand she hasn't been the nicest, but eventually she'll come around."

"When? She acts like I'm letting Brady shoot up heroin and taking him out to the strippers when I'm watching him. She purposely undermines me in front of him. And you just sit there in la-la land."

Okay, strike that last sentence. Tell him to strike the last sentence.

"La-la land?" he asks, his voice as cold and smooth as a bottle of vodka resting in a freezer. "It's not her decision to decide who I'm with, Lennon. It's mine."

I shake my head. "That's what you think. She continues to throw me under the bus and nitpick everything I do and you'll start believing it. It's inevitable, Jasper. One day you will have to choose between us."

His hand slams down on his desk, his business card holder falling down. "Goddamn it! Don't do this. Don't make this an issue before it is one." His voice rises and I swear I never thought this conversation would get this kind of reaction.

What do I do? What I do best. Get angry right back.

"If you heard what she said about me—" I shake my hand and raise my hand. "Never mind. I need to go."

I turn around to walk out of his office. My one hand is on the doorknob, Drew's coffee is in the other when his arms wrap around my waist again like they've found their home.

"Don't," he whispers in my ear and goose bumps ignite across my skin.

"I'm already late." But I don't move. Instead, I stand there while his arms tighten.

"We'll figure this out. I'm sorry for getting angry," he says, sounding a little desperate. I've never encountered this side of Jasper. Almost like he's fearful I'll leave him.

I swivel around in his arms, placing Drew's coffee down on the side table near the door. "Pretty soon my mouth is going to open and she's not going to like what comes out," I warn.

His eyes are distraught but he shakes his head. "I promise, it will never come to that." He pulls me into him, his arms so tight that I fight to breathe for a moment. "Just give me some time," he says softly.

I will, but after the hospital and his condo, I'm unsure if we can ever co-exist. I hate the thought of putting both Jasper and Brady in the middle almost as much as I hate the thought of having to deal with her bullshit for eternity.

chapter THIRTY-FOUR

"SO, HIS MOTHER SAID what?" Whitney says, her mouth hanging open.

"'Fun toy' were her exact words."

"Well, she doesn't sound so fun herself."

"Sorry, girls." Tahlia runs in with ten bags hanging from her arms. She drops them on the neighboring table and sits down in front of the coffee we already bought for her. "Whatcha chatting about?"

"Jasper's mom's a monster," Whit informs her.

"Oh, my God, have you ever seen that movie *Monster-in-Law*?" Tahlia asks.

"Of course you have a movie to compare it to." I roll my eyes.

Whitney laughs. I'm not sure there's a romantic comedy that Tahlia doesn't know.

"Her mother-in-law was such a bitch. Did you know it has Mary Fiore in it?" Tahlia asks us.

"You mean J-Lo?" I correct her.

"I only see her as Mary Fiore," she singsongs.

For those of you who don't know, Mary Fiore was the main character in *The Wedding Planner* and since Tahlia's wanted to be one since forever I'm guessing she's got a little girl crush going for J-Lo. Me? I'll take J-Law any day. She's much more my speed—a say-what-you-think-and-not-take-things-too-seriously kinda gal.

"You realize your obsession with Mary Fiore isn't actually healthy." I sip my coffee.

"Hello? You used to look up to that Kat woman who has her own tattoo company and was dating Jesse James, remember?"

"Um, Tahlia . . ." Whitney cringes, knowing she did not just school me.

"Kat is a real person who really tattooed people. Jennifer Lopez played a wedding planner along with a dancer, an abused wife, and Selena."

Tahlia shakes her head as if I'm not telling the truth. I won't completely burst her bubble today. Especially since I feel like my love bubble is slowly depleting of air the more Mrs. Banks wedges her way between Jasper and me.

"Forget all that," Whitney says, waving her hand at Tahl, "what does Jasper say?"

I shrug. "He says it will take time. That he's sure she'll come around." I roll my eyes, because I'd put money on hell freezing over first.

"Hmm," Whitney murmurs, agreeing with me.

"It could happen. She'll see how great you are with Brady. She's probably worried." Tahlia offers her glass-half-full advice.

"No." I shake my head. "This woman wants me out. I doubt anyone would be good enough for her son, but I'm her worst nightmare."

The side of Whitney's mouth lifts, attempting to show support. "Well, I'm sure Jasper will choose you."

I sip my coffee and place it down on the table. "That's the thing. I don't want him to choose. I mean, Brady loves his grandparents. Even if Jasper did choose me, he'd end up resenting me." I tell my friends the truth.

"God, I'm glad I don't have to deal with that. I'm sorry." Tahlia pats my hand.

"Cole doesn't like his family any more than I do, so it has yet to be an issue with us." Whitney places her hand on top of Tahlia's and I'm wondering if we're about to say, "Go, team," and disperse.

"You'll prove it to her," Tahlia says and they each take their hands off of mine.

"That's the thing, I don't want to prove myself to her. Actually, the more she expects me to kiss her ass the less I'm inclined to. You know how I am."

They both laugh.

"Yeah, we know, but you have to remember . . . you've never had this much to lose." Whitney's eyebrows lift.

Lose. Yeah, my heart aches thinking about losing Jasper and Brady. When the hell did that happen?

"Well, if they can't love me for me, they aren't worth my time."

"Classic Lennon." Tahlia shares a look with Whitney.

"What?" I ask.

The two share another look and then Tahlia's gaze meets mine while Whitney sips her coffee.

"The more you care, the more you've got one foot out of the relationship. The problem this time is we're not just talking about some fling with a guy who will eventually move on. We're talking about a kid . . . who wants a mom."

"Maybe that's not me," I say and they each shake their heads as though I'm a lost cause.

"I think all three of us know you are, Lennon," Whitney says. "For the first time in your life, you might have to let that defense mechanism of indifference fall. I think you're just scared that if you give your whole self to someone, they might not choose you back."

I push back the feeling that I'm not good enough, not strait-laced enough, not in the box enough. It's a feeling I've worn like a second skin my entire life and if I'm honest with myself, maybe there's something to what Whitney's saying. But I don't want to be honest with myself. Right now, I have a whole other mess to deal with.

"I better go. I'm meeting my brother at his office to tell him about Jasper." I change the topic fast and rise to my feet.

They each huff again.

"Lennon, we're talking," Tahlia says.

"Right now, I don't plan on seeing that woman for a while," I say, grabbing my purse.

"Why doesn't your brother know about you and Jasper?" Whitney asks, letting the topic of my insecurity fall to the wayside, for which I'm grateful.

I slide my chair into the table and grab my coffee cup. "Remember, he refused to introduce me so I took matters into my own hands?"

"He *still* knows nothing about you two?" Tahlia asks.

"Nope. So I'd better hop to it before the retirement party. Don't want the surprise to be on Jacob." I try to laugh but cringe instead, thinking about how pissed he's about to be at me.

"Well, good luck." Tahlia leans back, worry creasing her brow.

"He either accepts it or he doesn't." I shrug like it doesn't bother me and truthfully, it's Jacob's problem if he can't accept that I'm happy with Jasper. "Bye, girls. I'll see you there this weekend, right?" I ask and they both nod.

"Yep. We'll meet you there." Whitney nods. "And Lennon?"

I turn back around.

"Don't let the issues with his mother get between you and

Jasper," Whitney says, smiles and leans back in her chair.

"Thanks, Mom." I roll my eyes and then do what I do best—bolt.

chapter

THIRTY-FIVE

"JACOB? WHERE THE HELL are you? Call me."

I click the phone off, dropping it on the bed.

I went to his office that day.

He was out. Probably screwing Megan.

I've called him no less than five times every day, texted just as many and . . . nothing.

What the hell?

Jasper walks into the bedroom. A low whistle leaves his lips and when I look behind me, I find him leaning against the wall, ankles casually crossed and his gaze slowly moving up and down my body.

"Are you just going to gawk?" I ask, putting my other earring in.

He pushes off the wall and I hear the clicking of his dress shoes on the hardwood floor until his warm hands wrap around my bare shoulders. As always, his lips find that sweet spot between my shoulder and neck.

"I'd like to eat you up, but we're going to be late," he whispers, his hands sliding down my body until they rest on my hips.

"Tonight though, I plan on sliding this zipper down. Don't tell me what's underneath. I want to be surprised."

"What makes you think there's anything underneath?" I ask. He chuckles. "I'm looking forward to being able to use my vocal cords tonight," I say.

He grinds his already hardening erection into my ass and I close my eyes on a moan.

"I plan on making you hoarse by tomorrow." He kisses that spot one more time and then trails his lips down my shoulder until he hits the spaghetti strap of my dress.

"And I look forward to it." I dip my head back to his chest and his hands graze up my torso until his palms are massaging my tits.

"We should really get a babysitter more often." My own hand slides between us, rubbing his erection. "How were your parents anyway?"

He steps back from me and I wobble until I regain my balance.

"She didn't say anything," he says, walking to his dresser and placing his watch on.

"I didn't—"

"Didn't you?" he fires back before I can even finish my sentence.

From his reaction, I know that she did say something. Witch.

"I just wondered if they were excited to have Brady for the night," I say, lying through my teeth because truth is, I do want to know what she's saying about me every time he talks to her.

"Lennon." He says my name with an exasperation that reminds me of my own tone when a bachelorette party comes into the tattoo parlor. He turns around, shoving his hands in his slacks. "I don't want to talk about my mother tonight."

"Fine." I grab my clutch, smooth out my dress and walk out of the room.

"Let's not do this, please," Jasper begs one step behind me. "We're kid-free, and it's the first time I get to meet your family as your boyfriend."

I stop at the breakfast bar, taking a swig of Jasper's open Stella Artois. "Fine, it just bothers me so much because she doesn't even know me."

He cages me in, his hands clamping on either side of the breakfast bar, then sighs and stares down at me. I meet his gaze, his own as exhausted over this topic as I am. We continue to stare at each other until a smirk crosses both our mouths. "So, no more talking about her until tomorrow morning." He places a hand out in front of me.

I give it a half-ass shake. "Can I really trust your handshake?" I flutter my eyelashes.

He smiles, one of those rare full-wattage ones that reach his eyes. Dipping down, he takes my lips and plunges his tongue in, kissing me with so much want, I'm unsteady and heaving for a breath when he's done.

"Deal," I say faintly and he chuckles, grabbing his keys and walking to the door.

My own heels click on the floor and I smack his ass on my way out to the hallway. He locks up his door and we wait by the elevators.

Shortly after we step inside he turns to me. "Hey, is your brother back yet?" he asks and I stare up with ruffled brows. "He was in Europe. London, I think, on business."

"I had no idea." I stare down at my feet, my stomach gnawing with the fact I have to hurry up and corner Jacob as soon as I get to the party.

"I had to call his office and that's the only reason I knew." His hand lands on the small of my back and usually that ignites a rush of goose bumps, but my blood is running so hot right now, it's numb. "You have told him, right?" He peers over to me.

Ding.

The elevator saves the day.

"Oh, we're so late." I point to the clock in the lobby, but before I can completely escape, he grabs my arm.

"Lennon?" he questions, his eyes telling me he already knows the truth.

"I tried, but I guess he was in Europe. How was I to know?"

You'd think I was a five-year-old making excuses for hitting my brother. Easy to put myself there since I used to beat up on Jacob a lot. Hey, give me a break. Three brothers? I had to show them not to mess with me.

"You've had more than just this past week to tell him." He does the whole head-tilt fatherly thing he does to Brady when he's saying maybe it's not a good choice to jump off the furniture when your arm is in a cast.

"As soon as we get there, I'll corner him. It'll be fine."

As long as Jacob keeps his mouth shut before I can tell Jasper how exactly I ended up at that bar. No, I should tell him tonight. I was planning to do it in the morning, but maybe pushing up the timeline is a better idea.

I look up at his love-soaked eyes. Now, I should do it now. "Jasp—"

My phone rings and I dig it out of my purse to see my mom's name flashing across the screen. Jasper covers my hand, wanting me to ignore it, but nobody ignores my mother.

I hold my finger up. "One sec."

He steps back, fishing his keys out of his pocket. I nod for us to start through the doors and he releases a sigh before ultimately moving forward.

"I'm coming," I answer.

"Lennon. You are late and if you're late, your father will leave. You know him." I can hear the chatting of many people in the background.

"We're picking him up right now."

"You and Jasper?" she asks, excitement in her tone. She probably always assumed I'd end up with a starving artist, or a freeloader. I'm not even sure I saw a man like Jasper as a possibility.

"Yes," I say.

"Brady?" she asks.

"No, he's with the evil witch." I can say that since I'm tucked into Jasper's car and he's in front of the car waiting for a line of traffic to pass before getting in on the driver's side. "Hey, Mom, don't tell Jacob about Jasper."

"Lennon," she warns.

"Relax. What does he care anyway?" I cross my legs, laughing at Jasper's quick Frogger movements as he dodges the traffic.

"Lennon, you should have told him."

Jasper hops in the car and a long sigh leaves his lips.

"Watch out for those lily pads," I say, muffling the phone.

"It was the alligators that worried me." He smiles, turns the key in the ignition.

He so gets me.

"Gotta go, Mom. See you in a bit." I hang up, still hearing her call out my name.

"Your mom?" Jasper asks.

"Yeah. Hit the gas because my dad is probably about five minutes from leaving the station."

The last thing I want to do is screw up my dad's surprise. The list of my screw-ups is already long enough.

chapter THIRTY-SIX

FIFTEEN MINUTES, AFTER AN amazing job by Jasper, we pull up outside the police station my dad works at. He's outside laughing with some of his friends. That's the problem with civil jobs, some of his closest co-workers can't come to the party because they have to serve and protect San Francisco.

I climb out of the car and walk toward my dad. "Hi, Dad," I say, leaning in to give him a kiss on the cheek.

His hand lands on the small of my back and he leans in, allowing me to kiss him. "Lenny," he says his nickname for me. "You remember Cal and Nikki?" He opens the conversation to a man and woman who must be partners in the force.

"Hi," I say. Do I remember them? No. But they don't need to know that.

My dad's eyes shoot to Jasper's Range Rover. "Who's Daddy Warbucks?" My dad cocks his eyebrow.

"It's my boyfriend, Dad. Be nice."

My dad looks over for too long of a beat. Jasper's probably pissed that I made him double-park so he has no choice but to stay in the car. Just as I'm about to tear my dad away, a car parked in front of a parking meter drives off and Jasper slides into the space.

Nikki observes Jasper climbing out of his truck, inserting money into the meter and sauntering over to us.

"That's your boyfriend?" Nikki asks, her eyes still glued to him.

Can I blame her? No. He's nice to look at for sure. But he's mine.

"Mr. Hart," Jasper says, holding his hand out to my dad.

My dad looks down at his hand and then to me, his eyes wide. Finally, he shakes his hand.

"Your boyfriend is Jasper?" my dad asks, and I'm shocked my mom kept this secret.

"Nice to see you again." Jasper does the whole nervous meeting-the-dad thing to perfection. He turns his attention to the other officers. "Jasper Banks." Cal shakes his hand while I think Nikki's breathing might have stopped.

Cal slaps her on the back and she jolts, finally blinking. "Pleasure," she says.

"Well, let's get this over with," my dad says, shaking hands with Cal and Nikki.

After he starts walking to Jasper's car I rush to catch up while Jasper is telling Cal and Nikki how nice it was to meet them. Kiss-ass.

"Dad?" I question and he stops at the passenger side of Jasper's car. The spot that should be mine, but I'll take a backseat to my dad.

"The party?" he deadpans.

Everyone knows my dad hates parties.

"Yeah," I answer and he shakes his head.

"How many people?"

"One hundred, I think."

"Great." He couldn't sound more unenthused.

The doors unlock and Jasper comes over with the key fob in his hand.

"Nice guy." He nods to Jasper and a smile forms on my face.

Jasper comes over and opens the door for me. He is a nice guy.

Once I'm tucked into the backseat, next to Brady's car seat, Jasper goes to the front and starts the car.

"So, Jasper, how have you been?" my dad asks and Jasper laughs.

"I've been good, Ben. You ready for the party?" Jasper asks.

"No, but what Eva wants, Eva gets. And she wants a party, I guess," my dad says.

Jasper starts the car and pulls into the traffic.

"So, you never told your brother, huh?" my dad says and Jasper gives me the stink eye from the rearview mirror.

"You know me, I like to surprise people." I use my singsong voice as though my insides aren't tumbling like a dryer full of laundry, worrying about Jacob's reaction.

"Don't we all know it," my dad deadpans.

Here goes nothing.

chapter
THIRTY-SEVEN

WAY TO DISGUISE A party. We pull up outside the restaurant and Jasper can barely find a parking spot.

"Why don't I drop you two off?" Jasper offers and I'm all for that plan. It gives me time to drag Jacob off to talk. "I'll sneak in and find you." His eyes find mine in the back seat and my stomach purrs before it drops.

I need to find Jacob first and then we can live happily ever after. "Perfect," I remark.

Jasper stops outside the doors.

"Here goes three hours I'll never get back," my dad complains and opens the door, climbing out.

"See you in there," I say, leaning forward to kiss Jasper's cheek. "Thank you for always understanding."

He could throw a fit that I'm putting him in a bad position, but he understands that's just how I roll. I wait until the last possible moment to do what needs to be done. I just hope he's as accommodating tonight when I tell him about how I ended up at the speed-dating evening where we met.

Once we're out of Jasper's truck and he pulls away, I slide my arm through my dad's and we walk toward the restaurant doors.

"He really is a good guy, that one," my dad says and I smile, knowing my dad doesn't mix words, so, he really does believe Jasper is great.

As do I.

"We finally agree on something," I joke, leaning into my dad and laughing.

"Only took twenty-six years." He smiles and opens the door for me.

"So I have to answer a call. You enter first." I roll my eyes and he lets out an exaggerated sigh.

"Yeah, have a nice call."

We both know what's going on and he walks in through the private room in the back of his favorite restaurant to an enormous rendition of *For He's a Jolly Good Fellow*.

My mom runs over and he smiles and laughs and hugs her close to him. He loves her that much that he puts himself through hell for a few hours to make her happy and pretends to be surprised. My dad is a pretty great guy.

I walk in right after and my mom hugs me. I resist the urge to say, *Ha, I did it. I got him here and you all thought I couldn't do it.*

"You look gorgeous," my mom says.

I glance at her lovely red dress and think many people wouldn't even believe she was my mother with her youthful appearance. Then I spot Jacob talking with some friends.

"You too, Mom." I smile down at her.

"Where's Jasper?" she asks.

"He's coming," I say. "I need to catch Jacob though." I don't wait for her to respond. Instead I run over to Jacob.

I dodge all the family and friends who try to stop me to talk. Later, later, later.

"Jacob," I whisper to interrupt him, but he ignores me.

Typical.

I wait patiently for a few more seconds while Jimmy Twendle from grade school, rambles on and on about baseball.

Who gives a shit, seriously? So you're some superstar ballplayer. Whatever. Some of us have more pressing issues.

"Excuse me." I hold my hand up.

"Lennon, man, you're looking hot," Jimmy flirts and I look to Jacob, rolling my eyes.

"Too bad you're not," I remark and they all laugh, thinking I'm joking.

Truth is Jimmy was my crush in high school. Along with Whitney and Tahlia's. One night after my brother went to bed, Jimmy Twendle joined me on the couch. He kissed me and then got a little handsy. That is until I kneed him in the nuts and broke his nose.

"Oh, Lennon, always a joker," he says and gives me the once-over.

"How's your nose?" I ask and he turns beet red, his eyes suddenly finding his beer. Jacob looks between us, puzzled, because I never told him about what happened and I don't have time to worry about any of that right now. "I need to talk to you," I say to him and drag him away by his arm.

"What the hell?" he complains.

"Why didn't I know you were out of the country?" I ask.

"What?" His face contorts like I'm a fly buzzing around his food.

"Anyways." I wave my hand in the space between us. "I need to tell you something, and try to act mature about it."

He stares down at me, with a bored look on his face. "I am the mature twin," he deadpans.

True.

"I have a date with me tonight." Let's ease into this.

He focuses forward over my shoulder. "Why is Jasper here? Did Mom invite him?" He touches my shoulder to move me out of the way, like we weren't just having a conversation. "I'm going to say hello."

I step in his path, my hand on his chest. "Um, Jacob."

He glances down and then back up to where I'm guessing Jasper is. "What?"

"He's here with me," I say, my voice losing all its usual confidence.

"What!" he yells and I push him back into the corner to get away from the nosy family members now looking our way. "Lennon, I told you to stay away from him."

I hold up my hands. "It has nothing to do with that. We met and . . . I don't know, a spark kind of ignited." I smile, thinking about how happy I am when I'm with him.

"A spark? You? Give me a break, Lennon." He grabs my arm and guides me to a small alcove where the wait staff gets drinks. "I can't believe you'd do this. He is not one of your usual boy toys." There's so much anger in his voice that venom could slide through his clenched teeth and singe me.

I shrug my arm from his hold. "I like him, Jacob."

"You like him?" He laughs a hollow and empty laugh.

"Yes."

"You like his money. You like his connections. You like what he can do for you," Jacob accuses.

"I like him. All of him. It has nothing to do with his money or his connections." I fight back, glancing out the small cut-out section in the wall, finding my mom introducing him to people.

"God, Lennon, this is an all-time low for even you. I told you to stay away from him, and now you're saying you like him. You bring him to Dad's retirement party. Did you even know he has a son?" Jacob's voice is rising and his face is growing redder.

"Yes, of course I've met Brady and I love him."

He rolls his eyes. "You're seriously demented. You aren't capable of loving anyone but yourself."

"Listen, I might have gone to Jasper to get him to invest in my business, but things changed."

"So you admit that's the entire reason you met him? To get him to invest in your company?" Jacob clarifies.

"Yes, but if you would have just introduced m—"

"Don't pin this on me. You sought him out."

Jacob's right. I know it, but we're twins. I'm not going to let him know it that easily. I let out a deep breath. "Yes, I saw on your phone that he was going to be at some bar, so I went there that night to get him to invest in my company."

"What?" Jasper asks behind him and my entire body freezes.

I spin around to find his face pale and that sparkle that's always in his eyes missing.

"No, it's not what you think," I say.

"Classic Lennon. You never even told him your meeting wasn't coincidence but a calculated plan on your part." Jacob shakes his head and slides past me. He clasps Jasper on the shoulder. "I'm sorry, man. I wish I could say I was surprised."

Jasper disregards him, his gaze remaining solely on me.

"You knew who I was the entire time? This whole thing was a charade to get me to invest in you?" His hand flies through his hair.

"No." Why won't my words come out now? Tears well up in my eyes that he's this upset with me.

"And I fell for it all. I set you up with Drew. Were you just going to be with me until your business succeeded and then you'd kick Brady and I to the curb?" he asks and begins to leave, but I pull on his coat sleeve.

"No, Jasper. Don't leave."

He shrugs me off and turns around, staring down at me, his hands tucked into the pockets of his slacks.

"You pretended to be as surprised as I was to find out we had Jacob in common. Tell me you didn't plant your friend to call about the sex toy when we were together, knowing that I'd bite. Tell me you didn't show up at that Starbucks before the speed-dating to have a leg up."

"No, I didn't."

"So, I'm imagining all those things or I misunderstood somewhere along the way?" he questions. His tone and his body are all calm and collected while my mind is bouncing around like a deflating balloon.

"Yes and no. I knew you were going to be there at the bar that night, but Starbucks was not planned and when I realized there was something between us I gave up asking you about the business," I fight back, finally finding my words.

He leans down and lowers his voice. "In the end you got what you wanted, an investor for your business. Maybe you should've been fucking Drew this whole time and not me." He shakes his head and looks at me with disgust. "I hope your dildos keep you warm at night and screw you as well as I did, because I'm out." He turns around and I cling to his sport jacket, ready to fall to my knees, but he shrugs me off, leaving me in tears.

I wait for him to return. Because if he loves me like I love him, how can he just leave me?

He doesn't come back.

chapter
THIRTY-EIGHT

IT'S BEEN TWO WEEKS.

Two weeks with no word.

He hasn't reached out and I haven't reached out to him.

I sit on a bench at the park, watching Brady play across the street at the school. He's there for day camp and I wonder where he thinks I've gone. Did Jasper tell him that I was away on business? Or did he break his heart and say I wanted to leave? The thought of Brady thinking it has anything to do with him has brought me to my knees sobbing more than a few times.

He's running around, playing tag with a group of kids. He's full of life, running and laughing, which means that he might not know anything.

"What are you doing here?"

I think I could pinpoint Natalie's voice from across the Bay Bridge. I turn to find her glaring at me with her hand on her hip. Boy, am I ever glad I wore my 'Friday Is My Second Favorite F-Word' shirt today. Not.

"I was just walking by," I lie. I came here on purpose, needing to see Brady. To see if Jasper told him I'm out of their life for good. I figured I'd be able to tell by the look on his face. Or maybe that was wishful thinking. Maybe he just as easily tossed me aside as his father did.

"Another lie? Shocking," she says. "Haven't you done enough?"

She must know. Jasper told her.

"I had to see Brady. I'll go now." I stand and spin on my flats and start walking down the sidewalk.

"Stay away! You're no good for them," she calls out and I glance to the playground, finding Brady still playing with his friends.

When I turn back around, my eyes fix on her. "You know nothing about me. I love both of them." I push back the tears that have been threatening to fall all afternoon. "I understand you think that because I look a certain way and because I'm not Suzy Homemaker, I'm not good enough for your perfect boy and grandson. You'll probably run off every woman who ever wants in their life, and if you win kudos, but all you'll do is make them unhappy in the long run. I love your son and your grandson. I would've made them happy."

"But you screwed it up, didn't you?" she asks.

My head falls between my shoulders and I try to slyly wipe the tear from under my eyes. He never told her. "I did."

With my admission, I turn around to walk away from the Banks for good this time.

"Brady is getting his cast off this afternoon. Jasper is out of town. Would you like to say hello?" she hollers and my footsteps halt.

"Really?" I ask, not sure if I should see Brady. It might only piss off Jasper more.

She smiles. The gesture looks foreign on her. "Brady and I had a long talk the night of your dad's retirement party."

I walk back toward her, unsure if I can really trust her. I mean, this is the first time I've even seen the woman smile.

"You did?" I ask and she nods.

"He asked me why I hated you." Her head falls and she shakes it while walking back to the school building. "I'd been giving Jasper hell for being with you and I never realized Brady would see it. You need to understand how much it broke my heart to see Brady's mother just toss him aside like he didn't mean anything. Her own child."

She pauses and presses her lips together, gathering her emotions, I think. For once I know when to stay quiet.

"I may be his mother, but I know how Jasper must look to single women. He's handsome, successful, he has more than enough money, and he's a good person. I've always been afraid that some money-hungry woman would try to swoop in, take what she can from him and then leave them both behind. I didn't want to see either of them go through that again."

I nod. I can understand why she might have felt that way, but it still doesn't excuse the way she treated me.

Her hand lands on my forearm and I look up at her. "I want them to be happy and you seemed to make them happy. I don't know what happened between you two, besides the fact that Jasper told me you lied to him. But, I believe you when you say you truly love them."

These are the words I've been longing to hear from her, but they're too late to make a difference. "You're right. I messed it all up." Tears well in my eyes again and I blink a few times to get them to stop.

"The one thing about my son, he's forgiving." She pats my arm and we enter the school.

"I'm not sure."

She shakes her head. "Then you don't know him at all."

She signs the form from the office to get Brady and a few minutes later, he runs out with his backpack bouncing on his back.

His sneakers skid to a stop when he sees me. "Lennon," he says so quietly and with such disbelief that my heart shatters. "Lennon!" His voice picks up and he runs into my arms, gluing my shattered heart back together.

I hug him tight to my body, picking him up. God, he feels so good in my arms.

"I missed you," I say softly and then I hear the quiet sobs and a hiccupping from his chest.

"You left," he whispers and I shake my head.

"I'm sorry, Brady," I say, setting his feet back on the ground.

"Hi, Grandma," he mumbles, looking away.

"Are you surprised to see Lennon?" she asks.

He nods, a smile crossing his face and the tears fading. I wipe my own wet cheeks and he grabs my hand. "Are you coming to see my arm?" he asks and I laugh.

"I hear you're getting your cast off." I stare down at him. "I've never seen your entire arm." I nudge him with my hip and he laughs.

"So, you're coming?" he asks.

"No." I look over to Natalie. "I'm not. I just wanted to say hello."

"Come," he whines, both his hands on my arm now.

I should have predicted this.

Natalie's lips are sealed together, watching from afar.

"I can't, buddy. I wish—"

"Did Dad tell you not to come?" he asks and my shoulders fall. I squat down to his height, taking both his hands in mine.

"No. He didn't. I just—" I trail off, unsure what to say. I could kick myself for coming here. I'm only going to make it harder on him.

"Then come. I want you there," he whines and I look to Natalie who nods.

I stare up at the ceiling. I could see him get his cast off and then say goodbye the right way. Maybe we just need some closure.

"Okay, I'll come," I say. He screams, jumping up and down. "But"—I hold my hand up—"I have to leave right after."

He nods his head. "Okay, okay." He runs over to Natalie. "Did you hear? Lennon's coming." He grabs both of our hands, bridging the gap between myself and a woman I never thought I'd have a kind thought for. But it must be a full moon because I feel like I understand Natalie a little better now. If things had worked out differently perhaps we might have been able to have a cordial relationship.

Now I'll never know.

chapter THIRTY-NINE

FORTY-FIVE MINUTES LATER WE'RE all in his doctor's waiting room. Brady seems super nervous and Natalie and I have both tried to calm him down. But he's quiet and from the small amount of time I've known Brady when he's quiet, he's anxious.

"It's okay, bud, I promise." I smile, but he sits on the table not looking like he truly believes me.

The nurse knocks and comes in with the doctor. "The day is here, Brady, are you excited?" The fifty-something doctor who dresses trendier than Drew walks in the office with a smile on his face. He quickly explains that Dr. Bierdman was called away on an emergency and asked him to take over.

Brady stares over at him.

"He's a little nervous," Natalie says.

"Oh, it's easy. You'll feel nothing." The doctor logs onto the computer and starts typing in things and scrolls through Brady's information.

The door opens again and I assume it's another nurse, and it isn't until Brady yells, "Daddy," that I look up, finding Jasper in the doorway.

His wrinkled suit hangs off him and he grips the doorknob, probably wondering if he has the right room. The eyes that used to look at me with such love are flooded with hatred.

"You think I'd miss this?" he says to his son.

I slide off the bed, giving him room to say hello. He goes to the other side, taking Brady's hands, and kisses the top of his son's head.

"Okay, are you ready?" the doctor says, pulling out a huge pair of scissors.

Brady stiffens and the doctor looks between us. "Maybe if Mom and Dad each take a side." He glances between Jasper and me.

"She's not his mother," Jasper says coldly.

Brady's eyes are fixed on the scissors, not really paying attention to what's going on around him. Natalie remains quiet.

"Well, then Dad, hold him tight," the doctor says and slides the metal scissors under his cast.

Jasper does that and as I sit there watching Jasper calm his son, telling him it will be all right, getting him excited for everything he can do now that the cast is off, I realize—this isn't my place. Not anymore.

"Done," the doctor says and the nurse gives Brady a lollipop.

"My arm is so small," Brady says, staring down at his wrinkled arm.

"And smelly," Natalie says, ruffling her grandson's hair.

"Your dad will have to wash it good tonight," the nurse adds, taking wipes and sliding them down the length of his arm.

Brady, calm now, looks up to me. "Now you've seen all of me, Lennon." He beams and a pang of regret hits me that this is the last time I'll probably get to see that expression on his face.

"Yep. I'm so happy for you, but I better get going," I say. Jasper slides over on the bed as though he'd catch the flu by being near me. I bend down and kiss Brady's forehead. "Bye, Brady." My voice cracks, and I push back that tingling in my nose and the wetness pooling in my eyes.

"Wait," Brady says before I can leave the door.

I turn around, smacking on a fake smile. Jasper looks over to me, but then concentrates on his phone.

"Grandma, can you get me my backpack?" Brady asks and Natalie smiles, handing it over to him.

"Here you go." She opens the pocket he wants her to and his healthy arm digs into the zipper and he pulls something out.

The pin.

A heart-shaped pin with fake pearls and rhinestones glued to it.

"This is for you," he says, placing it in my palm with a smile.

Jasper looks up from his phone, his mouth hanging open, his eyes flashing between me, Natalie, Brady and back to me.

"It's beautiful." I smile, pinning it to my shirt. "I love it."

I lean over again and hug his small body to mine. My tears, unable to stay away, fall freely down my cheeks now. "Thank you so much," I say. "It's the best present anyone has ever given me."

"Don't cry, I didn't want you to cry," he says and I shake my head.

Natalie laughs.

"I'm crying because I love it so much. They're happy tears."

Okay, I may have just half lied to him, but I've been skipping mommy training classes lately.

"I'll see you soon," I say. Another lie.

I run out of the room as fast as I'm able, feeling bad for not staying with Brady, but there's no way I can remain in that room with Jasper either. I stop in the lobby to compose myself for a second.

"Lennon," Jasper calls after me and I look up, the tears that were waning rushing back.

I turn and he's standing there with his hands in his pockets.

"I'm sorry," I say, unpinning Brady's gift from my shirt. "You save this for when you meet his real mom." I hold it out but he doesn't take it from me. "Just take it, Jasper." I hold it out a little firmer this time. When he still doesn't take it but remains silent, I slip it into the pocket of his shirt.

"Lennon. Stop." His voice is cold and nothing like the one I'm used to.

"Just so you know, I did love you. I know I lied and deceived you, but my feelings for you and Brady are real. So, please, never doubt that." I step forward and press my lips to his cheek.

His hands never leave his pockets and I fall back to my heels.

"How can I ever trust you?" he asks in a ragged voice.

I shake my head. "I guess you can't."

I turn around and run out of the doctor's office and it isn't until I'm in the elevators that I'm able to release the sob I've been holding in my chest.

chapter FORTY

"YOU'RE INSANE. DON'T DO this," Whitney says through the phone.

"I can't in good faith take this deal."

I'm on my way to Jasper's office because Drew has some huge deal that came through for me. It looks as if one of my patents is going to come through and one of the largest distributors of adult products in the country wants to license the product.

"Yes, you can. Who cares. If the prick can't face the fact that you love him and accept your apology, screw him." Whitney has a fierce side that many don't see. But when she feels strongly about something it's hard to get her to back down.

"I'm fine. Really. It's for the best. I'll figure something else out."

Maybe I'll be tattooing forever, but who cares? At least I'll have proven to Jasper that I wasn't with him for his connections. It won't change the outcome, but I'll feel some satisfaction knowing that when he thinks of me, it's not to think that I'm a gold-digging opportunist. If he even thinks of me at all, that is.

"Oh, Lennon." She says it like I'm attending a funeral.

"Whit, I'm fine. This is the last time I'll have to maybe run into him. And I can try to get past all this." My subconscious nudges me, knowing that'll never happen, but a girl can dream.

"Call me when you're done," she says, defeat thick in her voice.

"Will do."

I hang up and shove my phone into my purse. My stomach knots and I release a breath as the elevator rises. I step off and open the doors to the office. Brittany smiles and picks up the phone.

"You better be calling Drew." I point my finger, my feet moving faster.

"Mr. Banks." She shoots me a tight smile, but I reach over the receptionist desk and press the button to end the call.

"No. No Mr. Banks. I just need to see Mr. Ashland," I say as nicely as I can manage and she scrunches her eyebrows and then nods.

"That explains Miss Schmidt."

Miss Schmidt? Jasper's seeing someone else already? I ignore the twisting in my gut.

She picks up the phone. "Hi, Sue, Miss Hart is here to see Mr. Ashland." She pauses for a second. "Okay, I'll just send her back."

She hangs up just as Jasper comes out into the reception area.

"Brittany, why did you han—" He stops when he sees me.

Brittany's gaze moves back and forth between us. "Awkward," she says, her teeth clenched but her eyes fixed on what she thinks will be a show.

"Sorry, it's not Miss Schmidt." I walk by him, the smell of his cologne filling my senses, and I lose my footing for a second, but get back on track.

"What?"

I ignore him and continue down to Drew's office. Sue smiles when she sees me approach. "He's ready," she says, holding her hand to the door.

"Thank you, Sue." I smile and grip the doorknob.

"Are you joining them, Mr. Banks?" she asks and I glance over my shoulder, finding him in the hallway, his narrowed eyes on me.

He shakes his head. "No."

I open the door, no longer able to look at him. It only brings me pain and I'm so tired of being in pain.

Drew sees me enter and smiles before he rounds the corner, wrapping his arms around my waist and swinging me in a circle. "Congratulations!" he says so loudly I wish he'd quiet down.

A second later, there's a knock on the door, and Jasper comes barging in, finding me in Drew's arms.

He huffs. "I see you move fast," he sneers and slams the door.

Drew sets me back down. "What is he talking about?" His forehead creases and he scratches the side of his head.

"I'm not taking the deal, Drew." I stomp out of Drew's office, down the hall and into Jasper's.

I slam the door behind me and he's there waiting for me, leaning back in his office chair, his intent gaze on me. He knew I'd follow and fuck if I didn't take the bait.

"What is your problem?" I ask, my hands on my hips.

"I just find it convenient that we break up and now you're in Drew's arms. You can sure shift gears fast."

My blood boils. I love this man, but I'm done being a punching bag. "Fuck you, Jasper."

He stands up, his hands pressed on the desk in front of him. "Been there. Done that. First you fucked me, then you fucked me over." The anger and hurt in his voice shakes every bone in my body.

"How many times can I say I'm sorry? I wasn't expecting to meet you and feel something for you."

"But you went on a date with me to try to get me to invest in your company?" he asks, leaning on the edge of his desk, and damn if I don't notice how impeccable he looks in his suit.

"Yes, but when I accepted I decided at that point that I wouldn't approach you on the business part of it."

"You could've been truthful with me from the start."

My shoulders fall. "I can't excuse my behavior. I said I was sorry, but I don't have a time machine to go back and change what happened."

"When do you think you'll grow up?" he asks, raising his eyebrows.

I hold my hands up. "Forget it. I'm out. Enjoy Miss Schmidt."

I walk toward the door and his fist pounds on his desk. "Goddamn it, Lennon."

"What?" I turn around. My eyes lock with his angry ones. "There's nothing else I can say or do."

He blows out a breath and steps forward. "Stop running."

I fall to my knees and place my hands in prayer. "Is this what you want, Jasper? Please forgive me. I was wrong, I promise to never do it again."

He grabs me and pulls me up from under my arms. "Don't make a joke out of this."

"I'm not." Tears falls down my cheeks once more. God, when will they stop? "I don't know what you want from me. I'm sorry, I *don't* wish I could go back to that first night and tell you exactly how I ended up there, because what if you would've walked away from me? I can't say I truly feel that way because what we have . . ." My head falls. "Had." I take a deep breath at hearing us referred to in past tense. "As much as it hurts, I love the time we spent together and I would never want to change anything and risk that it wouldn't have happened." I wipe the tears from my cheeks. "I fell so madly in love with you and Brady . . . I can't regret anything that made that time happen." He looks away and I take that as my cue to leave. "I am sorry that I hurt you. You just snuck into my heart and I was too afraid of losing you both."

I grip the doorknob. "Take the deal, Lennon," he whispers.

I shake my head, turning around, tears blurring my vision. "It's just not important anymore."

I open the door, passing Drew and Sue, who look like they've been out here listening to our argument.

Drew catches up to me at the elevator. "You have to take this deal, Lennon. We're both going to make a lot of money."

I press the elevator button and give him a sad smile. "I'm sorry, Drew. I appreciate everything you've done."

I step into the elevator and leave behind all the hopes I'd had for my future behind the steel doors.

chapter FORTY-ONE

I'M IN MY CURTAINED-OFF room in the back of my tattoo parlor eating a quesadilla when Michelle peeks her head in. I startle and a drop of salsa lands on my 'I Hope You Step On A Lego' shirt.

"Shit," I say, using a napkin to wipe it off. I really like this shirt. I saw it a while back but until I actually stepped on one of Brady's Legos, I didn't really get it. After experiencing the kind of catastrophic pain at the hands of a child's small plastic toy I went and brought it the next day.

"Lennon," Michelle says. "Your appointment is early."

I put my food down in the takeout container and shove it on the counter then begin to wash my hands. "Send him in."

"Okay."

She disappears and someone walks in behind me. I take the paper towels, drying my hands.

"Hi, I'm Lennon." I turn around to find *him* on the table.

You know which *him* I mean.

Jasper Banks.

"I have an appointment," I tell him, crossing my arms over

my chest.

"Me."

"You?"

That playful smile crosses his lips. "Yes, me. See, I figured I could come here and grovel. I could fall on my knees and beg you to take me back. I could apologize for storming out or for not running after you at Brady's doctor's office."

I swallow past the dryness in my throat and try to act like the words he's saying aren't exactly what I've wanted to hear since we broke up.

"Most of all I could tell you how deeply your words reached me. How you not taking the deal showed me how much you loved me. And how ashamed I am that I would need that reassurance to know you love me because when I'm with you . . . I *feel* it. I fell in love with you long before you ever chose to admit you loved me, but I found comfort in knowing that you loved me, too. When I thought it was all a sham . . . I was hurt and pissed off at myself that I put Brady in the position to lose someone again."

"And now? You said you could never trust me again."

He hops off the table, stepping into my personal space, and places his hand on my cheek. Instinctively, I lean into his strength, somehow still needing it.

"I'm giving myself to you."

"Oh, sweetie, but you already did that." Sarcasm drips off my words.

His hands drop and he backs away from me. A devilish gleam in his eye, he lies down on my table. "I'm yours."

"You came to apologize and beg me to take you back by letting me have sex with you?" I ask.

He rolls to his side, propping his head up with his hand. He could be on a commercial. "No, my body." He shakes his head. "You tattoo me, whatever you want."

I stare at him for a moment. "Anything?"

"Anything." He doesn't flinch.

"Maybe I'll put a unicorn cock on you," I say, sitting on my chair.

He crooks his finger to me. "I'm not even sure what that is, nor am I sure I want to know." He chuckles. "Come here," he says and I roll over to him. "I trust you. This is me showing you that I trust you. That I'm ready to put it behind us and move forward."

"You're giving me all of the control?" I ask, still unsure exactly what his point is.

He nods. "Some would say I'm crazy, but I like to think I'm crazy for you." He chuckles.

"Okay." I hold my hand up in the air. "Where is Jasper Banks?"

"I'm right here." He laughs like I'm talking gibberish.

"Me tattooing a unicorn cock on you isn't going to put a Band-Aid on the problem."

He sits up and pats the seat next to him.

"Jasper," I sigh.

"Come here."

I climb on the table, my legs swinging back and forth. "I need to tell you the whole story," I say, my voice small.

He slides closer, his hand landing on my knee. "Why don't you tell me while you ink me?"

"I can't tattoo you, Jasper," I say.

"Yes, you can." I look over and his hand tightens on my thigh. "Come on."

I look into his eyes. He's serious. If he thinks this will put it all behind us, I'm game. "Give me a few to draw it up."

"I'll just lie here." He lies down on my bed once I hop off and roll my chair over to the table. "And admire you."

I glance over my shoulder and that grin on his lips makes my stomach flip. He truly is the most gorgeous man I've ever seen.

"How's Brady?" I ask, searching on my phone for exactly what I want the tattoo to resemble.

"He misses you. He hasn't said much to me after the doctor's office. I messed that up pretty big."

My gut wrenches thinking about Brady, an innocent victim in all this.

"He'll be happy to have you back," he says, full of confidence.

"Jasper," I sigh because he hasn't heard the entirety of what I did. How premeditated my actions were. There's a possibility he won't be able to move on and I don't want to get my hopes up.

"You almost done? I'm eager to put this behind us."

"You're relentless," I say, standing up to take my picture to the front to get the stencil made.

"That's why you fell in love with me." He winks and my face heats.

"I'll be right back." I walk past Sebastian, my next-door neighbor, who's piercing a girl's tongue. Weaving by the open tables in the front, I slide by Michelle to make the stencil at the thermal fax machine.

It scans and I look out the window while I'm waiting. Can we really move on?

"He's hot." Michelle taps her pen to her lips.

I stare blankly, not about to give her the gossip she's looking for. I've kept Jasper away from this place except for the time I brought him here one night after coffee. Michelle wasn't here then and there's a reason for that. She tends to flirt with anyone with a twig and berries between their legs.

"He yours?" she asks, the pen cap hitting her teeth.

"Nope."

"Hmm," she mumbles. "He didn't seem interested when I tried to flirt with him earlier."

"So you figured he was with me?" I ask.

She smiles. "That and the fact he had this look in his eyes when he asked for you."

"What look?" I roll my eyes, wishing this antiquated piece of equipment would hurry.

"I don't know how to explain it. He actually looked me in the eyes." She purses her lips, her head dipping to the cleavage busting out of her shirt, seeming confused why it didn't work on Jasper.

The machine finally finishes and I pat her on the shoulder. "Don't think too hard, otherwise you'll lose those brain cells."

She says nothing, still trying to figure out why her secret weapon didn't work for her.

I walk back through the curtain to find Jasper is now shirtless, lying on his back with his phone in his hands raised above his head.

Seriously, this man is temptation with a capital T.

"Making yourself comfortable?" I ask.

He peers at me through the opening of his arms, placing the phone down by his side. "I assumed you'd tattoo my chest or back."

"You assumed wrong, making you an ass. So drop the pants and bend over." I busy myself grabbing all the supplies.

"What?"

"I doubt you want a big old rooster with a unicorn horn on its head on your pec. I'm throwing you a bone by putting it on your ass."

I keep my voice even, which is hard with the expression on his face. I turn back around to ready my supplies and a thud hits the floor. I peer over my shoulder to find his jeans in a pile at his feet and one side of his boxers exposing an ass cheek.

"Can you do my right? Because you know I'm going to want to spoon you tonight." He winks and if I wasn't so speechless at the sight of his perfect ass, I'd have a comeback.

"Pull them up, hop on the table again and give me the inside of your bicep."

I wash my hands and put my gloves on while he does as I direct. Sitting down, I roll over to the table he's on and wash the surface. "You're sure?" I ask and he nods, not a worry line etched on his face.

The stencil goes on perfectly and as I stare down at it, I find the excitement I had when I first started. Back before tramp stamps and tribal arm bands were all the rage. When customers allowed the artist to draw and use their talents. Those customers are rarer than you think.

I prep my gun and buzz it for a second. "Ready?" I ask.

"Go for it," he says.

I hold the needle over the skin and he waits patiently for me to start. He's always been patient with me.

"I knew you before I knew you," I tell him as I press the needle into his skin.

"Glad to know I'm notorious." He laughs, but I look at him and he stops.

"Jacob told me about you, but refused to set up a meeting between us. He was embarrassed that my business was sex toys and thought you were too straight an arrow to ever be interested in something like that. Little did he know what you can do with a string of anal beads."

I smile at him, remembering the first night he used them on me. He meets my smile and raises it a few notches.

"Anyway, I was at his office, desperate because my grandma's inheritance was dwindling and this company was going to be dead in the water. He refused again and then you happened to text him. He was too busy to notice and I saw the time and place you'd be at that bar."

"And you made sure to meet me there."

I nod. "But I didn't know it was you. All my Google searches gave me nothing. Not one picture or any personal info about your life."

He blows out a breath of air and I don't know if it's because of the needle or something else. "I pay someone to check the internet and remove any personal information about me. You were desperate to get in contact with me, right?"

"Yeah."

"So are a lot of other desperate people whose dreams are failing. I can't take on everyone and there are people out there who are disgruntled. The last thing I want them to find out is where I live, or that Brady even exists. Nor do I want his mother deciding to suddenly pop into his life unannounced."

"That's why you have no pictures of him in your office." I swear someone just turned the light switch on in my brain.

"Yeah. No one needs to know anything about my life."

I nod, thinking all that makes him a wonderful father.

"The Starbucks thing was a coincidence. I had no idea who you were then. Not that you showed me a ton of interest." I raise my eyebrows, wiping the ink off his skin.

He laughs. "Believe me, I noticed you and I wanted nothing more than to fuck your brains out that night. But Brady had just left for camp and I'd promised myself that I needed more than just fuck-and-chucks. That I needed to look for something more serious. Hence, the speed dating. You know how I spent that night and who I was thinking about." He makes a hand job gesture with his hand.

I shake my head, a rush of heat to my cheeks and between my thighs. "Thanks for the reminder."

He winks and my stomach flips.

"I felt something both times we met and after the speed-dating night I didn't want you to think I was with you only for the business. I still think if I had come clean that first night you would've stopped what was happening with us."

He nods and I go back to tattooing him. "Probably."

"The longer we were together, the more I couldn't jeopardize losing you. I was scared of losing both you and Brady." I finish the tattoo and sit back so he can see me. "Whit calling me about the vibrator wasn't planned. I was never going to bring the business up to you after we'd slept together. I swear." I hold up my Girl Scout honor sign and he moves to come over. "Not yet." I wipe it down one more time. "Go look in the mirror."

He stands up and I rise from my stool, waiting to see what he thinks. This is always the most nerve-racking time for a tattoo artist, when you're waiting to see if your client loves it.

He stares at it for a long time and then finds me in the mirror. "What does it mean?"

"It's the Celtic tree of life. Trees signify strength and longevity. The leaves represent rebirth and the roots and branches are strong and resilient. It's how I see you." A tear slips down my cheek and Jasper turns, his hand the perfect fit for my cheek.

The next tear can't fall because he catches it with his thumb. "I love you, Lennon Hart," he says.

I look up into those eyes that have nothing but more love for me. "I love you. And Brady."

"Can you do me a favor?" he asks and I nod. "Can you add a colored leaf to the tree? One for each member in my family?"

I smile. "That's a great idea. Sit back down."

He lies down in the same position again and I grab the bright green ink container from my shelf. It only takes me a couple of minutes to add the two leaves. One big one for Jasper and another smaller green leaf to represent Brady. I wipe away the blood and excess ink and sit back to admire my work.

"It looks perfect now," I say.

"No, it doesn't," Jasper says, shaking his head.

"Is there something you don't like about it?" I ask as I

examine it again to see if I missed something.

"You forgot to add another green leaf."

I crinkle my forehead. "No, I didn't. I've got you here and Brady right here." I point to both spots and Jasper grasps my hand in his.

"If we're really going to put this behind us, we need to add your leaf on there too, Lennon."

My heart swells with joy and I think it might be in danger of bursting through my chest.

"So, can we put this all behind us?"

I gaze into his eyes and know that with all the love and affection I see there, I'll never feel like I'm not enough again. I nod slowly and then go about the business of making myself a permanent mark in the lives of the two boys I love most.

EPILOGUE

IT'S BEEN TWO MONTHS and Jasper's tattoo has healed nicely. Brady went back to talking to him—once I moved in.

Yep, I'm out of my hellhole of an apartment and living in Jasper's condo. At first it was scary because what if we don't make it? I mean do the research, many couples don't. But I like to think there's something special between us. And Brady comes first, before us, that's the agreement we made.

Speaking of, Brady's hand slides into mine as we walk down the sidewalk, all three of us exhausted from another day spent at the zoo.

He looks up to me, eyeing the pin on my shirt, and then falls back to my side. I made a mistake giving Jasper the pin back and I'll never hurt Brady like that again. Jasper had returned the pin to him and explained why I felt the need to return it at the time. The first night after we reconciled, I tucked Brady in before Jasper came to read him a story and I told him how much it means to me that he gave me the pin and that I was sorry I hadn't kept it.

Like most six-year-olds, he was able to forgive easily with

no hurt feelings, but he checks up every once in awhile, wanting to know where it is.

"Coffee," I whine as we approach a Starbucks.

"There's nothing there for me," Brady says.

"How about a cookie?" I bribe and he smiles.

"Cookie? On top of the popcorn, pretzel, and nachos at the zoo?" Jasper's back to his stick-in-the-mud status, but he's my stick in the mud. "You're cleaning up the puke," he says as I open the door to my nirvana, letting the aroma of coffee beans infiltrate my veins.

"I've done it once. I think I can handle it again," I say with confidence I really feel.

"It truly is a sick obsession you have with this place," Jasper says, passing by me. "Sit down and I'll get the coffees."

Brady and I don't object, finding a table by the window. We talk about the elephants, the lions and how exactly the momma kangaroo gets that baby that's in her pouch.

"Um, I'm not sure," I lie because surely I am not the one who should be having this conversation with him.

"One day it just shows up?" Brady asks and I check on Jasper who's paying the cashier.

"Well, the mommy and daddy . . ." I start, realizing that's a bad path to go down. I look up to the ceiling.

"So you and Daddy will have a baby who shows up one day?"

"Okay . . ." Shit. Where's the *Parenting for Dummies* book now?

"People say you're half your mom and half your dad. What does that mean?" he continues on.

I pat his hand, about to rip the cookie from Jasper's hands as he chitchats with the barista, pointing to things in the glass case.

Seriously?

"Lennon, are you my mommy?" he asks and my eyes shoot

to him.

In the months that I've been with his father, he's alluded to it, but never asked.

"Because Sara at school asked if I had two dads when I told her I didn't have a mommy." He smiles proudly. "I told her I had a daddy and a Lennon."

I smile back at him, wetness filling my eyes. "I will always be *your* Lennon."

"But not my mommy?" His lips turn down slightly but he's not in full-on pout mode.

I glance over and Jasper's waiting for the coffee. "Jasper!" I call out and he smiles, holding his finger up. Understanding that he's useless in this moment, I look at Brady for a minute. "Technically, according to the law, I'm not your mom. I can't be your mom until your daddy and I get married. Well, if we get married." *Treat the kid like an adult,* I tell myself. *None of this 'hoo-haa' and 'dinky' shit. Call it what it is, a vagina and a penis.*

"So once you get married, then you're my mommy," he clarifies and I give it to the kid, he's inquisitive.

"Yes."

"Do you want to marry my dad?" he asks and of course, *now* Jasper's finally coming over with the cookie.

He's almost to us and I smile, eager for Brady to have his cookie so the spotlight can be removed from over my head.

"Mr. Banks," the barista calls out and he stops.

No! I need the cookie.

He turns back around, grabs his coffee and moves to the station and then waves me over because his hands are overfilled with the entire collection of bakery treats.

It's an exit and I'll take it. "I'll be right back. You stay here," I say to Brady, thankful for at least some time to think of answers.

Jasper's getting his coffee ready, stirring the sugar as he focuses on Brady behind me.

"You complain about a cookie and then buy all this," I comment, scooping all the baked goods in my hands.

"Leave those, just grab your coffee when she calls your name."

"Speaking of which, I'm very disappointed by your choice of name. Tell me we haven't lost the spark already," I joke, my hip resting on the coffee station.

"Cut me some slack, it's been a long day. I promise to knock your socks off the next time." He bends down, kissing my lips.

"You're off the hook for today only. But you still have to woo me," I call out as he passes me by and I wait for my coffee.

Not only does he not do the name thing but he gets his coffee first. If this is what relationships are about, then I understand why people complain about them.

A lifetime later—okay, not a lifetime, but it feels like it—the barista comes over to the counter and I step forward, knowing it's for me.

"Mrs. Banks," she calls out and places it on the counter.

Oh, my God, is Natalie here? We're getting along better these days, but she's not the type of surprise I'd appreciate.

I scan the small cafe, but no one is getting up and I don't see Natalie anywhere. Glancing over my shoulder, I see the table where Brady and Jasper were is empty. Just the pile of pastry items and one lone coffee sit there. Brady must have had to go to the bathroom.

So I wait and watch the coffee cup sit there.

"Are you going to get your coffee?" Jasper says from behind me, his voice soft and loving.

I turn to find him and Brady on bended knee.

"What?" I ask, looking down at my cut-off shorts and tank top that says 'Jesus Loves This Hot Mess.' Not exactly ready to be proposed to.

"Lennon, we love you."

"Yes," Brady adds.

"We want you to spend the rest of your life with us."

"Yes," Brady says.

"We promise to put the toilet seat down and not drink out of the cartons."

"Yes," Brady says, slowly leaning to the side, growing tired of being on his knee.

"We promise to worship you. To love you. To protect you."

"Yes." Brady nods and loses his balance.

"Will you marry us?" Jasper asks and the few people in the cafe all "aww."

"I have to take both of you?" I joke, staring between them.

"Afraid so. Package deal." Jasper smiles.

"What if I only want the little one?"

Jasper looks down to a smiling Brady and shrugs.

"Then I'll be heartbroken." He covers his heart with his hand.

"What do you say? Do we let him live with us?" I say to Brady. "Can I be your mommy and his wife?" I turn the tables and Brady runs over to me, and I squat to catch him. His arms are so tight around my neck I'm almost terrified of finding my next breath.

"You're my mommy first," Brady says softly.

Jasper comes over and wraps his arms around us. "I'll be second place this time." He kisses my temple and then finds my lips, giving me a nice, short kiss that still makes me tingle from my head to my toes.

We both stand after a minute and Jasper picks up the coffee. "So, I have no ring. I wasn't planning on this until I walked up to that barista. I saw you and Brady and somehow I knew. You're our missing piece." He holds it out to me. "So do you accept your coffee, Mrs. Banks?"

"Every morning for the rest of my life."

Brady finally unwraps himself from me and I let him down. He runs over to the table of goodies.

"You pick the date and in the meantime, I'll make sure you have one hell of a rock on that left finger," Jasper says, clearly surprised himself about the impromptu proposal. I'd have it no other way.

"Why not now?" I ask. "I mean, why wait? All I need is you and Brady there. We can do a reception or something for friends and family some other time."

Jasper looks down at me, unsure if I'm serious.

"I'm serious, Jasper. Let's just elope. The three of us can go somewhere."

His full of life smile spreads across his lips.

"Let's go, Mrs. Banks." He holds his hand out for me.

I take it and he grips mine in his much larger one and I know I'm never letting go ever again. He's stuck with me for all eternity.

"Lead the way, Mr. Banks."

The End

A note to READERS . . .

We have to admit, we're a little sad that this series is coming to a close. This gang has been so fun to write and we hope you enjoyed seeing the softer side to Lennon as much as we enjoyed writing it. But if you head into our next series (The Single Dad's Club) you're going to see some cameos from your favorite Modern Love couples. Ooops! Were we supposed to keep that a secret? Oh well.

If you made it this far in the series we're going to take a guess and say, "You like us! You really like us!" ← Sally Field's Oscar speech anyone!? No? Anyway, we were blown away with how open and accepting readers were of the new (but not new) kids on the block. We didn't anticipate all the enthusiasm readers have shown us and to say we're grateful is an understatement. This is a tough, tough market and it's near impossible to get noticed and having you shout your praise from the rooftops has helped so, so much! Each and every one of you is a special unicorn to us. *throws unicorn glitter on all of you*

We have to thank the team behind The Banker

Djordje Grbic, our Cover Designer

RJ Locksley, our Editor

Behind the Writer, our Proof Reader

Linda Russell, our PR from Sassy Savvy Fabulous

Give Me Books, our promotional company

Blogs, who carved out scheduling time to promote us and/or read and review the book

IndieSage PR—Our Web Designer

Michelle New—Our graphics gal extraordinaire

Type A Formatting—Formatting the paperback

First Readers—Heather and Angela

And, of course . . . we thank each other. Because two heads are better than one. (Lennon just popped in and is dying to make a double penetration joke at that but we'll resist). ;)

Thank you again! We can't wait for you to meet our single dads—Marcus, Dane and Garrett!

xoxo

Piper & Rayne

about PIPER RAYNE

P PIPER RAYNE, OR PIPER and Rayne, whichever you prefer because we're not one author, we're two. Yep, you get two established authors for the price of one. You might be wondering if you know us? Maybe you'll read our books and figure it out. Maybe you won't. Does it really matter?

We aren't trying to stamp ourselves with a top-secret label. We wanted to write without apology. We wanted to not be pigeon holed into a specific outline. We wanted to give readers a story without them assuming how the story will flow. Everyone has their favorite authors, right? And when you pick up their books, you expect something from them. Whether it's an alpha male, heavy angst, a happily ever after, there's something you are absolutely certain the book will contain. Heck, we're readers, too, we get it.

What can we tell you about ourselves? We both have kindle's full of one-clickable books. We're both married to husbands who drive us to drink. We're both chauffeurs to our kids. Most of all, we love hot heroes and quirky heroines that make us laugh, and we hope you do, too.

WE'D LOVE IT IF YOU'D STALK US :

www.piperrayne.com

Facebook Page—facebook.com / PiperRayne

Reader Group—facebook.com / groups / PiperRaynesUnicorns

Instagram—authorpiperrayne

Twitter—@piperraynerocks

other books by
PIPER RAYNE

MODERN LOVE SERIES

Charmed By The Bartender

Hooked On The Boxer

Mad About The Banker

SINGLE DADS CLUB SERIES

Real Deal

Dirty Talker

Sexy Beast

DIRTY TRUTH SERIES

The Manny

Doggie Style

Chore Play

Printed in Poland
by Amazon Fulfillment
Poland Sp. z o.o., Wrocław

67702401R00197